The Deportation of Wopper Barraza

The Deportation of Wopper Barraza

A NOVEL

Maceo Montoya

UNIVERSITY OF NEW MEXICO PRESS ALBUQUERQUE

Library of Congress Cataloging-in-Publication Data

Montoya, Maceo.
  The deportation of Wopper Barraza : a novel / Maceo Montoya.
    pages cm
  ISBN 978-0-8263-5436-5 (pbk. : alk. paper) — ISBN 978-0-8263-5437-2
(electronic)
  1. Hispanic Americans—Fiction. I. Title.
  PS3613.O54945D48 2014
  813'.6—dc23
                                    2013036251

Cover and text design by Catherine Leonardo
Composed in Sabon LT Std Roman 9.75/14
Display type is ITC Kabel Std

For Lalo and Chucho, who live it.

Prologue

Julio Cesar Tamayo

I HAVE A SIGN UP IN MY BAR, DIRECTLY BEHIND THE TAP AND RIGHT NEXT TO the flat screen television, so you can't miss it. In neon pink and yellow marker it says: "If you're drunk, 1. Call a cab. 2. Walk. 3. Call your Mom! Now you have no excuse." I have one of the girls rewrite it every couple of weeks because it's written on an erasable board and it wears away. Every now and then we'll add a few more entries just to fuck around. A while ago we wrote, "Remember Wopper Barraza!" It was there until just two weeks ago. I erased it myself after seeing Wopper Barraza at the county fair. I was with my cousin Ralph. We had just passed the kiddie rides, and we were eating candy apples and talking about getting a churro or maybe a hotdog before we reached the beer garden. Ralph pointed him out—otherwise I wouldn't have recognized him. "Look over there, man, that's Wopper," he said. "I thought they deported him," I said. "He came back," Ralph said. "Two years he was gone. Became a big shot down there, like a real big shot, raking in money and everything, but he gave it up and came back." I asked Ralph how he knew. He said Mr. Beas, his counselor at the community college, told him. Then Wopper saw me and nodded his head to say what up. I went to the bar right away and erased the sign, you know, just in case he showed up at some point. But he still hasn't.

PART I

|

AFTER WOPPER BARRAZA'S FOURTH DRUNK DRIVING VIOLATION, THE JUDGE ordered his immediate deportation. Wopper, whose given name was Roberto, told the judge, "But I haven't been there since I was a little kid."

The judge, a gray-haired man with thick black eyebrows, looked for a long time at Wopper's round face, slowly shifting his gaze from the young man's shaved head to his full cheeks and broad nose and finally resting on his languid brown eyes. Then he replied, "Well, you should have thought about that before you got behind the wheel."

Wopper muttered his disbelief. Then he objected again. "But that doesn't make any sense, sir. I don't know anybody there. I came here when I was three years old! I'm American. You can't send me to Mexico—what the hell am I going to do there?"

The judge sighed but was unmoved. "Look, you were warned after your third drunk driving violation that there was a chance you could be deported. If that didn't scare you enough, then, well, you deserve the punishment. You're lucky you have your life. You're lucky you didn't kill someone." He scanned his papers. "Your blood alcohol level was your highest yet."

Wopper told him his defense from the beginning: "But I only live two blocks from the bar."

"Then you should have walked," the judge said. Before Wopper could protest, the next case was called.

His mother didn't take the news well. He and his father were seated at the kitchen table while his mother paced back and forth, opening and closing cabinets for no apparent reason. As she listened to Wopper's explanation, her pudgy face twisted in agony. She clasped her hands together. She stomped her foot. She even reached across and swatted his head. She then told him she'd never make menudo for the rest of his days. "Because with your lifestyle you'll be dead before long in Mexico. But even for the rest of my days I won't make menudo!" His father protested, as this was also his favorite meal to nurse a Sunday morning hangover. "Woman, calm down now. Let's not get carried away. That doesn't even make any sense. What does menudo have to do with anything?"

"I don't care!" she snapped. "I don't care! I punish you, too, Jorge, because if you had just been harder on him when he was a child, he wouldn't have ended up like this! You gave him everything he wanted! Everything! Whatever he wanted at the store, you buy! Whatever he wanted to eat, you give! And that's how he ended up like this! Twenty-four and still a child!" Once more she swatted the back of Wopper's head. Then she sat down at the table and burst into tears.

"Mom, don't cry—"

"You be quiet! I'm not crying for you. I'm crying for myself because no mother should have to wake up one day to realize she's raised a son like you!"

Wopper considered this for a moment and sighed. He had messed up and he knew it, but at this point the drunk driving seemed almost irrelevant. It was his punishment that troubled him. Wopper recalled the court-appointed lawyer's detached expression as he explained the terms of his release. "Three days, Mr. Barraza. That's it. You've got three days to leave the country or else face arrest."

Wopper groaned. "What am I going to do in Mexico? I've never even been there since I was three."

His mother didn't answer him.

His father, on the other hand, accepted the news favorably. He also didn't understand what was so bad about driving drunk if you didn't crash, or why imbibing five beers and two shots was cause for nights in jail, exorbitant fines, long meetings with Mothers Against Drunk Driving, and—who knew?—revoked green cards. But now that it had happened, he mulled over the situation, considered it with his optimist's bent, and announced to his son that he would turn over all his property to him.

"What property are you talking about?" Wopper asked.

"Oh, mijo, I never did tell you about my land, eh?" his father said, removing his cowboy hat and running his fingers through what remained of his stringy hair. With great pride Jorge Barraza told his son about the ten-acre parcel he had purchased on the outskirts of their hometown, La Morada, Michoacán. He had saved and saved and bought a choice piece of property overlooking the vast reservoir, the very one constructed by the government in 1972 to provide much-needed water to the villages on the outskirts of La Piedad. The earth was rich, the soil was red, and there was not a stone to be found. It was his piece of heaven, he said.

"No it isn't!" Wopper's mother screamed. "It's shit for a piece of land with more rocks than weeds! You couldn't grow crab grass on that land, let alone—"

"Woman, that's not true!" Jorge insisted.

"Tell him lies, then! Tell him and he'll go find out for himself!"

"Please stop with all of your negative talk!"

"He'll find out for himself. Then he'll know you're full of it!"

Jorge shook his head vigorously but said nothing.

His wife continued unabated. "Negative talk, you say! I'll show you negative talk. How about when he gets down there, not knowing a soul . . ."

Wopper left his parents arguing in the kitchen. Telling them was easy compared to what came next. He grabbed his bike from the side yard and pedaled over to Lara's house.

After Wopper looked up from carefully and noiselessly leaning his bike against the short chain link fence outside her parents' small one-story stucco home on Depot Street, Lara was already at the door chewing him out.

"I seen you from the living room window, and what did I tell you about calling before you come over?" she yelled.

5

Wopper ignored her and walked past her into the house. He could smell her perfume. It was the one that gave him a headache. She also wore more makeup than she used to, which he didn't understand, since she barely left the living room. At least she had stopped wearing the contacts that were supposed to make her black eyes look green but only made them look swampy. She had stopped that on her own; he never dared comment on her appearance.

Lara continued, "What did I tell you about calling before coming over?" Wopper turned on the television. She walked over and turned it off. He looked up at her. "What'd I tell you?" she asked again, her voice rising.

"Tell me about what?"

"About coming over without calling?"

Wopper couldn't remember.

Lara groaned. "You don't remember shit, you know that? I told you last time to call before you come because what if I want you to pick something up at the store?"

"What'd you want me to pick up then?" he asked.

"Stuff. Things for dinner. We don't even have soda."

"I couldn't pick it up anyway," he said, turning the television back on. "Because all I got is the bike now."

"Then take the bike with the basket!"

"I'm not riding around on that bike."

"Your dad does—drunk son like drunk father. Unbelievable!"

"Oh," he said quietly. "We gotta talk about that."

She nodded and then paused. "You know what I don't understand, Wopper, is how in the hell, with all these drunk asses leaving the bar, why it's you who gets caught every time? Why is that? Why does my boyfriend have to be the only idiot in town who has four DUIs—"

"I'm not the only one," he said. "There was this guy who had—"

"I don't care about that guy! I care about my boyfriend being an idiot. What's gonna happen now?"

In addition to a suspended license, weekly meetings with Mothers Against Drunk Driving, and significant fines, which his parents paid, his previous violations had resulted in Wopper performing community service, mostly involving trash pickup. The first and second times he was assigned highway duty. The third violation, however, had him working garden maintenance at the courthouse, smack in the center of downtown. He had to wear a bright orange vest, and, sure enough, several of Lara's friends spotted him and called her immediately to ask what had happened, feigning concern but hoping for juicy details. The first day she brought him lunch; after that she refused, telling him she was embarrassed to be seen with a convict.

"You gonna have to go to those meetings with the mothers again? I can't wait to see their faces when they see you come in *again*! This time you're not even gonna know what hit you! But for real, what did the judge say?"

Wopper sighed. "Well . . ." He sighed again.

"What he say?"

"*Shhh*, damn!" he snapped.

"Don't tell me to shut up!"

"I didn't tell you to shut up, just be quiet, damn, so I can tell you!"

"I'll leave the room, that's what I'll do! I don't care if they make you *live* with the Mad Mothers, I don't. I'll leave the room if you tell me to shut up again!"

"I didn't tell you to—" he drew in a deep breath. "Okay, okay, okay." He beckoned her to sit down. "Okay, just, just let me tell you. So the thing is—"

Lara was nervous now. She could tell by Wopper's face that it was serious, that it was something unexpected. Being nervous made her even more impatient. "Come on!" she cried.

"They're deporting me," he muttered.

Lara was silent. It took her a moment to register what he'd said. "Deported where?" she asked. "Out of Woodland? I didn't know they could do that—"

Wopper shook his head. "No, not Woodland, dummy. They're sending me to Mexico."

"Mexico! You're kidding, right? For how long?"

"Forever. They're kicking me out of the country. They're taking away my papers."

"But you haven't been to Mexico since you were a baby," Lara said, her voice trailing off.

Wopper was quiet. The television was suddenly very loud. There was a commercial on about a big sale at Sears. Smiling models wearing different outfits posed against a white background. They both watched it numbly. Suddenly the door opened and Lara's mother walked in, all bundled up in a coat, scarf, mittens, and a beanie. She saw the glum look on the young people's faces. She thought she knew why. "So you told him, huh, mija?" she said, as she took off her puffy purple coat and threw it onto the sofa chair. Lara remained staring at the television, dumbstruck. Her mother continued, taking off the rainbow-colored mittens and putting them in her coat pocket. "Well, so be it! You are going to be parents out of wedlock, but there are worse things in life." She loosened the scarf around her neck but kept it on. She tossed off the beanie, strands of hair full of static rising off her head. "I don't know how this could've happened. Seems to me like you guys are on the couch every night watching television. But what do I know? And yes, it's true, Wopper don't have a job, but he will find one, isn't that right? And me and Lara's father will do what it takes to help out when we can because that's what family is for, isn't that right?"

Wopper turned his head to her slowly, as if just now noticing her walk in. "What are you talking about?" he asked.

Lara's mother looked at him quizzically. "The baby."

"What baby?"

Lara's mother realized her error. "Oh, I just . . . I thought, I thought that . . ."

Without turning away from the television, Lara said, "We're going to have a kid."

Wopper was still confused. "What do you mean? Who is?"

"We are. Who else would I be talking about?"

"But I'm—" he stopped.

Lara then told her mother that Wopper was to be deported.

When Wopper left Lara's house he didn't feel like going home, so he rode his bike toward downtown. It was cold and he could see his breath in the air. There was no one around. The streets were empty, even of cars. He kept thinking of the look of disgust on Lara's face when he asked her if she was going to get an abortion. All she answered was, "I'd rather you cross the desert." He didn't know what she'd meant by that. "Maybe I will," he said. "Yeah, right," she scoffed, which confused him even more. On Main Street, he passed the Army Surplus store and peeked in. He hadn't shopped there in years, not since high school when all he wore were Dickies and Ben Davis. He'd have to buy clothes for his trip, he thought. No telling what they would have down there. He briefly imagined himself dressed like a vaquero with boots and a big shiny belt. He rode his bike across the street, then crossed back to the other side, and then looped around and retraced his zigzagged path. He paid close attention to the storefronts of Main Street's old buildings—antique shops, a variety store, a women's clothing boutique, a few restaurants, a diner—places he'd never entered, nor cared to. But now he realized he never would, and a part of him wanted to, just for the sake of knowing. He passed the pizza parlor; he had been there a few times, but he preferred Domino's.

At the corner of East and Main he rode past Jack in the Box. The lights were bright and from the street he could see Mr. Gregory, his racquetball partner at the sports club, eating a hamburger. The unlikely pair ended up together by default: during pre-league, when everyone chose playing partners, no one chose them. Mr. Gregory was too old and couldn't move fast enough to return shots. There were other old men, but they accepted their feebleness more gracefully. Mr. Gregory, on the other hand, complained, griped, instigated arguments, and called interference when no one was even close. He usually stormed off the court halfway through the match. In Wopper's case, no one asked him because he was overweight and lazy, or so slow that he appeared lazy, and, like Mr. Gregory, he complained to no end and called interference whenever possible. So they were left to one another. If anybody stuck around to watch their matches, they would've at least found them humorous—an old rail-thin white man dressed in all white with a headband playing against a fat brown kid dressed in khakis and a red 49ers jersey, arguing, insulting one another, half the shots unreturned—but no one watched: they were given the last slot of the night, after everyone else left to have beer.

Wopper parked his bike outside where he could see it and entered Jack in the Box. He approached Mr. Gregory's table and said, "That hamburger ain't gonna help you run any faster."

Mr. Gregory looked up, scowling and ready to return with an insult of his own. He was dressed nicely, but his eyes were bloodshot and he had trouble focusing. Wopper wondered if the old man was drunk.

"I was about to shove this hamburger where it don't belong," Mr. Gregory barked. "You're lucky I look before I act."

Wopper laughed. "Well, if you fight anything like you play racquetball, I'd be able to crawl out of your way."

Now Mr. Gregory laughed. He took a large bite of his hamburger and chewed slowly, smacking his lips. He sipped his coke and swished the liquid around in his mouth before speaking again. "What brings you around here? Have a seat."

"Just riding my bike. Needed to think," Wopper answered as he sat down across from Mr. Gregory.

"You want a hamburger?"

"Naw, that's all right. I ate not too long ago."

"By the looks of it, that never stopped you before. What, you on a diet? You trying to move up the ranks of the racquet league? I knew you'd get tired of playing this old fogey soon enough."

Wopper laughed and then grew quiet. He didn't know what else to say. They usually just played racquetball or cracked jokes about one another's playing ability. The old man continued eating, his chews and smacking lips the only sounds between them. Finally, Wopper said, "You know that's how I got my name?"

"How's that?" Mr. Gregory said after swishing around the coke in his mouth. He didn't appear too interested. In fact, it looked as though he was staring intently at his reflection in the window.

Wopper told him the story anyway. He was eleven, and he and his parents were heading to a soccer tournament in Redding. Before they left Woodland, his dad stopped at Judy's Grinders and bought twenty hamburgers for the entire team. Over the course of the two-hour trip, Wopper, alone in the back seat, quietly ate twelve of the twenty hamburgers. When they arrived, his dad held up the bag triumphantly and told Wopper's teammates that he'd brought them all "gwoppers" for lunch, because that's what he called every hamburger. The team cheered and gathered around, but when Jorge looked inside the bag, he found mostly empty wrappings. Meanwhile, his son had rushed to find a bathroom. When he returned, his teammates were cracking up, and his dad was yelling at him. "Twelve gwoppers, mijo, *twelve* gwoppers you ate!" But that day he scored the winning goal, a first for him. Everybody joked that it was because of the "gwoppers." By the end of the tournament it had become his nickname. Somewhere down the line the "g" was dropped.

When he finished his story, Mr. Gregory chuckled. "Gwopper, Gwopper," he mumbled. He took another bite of his hamburger and then again used his coke like mouthwash. "You told me that story before," he said.

"Really? Why didn't you stop me then?"

The old man didn't answer.

After another long silence Wopper told him that he wasn't going to be playing racquetball anymore. Mr. Gregory dropped his hamburger and rapidly wiped his fingers on a napkin. He looked hurt. Wopper realized that maybe Mr. Gregory thought this was the club's way of pushing him out of the league, so he told him his reason for leaving.

"Deported?" Mr. Gregory said. "I didn't know they could do that."

Wopper sighed and said he hadn't known either.

"So is that why you're out at this time of night—checking out your old haunts before leaving?"

Wopper hadn't thought about it. "I guess," he said. He rose from the table. "Maybe I'll be back someday."

"Sure thing, but tell me—"

"Yeah?"

"Did you let me win half those games? I just have to know. I just have to know whether the games I did win were won fair and square."

Wopper chuckled. "No, you beat me fair and square," he said, overemphasizing the fair and square, as if maybe he didn't mean it.

"I figured," Mr. Gregory said. "Well, we'll see if I find another partner who's as lazy as you."

"I doubt it," Wopper said as he turned to go.

"Good luck down there. If you need anything don't hesitate to call. You got my number, right?"

"Yeah, I think so," Wopper lied, assuming the old man was just being polite. He couldn't imagine what he'd ever need from Mr. Gregory.

He lingered for a moment. Mr. Gregory returned to his hamburger.

"Do you think I'll be all right?" Wopper blurted out. Mr. Gregory stared straight ahead, chewing loudly. He hadn't heard. Wopper didn't care to repeat himself. He didn't even know why he had asked. He turned around, and through the window he saw that his bike was gone. He hurried outside and circled the restaurant, looking for it, but to no avail. He kicked the brick wall and cursed. He thought of calling his dad for a ride but then decided to walk.

On the way home he felt sadder than he could ever remember feeling. He stared hard at everything he passed, as if taking it in for the first time. He noticed the shadows cast by the large dormant trees. He looked closely at the houses he'd walked by his entire life. First, the nice old homes close to downtown, dark and quiet, peaceful. Then the homes grew smaller, some run-down, others not, until finally he reached the dilapidated apartments and bungalows on Fourth Street. This was the beginning of his neighborhood. Men in cowboy hats and baseball hats, bundled in jackets, stood around their cars, drinking beers and listening to norteño music on the car radio. Children were still outside playing. On Fourth and Fifth Streets, children played at all hours of the day, even in the cold and late into the night, as if no one ever told them to come inside. In the distance, a group of men, women, and children surrounded the hotdog and corn-on-the-cob stand in front of El Buen Gusto, their faces hauntingly illuminated in pale green. He absorbed it all and wondered if he would remember this night. Would he even remember his neighborhood, or would it all disappear because he'd never paid close enough attention? Until that moment, he never thought he needed to. Why remember what's always been there and always would be?

He was leaving everything he'd ever known. He had never done anything by himself before, never gone anywhere alone. He hadn't even really left Woodland. He had an aunt in Dunnigan, an uncle in Antioch, another one in Vacaville, a few cousins in Fresno. He'd visited them a handful of times. He'd been to Los Angeles once for a wedding and to San Francisco for a quinceañera. But that was it: a day or two, a long weekend. But this was permanent.

His father was waiting for him at the kitchen table. The house was dark except for the ceiling lamp above him. He had a crudely drawn map spread out on the table and was inspecting it with a magnifying glass. Next to the map was a list of names and addresses, all in his father's scribbling hand. "Mijo!" he called out as soon as the door opened. "So glad you're home! I've found it. I've located our land so that when you get there you'll know exactly where to go."

Wopper walked toward the kitchen table and peered at the map. His father had covered it with indecipherable details. Wopper went to the fridge and poured himself a glass of milk. His father jotted down something else and then pulled a chair out from the table. "Sit, sit! We have to go over this!"

Wopper sat down. He was suddenly very tired and wanted to go to bed.

"Look, mijo. So here you see I've written down all you need to know to make yourself comfortable in La Morada. Here is where you buy groceries—from Doña Eusebia—and you buy milk—oh, milk like you've never tasted! Straight from the cow—from her husband who sells it at the corner, over here. His name is Don Pio. And then over here is where you need to go for all your work supplies, hardware, anything you should need to fix up the little house that's there. It's not much, I'll warn you, but it'll do for now until you can start saving a little from the crops—"

"Wait, Dad, what crops? What are you talking about?"

"Mijo, you're going to cultivate our land! You're going to grow corn! Good corn—corn like you've never seen before! At least that's what you'll grow mostly. You'll have a garden of your own for basic vegetables, and I'll tell you what—you see this house right here, this is where Don Martín lives—you go to him immediately, *immediately*, I say—he'll help you. He was your grandfather's compadre and he wouldn't deny the grandson of his compadre anything. He knows everything there is to know about La Morada. You go to him and he'll make sure you lack for nothing. Do you understand me? Mijo, are you listening?"

Wopper nodded his head slowly.

"This is an opportunity for you! I realized this is a blessing. This will change your life—you'll become a man now! A man! No longer your mom's little boy who can't fend for himself—no! You'll become a man down there, I swear to God."

"Dad."

"You'll love it down there—at first it will be different, very, very different, but you watch, you're a son of that soil, as much as me, as much as your grandfather and grandfathers before—the Barrazas are a strong family in La Morada, just ask Don Martín when you see him, he'll tell you. Watch and see the respect you command when you say, 'I am Roberto Barraza.' You wait—"

"Dad."

"What, mijo? Look, so here I've written down where you need to—"

"Dad! Listen to me!"

"What, mijo? What?"

"Lara is pregnant."

In a moment his father's excitement disappeared completely. His brow furrowed and a look of confusion crossed his face. "But mijo . . ." He paused, his expression fixed. He turned and looked at the map. He made to point at something but then stopped. He looked at his son and said, "What'd you go and do a thing like that for?"

Wopper looked at the map. He scanned the names, reading the scribbled details without comprehending them. "It doesn't matter," he mumbled. "It doesn't change anything. She isn't coming with me."

II

Raul Leon

The night before Wopper left, he was supposed to meet up with us at Zitios Bar. He told me he had plans with his girl, but he didn't think they would stay out all night, no later than eleven, twelve. So me and all these other fools we grew up with got together probably around ten. We sat at the bar and ordered a round of tequila shots, and then we got beers and made fun of Pete for ordering a bright blue mixed drink. We talked about playing pool or darts, but none of us made any move to do so. The night was slow and it was just us for a good while, then a few other fools we didn't know showed up, then some girls, nothing much to look at, but we looked at them anyway. Mostly, though, we just watched the television screens.

When I heard Wopper was gonna get deported I felt real bad for him, but more so I felt bad for his mom, because I couldn't help but think about my own mom and how she would feel if one day I got kicked out of the country. I love my mom. I love her more than anything else in this world. She's everything to me. And me and my brother and my little sister, we're everything to her, but me especially because I'm the oldest. What I mean is, I was old enough when my dad left that we both felt it together, and she knew that and I knew that. I was nine, but my brother was only three, and my sister was still in my mom's stomach. So my dad mainly left me and my mom, if you know what I mean, and even though it was hard for me, I had to be there for her, and she always loved me more for that, I feel like. I've fucked up along the way, got suspended hella times then finally expelled, never graduated even though all I had to do was fill out some study packet, got arrested twice, came home too many times to count with swollen foreheads, black eyes, and broken noses, but for all the worry I must've caused her she never held it against me. Shit, she's been there for me just like I've been there for her. I don't know what Wopper and his mom's relationship is like, but like I said, I couldn't help but feel bad for Mrs. Barraza.

While we were waiting for Wopper, these fat girls in skimpy-ass tube tops sat down next to us, and they were fucking ugly. Busted teeth, eyebrows drawn in all lopsided. I had no interest in talking to them, but I wasn't sitting next to them, Frankie was, and Frankie is about as ugly and fat as they were, so he started in asking them lame questions like, "You all come here a lot?" At some point they asked us what we were up to. *Drinking, bitches,* I thought to say, but

Frankie tells them that we're waiting for our friend Wopper. "Oh," they say. Then like five minutes passed and Frankie's dumb ass runs out of dumbass things to talk about, and there's just silence, all of us sitting at the bar—me, Frankie, Pete, Tony, José, Arty, Johnny, Oscar, Ruben, and these fat chicks—and we're not saying a damn word, and the jukebox had stopped playing, and it was the longest silence, I swear to God. We were just looking at the television, or at our beers in front of us, or at the shelves behind the bar full of tequila, whiskey, and vodka bottles, not saying anything. I even turned to my left and stared at the pool table as though there was a game going on. Finally, one of the fat chicks with dyed blonde hair asked, "Why you call him Wopper? He eat a lot of Whoppers or what?"

And dumbass Frankie just nods his head, his fucking neck jiggling, and he says, "Yup. Basically."

None of them know Wopper like I know him. We've known each other since Beamer Elementary. I came here not knowing a word of English, not one word. And so the teacher, she told me to sit next to Roberto Barraza because he was good at explaining things. And so everything the teacher said in English, Wopper told me in Spanish. And even though I wasn't the only one who didn't know English in the class, I knew I had the best translator, because Wopper wouldn't just repeat what the teacher said, but he'd add his own shit, like he knew more than she did. What was her name? Ms. Martinez, that's right. She was my first teacher, but sometimes I don't know what I learned from her and what I learned from Wopper. Because she taught me about letters and numbers, but Wopper, he would talk about Woodland, and the NFL and WWF, and shit on television I had never heard of, and he would tell me what we were gonna do at recess, and he would tell me about girls even though we couldn't have been older than eight. I swear to God I thought that fool was like the expert on the United States. I never forgot what he did for me, even though it was the most natural thing to do. Just be friends with the new kid. But I was that new kid, and I wasn't just new to the school, but new to the country, and Wopper took away all my fear. That's all I knew before. Just fucking piss-in-my-pants fear, and Wopper, he took that away. And I love him for that. I'll say that to the day I die. I love Wopper for what he did.

When we got older we stayed close, but we were never as close as when we were kids. My mom and us, we moved to Donnelly Circle, and I started hanging out with older fools who lived where I did, and they got me doing shit I wish I hadn't done. Not for my sake, but for my mom, because she couldn't have wanted me getting high and fighting and getting kicked out of school. But I was just doing what made sense to me. Wopper stayed out of it. He kicked it with a lot of Norteños, but he was never one of us. But not because he was a pussy; he wasn't. He'd just say, "My mom would kill me." And the other fools laughed, but I defended him because I could respect that. I remember one time he was about to be jumped by some Sureños just because he was wearing a red 49ers hat—fool loves the Niners—and I just happened to come by, and because those fools didn't want beef with me they left Wopper alone. But he would have fought them. He would've and everyone knew that, so it was cool that he kicked it with us without being one of us. He was a homie, and that was it. He just had his own way of doing things.

When we all got older, us friends from elementary school, we'd meet up at the bar, buy each other drinks like that was the nicest thing we could do for one another, and we'd talk about when we were kids. That's all anyone ever talked about, like nothing new was worth mentioning. But Wopper getting deported, now that was something new. That was something to talk about. But the truth is, none of us knew what to say. I guess we could've started with what the fuck he was going to do in Mexico. Where would he live? What kind of job would he get? I mean, seriously, I couldn't picture any one of us living in some ranchito. Visiting during the fiestas, that's all right, but forever? Couldn't imagine it. None of us could.

So we all sat there at the bar, waiting for Wopper to show up on his last night in Woodland, and it got later and later, and those ugly-ass bitches left, and we still waited, and we kept talking about old times, and we laughed even though none of the stories were that funny. We just laughed because we were getting faded, and it was better to laugh at old times than to pretend that what we were doing now was worth talking about. My job stacking boxes at the Walgreens warehouse? I swear to God I think we all envied Wopper. Maybe we all felt bad for his mom, but we all envied that fool. Why? Because he was getting the fuck out of Woodland, which I guess is an all right place to be from, but at the same time it's just fucking Woodland, and it'll always be Woodland, and I don't know how else to explain it. We envied Wopper because he had no idea what tomorrow would be like. And we all knew exactly what it would be like. Like yesterday and the day before. I already said this, but I'll say it again because sometimes people forget what others mean to them. I love Wopper for what he did when I was eight years old, when I came here afraid of everything and he showed me that I didn't have to be. I love him for that. I wish we'd stayed as close as we were at that age. To me there's nothing sadder than friends going their separate ways. Sometimes it's gotta be that way, it just happens, you know, but it's still sad.

That's why, when I heard Wopper was getting deported, I called that fool up and told him we were gonna drink to old times, but mostly we were gonna drink to his future. "Yeah, yeah, cool," he said. "I'll be there." But he never showed up. He never came, and everyone took off except me. I waited and waited, and I kept looking at my phone, thinking he was gonna send me a text or call. But there was nothing. He probably couldn't get away from his girl, I figured. So it was just me and the bar and the drunks getting drunker. I watched the television screens show the same sports highlights they'd been playing for hours. Before I left, I went into the bathroom and took a piss. I stared at the white wall, and you know what I wanted to do? I wanted to punch a hole right through it. I wanted to punch a hole in that fucking wall. And I was about to. But I stopped myself. I kept looking at the white wall, and it was spinning, but not like you think. It was spinning and spinning, and I swear to God I thought I saw Wopper's future. And instead of punching the wall I started laughing. I said, "Motherfucker, you the lucky son of a bitch!" I couldn't stop laughing. I only stopped when some drunk-ass wetback came into the bathroom and said, "Why you laughing, primo?" I told him to mind his own business, I wasn't his fucking cousin, and then I left the bar and drove home.

III

Lara Gonzalez

My bedroom window faces the afternoon sun, so that starting in April and all the way through probably September, by two, three in the afternoon, it's too damn hot to be in. I swear, my room doesn't cool down until two in the morning. But I'm used to it. Sometimes I'll open my window, and from my bed I can stare up at the stars or maybe the moon. My room is the same as it was in junior high, the same posters on the wall—Selena, *Titanic*—the same photos of me and my friends—our bangs teased so that they stood straight up—even the same pink comforter from *Beauty and the Beast*. I don't know why I never changed anything. Just got used to it, I guess.

It was on one of the last hot nights of September that Wopper got me pregnant. My parents had gone gambling at Cache Creek. It was late and I was tired and I just wanted to watch television, but Wopper convinced me. He said something like, "Who knows when's the next time they'll be out." So I gave in. Wopper came and then he just collapsed on top of me—as if he'd been knocked out cold—and I remember I was staring out my window at the stars, wishing I knew of constellations other than the Little Dipper and the Big Dipper. That's what I was thinking about, I swear to God. When Wopper got up from the bed, I heard him mumble, "Shit." But I didn't think to ask what had happened.

The evening before Wopper left we got a room at the Best Western off Highway 5. I told him to get a nice hotel in Davis so we could at least feel like we'd gotten away from things, but he told me he didn't want to be driving all the way out there. A ten-minute drive, fifteen at the most! *And* I was the one driving because he didn't want to risk it. I don't know what else they could've done to him. But anyway, the Best Western isn't too bad if you ignore the highway traffic outside your window. We went to our favorite place to eat first, not a fancy place, just a taqueria that we always went to with bright orange tablecloths and white plastic chairs. It was my idea to go there, but Wopper probably would've chosen the place as well, not for any sentimental reason though, just because it was the place we always went. I was freezing my ass off in my nicest black dress, and all he wore for the occasion was a parka, a black pocket t-shirt, and jeans. We were quiet as we ate our food: me, tacos de res; him, sopes. Funny the things you remember. Even though I tried to ask questions, I could see I was mainly annoying him, so I stopped. I looked at the paintings on the wall: scenes of Mexican villages with red tile roofs and cobblestone streets. In each one there was a beautiful Mexican girl with green eyes too large for her head, wearing a white blouse and carrying a ceramic pitcher of water on her head. I wanted to make some crack about those paintings being like the rancho Wopper was heading to, but I kept my mouth shut. As we were finishing, a man went to the jukebox and put on Pepe Aguilar's "Por Mujeres Como Tú." It wasn't our song—we didn't have one, of course—but it was a song I liked, and sometimes I wondered about it, you know, if Wopper heard this song—shit, if he heard any song about love—did he think of me?

Was I the one to lose him because I said I wasn't following him? How could he expect me to go? Even if I wasn't pregnant, this was his shit to deal with. I couldn't be dragged along. I never even gave him a choice. I told him I wasn't going as soon as he told me, and of course he let it be, probably knowing I was so stubborn that if he tried to fight I'd only fight back harder. But still I wanted him to beg me a little. I wanted him to at least ask, even though I'd already told him my answer. *Will you go with me?* he should have said. And I would still yell at him and tell him what an idiot he was and how never in a million years would I bring up my kid in Mexico, but still, I wanted him to ask. Instead, he just shrugged. He always shrugged. Never seen someone shrug as much as Wopper Barraza. You'd think he had no opinion on anything. Just went along with it all, or at least pretended to go along with it all. Because a shrug can mean, *Okay, sure*, or, *I don't agree, but whatever*, or it can mean, which was most likely the case, *I'll say I'm going along with it, but in the end I'll just do what I want*, which isn't much either way. I don't know how it fits here. Like I said, it wasn't like he had a choice. He had to leave and I told him I wasn't going.

When we got to the hotel we still weren't saying much. Our room was on the second floor and faced a Denny's and a bright Chevron sign. We could hear the cars zooming by on the freeway. He kept looking at his cell phone. "Who you expecting to call?" I asked. "No one," he said, "just checking the time." "Where do you have to be?" I asked. "Nowhere," he mumbled. I asked him a question about the good-bye party his mother was throwing the next day. He didn't even answer me, and I could tell his mind was somewhere else. Not with me on our last night together. I told him, "If you just want to go home we can. No use wasting money on a hotel if you're going to be in a bad mood." And all he said was, "Nah, it's all right, I'm good." I felt sick to my stomach, I really did. We'd been together for seven years, and even though it seemed like most of it we were fighting and I was bitching and he was shrugging his shoulders, the thought of him being gone for good, gone because I told him I wouldn't follow him, was just hard to accept. At that moment, I felt like I couldn't breathe. As much as I hated to do it, the only way to relieve myself of the feeling was to start crying. He'd seen me cry before, but usually when I was pissed off or something. It'd been a long time since he'd seen me cry from anything else. I think it brought him back from wherever he was. He didn't say anything. He just put his arm around my waist as I tried to get the damn key card to open our door. I continued to cry and hated myself for it.

The room was stuffy and smelled like strawberry air freshener. There were paintings of pink flowers on the wall. I took off my heels, and Wopper lied down. I lied down next to him, and we started to kiss. More because we thought we should rather than either of us wanting to. We hardly ever slept on a queen-size bed; we were usually on the couch or on my twin bed when my parents weren't home, which wasn't often. I undid his canvas belt and took his pants off. He was still wearing his fucking parka. "Are you cold or what?" I asked. "No," he mumbled. "Take off your parka then," I said. So he took it off. He left his t-shirt on, though. I took off my dress because he wasn't making any move to do it. He never did. We both got underneath the covers and he crawled on top of me. My eyes were closed and I was waiting for him. Waiting like I hadn't waited in a long time. I wanted to feel him, and the longer my eyes were closed and the longer he took to touch me, the more I wanted his hands on me.

But his hands never touched me.

"Lara, I can't do it," I heard him say.

I opened my eyes. He was staring down at his plaid boxers. There was nothing. I felt like yelling at him. I felt myself getting mad, and I wanted to say something mean, really mean. For doing this, because I just knew he was doing this on purpose. But then his eyes met mine, and I saw how bad he felt. There were times when he looked at me and I remembered him when we were younger and all the years we had been together. Maybe it had all been a high school crush that should've ended there. Maybe I should've broken his heart five years ago when I had that crush on Rigo, this guy I worked with at Food 4 Less. But I remember Wopper gave me that same look then, and I felt so close to him, like I'd never know someone better than I knew him and like he knew me better than anyone else, and even though we'd just been together two years at the time, it felt like I'd shared my life with him. And that counted more than anything. Counted more than Rigo, at least. So we stayed together, and now I'm pregnant and he's leaving and he can't get it up on our last night together and he's giving me the look again, so instead of yelling, I told him, "Wopper, I don't care. Just hold me."

So he lay behind me and cradled me in his big arms, and I began to cry, and he told me, "*Shhh . . . shhh . . . shhh.*" Wopper was comforting me. He was comforting me! I'd never let him do that before. He'd never been allowed. I'd yell at him first. But this time it wasn't me who let him. He just did it. And when I look back and think about how Wopper changed, I remember this moment, and I think it was then that he began to grow away from me, from Woodland, from his life here. I vowed right there never to let anyone comfort me again, but I gave myself that night. So I cried some more and he held me until we fell asleep.

In the middle of the night I heard him call my name. "Lara, Lara."

"Yeah," I whispered.

"If it's a girl can we name her after you?" he asked.

I nodded, then realized he couldn't see me. "Yes," I said. Then he was silent.

"And if it's a boy?" I asked.

"I don't want a son," he said.

"Why?" I asked him.

I don't remember now whether I was dreaming all of this. Maybe I was. I really don't remember. No, he did. He must have. This is what he said: "He would be ashamed of me just like everyone else. And I don't care about everyone else, but I know I would care if it were my son. I wouldn't be able to take it."

IV

Jorge Barraza

Did I stunt him? Did I keep him from growing? That's what my wife always told me. "Jorge, no more!" she'd yell at me when I'd walk in the door with Roberto holding an ice cream. "Jorge, no more!" she'd yell at me when she'd see him approaching with stuffed animals or toys, eating a candy apple. "It's the county fair," I'd say. "It's only once a year." And she'd yell some more, telling me that for *my* son it was always the county fair. She never claimed Wopper as her own. The girls were hers, but Roberto was *my* son, *your* son, the son *you* raised! Maybe she's right. She is right. She'd yell and swat him for some stupidity—she was always the one to scold—and I'd wait for her to leave the room, then I'd take him into my arms (the girls too but she wasn't as rough with them) and tell him, "Don't cry, don't cry, my little boy, your dad is here to protect you." Then later she'd yell at me, tell me I was going to raise a son just like myself. "Which is what?" I'd ask. "A weakling!" she'd yell. And I'd laugh. I'd laugh because it struck me as funny to be called a weakling. I lived with her, and I dealt with her for how many years? And I'm the weakling? I consider myself strong as a pack mule.

No one shares this high opinion. Not my wife, not my daughters, not even my son. They never listened to me. You'd think they'd return my kindness. The kind father who always gave them their way. But no, I rarely cared enough to assert my authority, and when I did, they just ignored me. And sometimes, as hard as it is for them to believe, I'm right. Why wouldn't I be? I've lived life, I've seen many things, I know a situation when I see it. But if you want people to listen, you have to be stern from the beginning, from the very start. Once you let them push you over, they will continue until you're dead. Which is the story of my marriage. But that makes it seem like I live a miserable life. I don't. I'm comfortable with what I have. I am a simple man. I deal with what comes my way, always have. My father was a simple man. I adored him. Does Wopper adore me? When he's older he will. Right now he can't separate me from his failures. I say, what failures?

When I brought Wopper to the airport, I spoke the entire way, reminding him to go see Don Martín as soon as he arrived and bringing up other details about the property that I'd already told him a hundred times. It was dark, but the moon was low in the sky, and dark clouds must have covered the lower portion because it looked like a huge orange that someone had stepped on. It was cold outside, and Wopper turned on the car heater full blast. My little Toyota's air conditioning hasn't worked in a decade, but the heater might as well be a furnace. I felt sweat build around the brow of my hat, and my face and ears were hot, too, so I cracked the window for fresh air. But then a minute later I rolled it back up because the wind was so loud that I feared I wouldn't be able to hear him if he actually responded to one of my questions. Wopper finally turned off the heater, but I was still sweating.

I kept asking him if he had put the money I'd given him in a safe place. When he just shrugged, which I assumed to mean yes, I invented other questions to fill the silence. I don't even know what I said or what I asked. I spoke out of nervousness. Woodland is only ten miles or so from the Sacramento airport, just a few corn and rice fields away, so we didn't have much time. I wished we had hours more to go. I parked right in front of the Mexicana Airlines sign, and already he had his door open. I told him, "Wait, wait! There was something else I was going to tell you . . ." But I couldn't think of anything else to say. I had run out of questions. Finally, he said, "Dad, I have to go now." Then something came to me: I cautioned him about the conniving ways of taxi drivers, but as I was doing so I felt my voice grow weak until I realized that I was crying.

He stopped me. "Dad, don't cry," he said in English. I heard the irritation. I looked up at him. I recognized the embarrassment. I stopped my crying. I wiped my eyes even though no tears had fallen except maybe a few, and when he stepped out of the car I cursed myself, which is something I never do, because I've never seen the point. I just said, "Goddamn you, Jorge. Goddamn it."

I got out of the car too and rushed around the front to give him a hug, but then I saw that he had moved to the rear and was waiting with his hand on the trunk. "I need to get my stuff," he said. I hurried back around, opened the driver side and popped the trunk, and then rushed to help him with his luggage. I reached for his suitcase and he told me, "I got it, Dad." I wanted to help anyway, so I grabbed one side, but then I ended up dropping it because all I had to hold on to was a wheel, not to mention my hands were sweaty. "Sorry! Sorry!" I said. "It's okay, just leave it alone," he muttered under his breath.

His bags in hand, he stood on the sidewalk as if unsure what to do next, or as if he didn't know how to say good-bye. I thought maybe he was waiting to see what I was going to do, so I lunged toward him, grabbing him as tight as I could. He was a child full of laughter the last time I'd hugged him like this. He just stood there at first, but then after a few seconds I felt his arms around me, too. Then he said, "Okay, Dad." So I let go, stared into his eyes one last time, and tried to remember my son's face at twenty-four years old, because who knew how old he'd be when I saw him again? Then he turned around, and I watched him disappear into the terminal.

V

Wopper Barraza entered the airport terminal and had no idea where to go. He gripped the handle of his large bag, holding it at his side as if he were about to head somewhere specific. But he found himself frozen in place, unable to move. Finally, he turned around, half-hoping to see his father behind him, instructing him, pointing him in the right direction. He regretted telling his father to just drop him off. But then he imagined the two of them stuck in the middle of all these people, neither of them knowing what to do. His father would have at least pretended.

He turned back to face the rest of the terminal, and several people stared at him rudely or confusedly, as if he were blocking the only way from one side of the concourse to the other. He moved aside and followed a Mexican family: a short round man with a cowboy hat, his short round wife, and their three young kids, who looked like miniature versions of their parents, each with suitcases as large as Wopper's and two oversized boxes precariously tied with rope. After following them for a few yards, stopping when they stopped, checking his documents just as the father did, and moving forward when they did, he realized they were as lost as he was. At one point his eyes met the father's, and he recognized not his own apprehension, but an expression similar to one his own father would wear. It said, *I have no idea what I'm doing, but I'll figure this out!* Wopper could muster no such expression. And at that point, no one would have cared if he did.

He smiled, and the man said, "Guadalajara?"

Wopper nodded.

"Over there?" the man pointed. "Right?"

Wopper looked in the direction they were headed. Now he saw the signs. Now he saw the snaking rows of people. "Yes, over there, it looks like," he said.

He and the man struck up a conversation. The man did most of the talking. He introduced his wife and children. He told him where they were heading, explained the reason for their trip, briefly wondered about the weather in Guadalajara, and informed Wopper of how long it had been since his last visit. He even felt the need to describe the contents of the two boxes tied with rope. Wopper was too nervous to give much of his attention. He registered nothing except that the man was from Woodland.

The family was held up at the ticket counter because their bags weighed too much. They emptied the contents—countless pairs of shoes, boxes of packaged junk food, a toaster, a game station—and the man kept saying something about, "I told you, the scale, the scale," and the wife mumbled, "I know, I know you did, you're right." Wopper watched them from the front of the line and tried to piece together what was happening. A space opened up and he was beckoned forward. His bag was over the weight limit too.

"Do you want to move stuff into your backpack or another bag?" asked the woman behind the counter.

He didn't understand what she was asking. She repeated the question, and this time he saw what the family was doing, the mother on her knees, frantically unzipping bags, handing belongings to each of the children to hold while she reorganized each suitcase to fit under the weight limit.

"You can just pay the fee. Would you prefer that?" the attendant asked, clearly noticing the dread on Wopper's face as he imagined himself doing the same thing.

"Yes," he said.

When the bag was checked, she handed him his boarding pass and pointed him in the direction of security. He followed others who seemed to know where they were supposed to go. He felt freer without the huge suitcase that his parents had so diligently packed with gifts. They had given him detailed instructions about what was to go to whom; instructions he had barely listened to.

He passed through security, following the actions of those around him, and he removed his jacket, wallet, and belt, hesitating before taking off his tennis shoes. The man before him passed through the monitor and it beeped loudly. The security agent asked the man if he had anything else in his pockets, but the man didn't speak English, so the agent asked him more loudly and pointed to the man's pockets. Still confused and merely following the hand gestures of the agent, the man dug into his pockets and removed some change.

Wopper felt his body heat rise as he wondered what he had on him that might cause the alarm to go off. He braced himself as he walked through, and he was almost surprised when there was no sound and the security agent pointed him toward his belongings. As he was putting on his shoes, the man who'd been ahead of him was guiding his orange leather belt through the loops of his brown slacks. He heard the man muttering in Spanish, "That was tough, man. What a bitch that was. What was the point of that?" Wopper thought maybe he was talking to him. He looked up, but the man was still looking down at his belt, making sure the buckle was centered.

Wopper found his seat and waited nervously for the plane to take off. He had the window, and an old couple soon joined him in the adjacent seats. The old woman wore a colorful shawl; the old man a wide-brimmed straw hat.

"Where are you headed?" the old man asked him.

"Outside of La Piedad," Wopper said. "How about you?"

"We are headed to Cuatla, Jalisco," the old man answered. "That's where we're from originally and where we now live for half the year." After a pause the old man continued unprompted, explaining that they had come back for medical appointments and to visit their children.

"How long are you planning to be in Mexico?" the old woman leaned over and asked him.

Wopper paused a long time before answering. "Forever," he said finally.

They looked at him oddly, until the old man said, "When you're young it's good to just see how things go, right?"

Wopper nodded and forced a smile.

The airplane started to move and then picked up speed, the roar of the engine growing louder and louder. He clenched the armrests and held his breath. He glanced at the old man and woman. They didn't seem the least bit worried. He felt embarrassed. He tried to relax a little and even turned to look out the window. After a second of confusion, he realized they were already in the air. He stared out into the darkness and saw a thin strip of lights in the distance. It took him a moment before he recognized the moving cars. He wondered if it was Highway 5. As they rose higher and higher, he noticed thousands of lights clustered closely together, surrounded by blackness. Woodland, he thought. And he wondered if that would be the last time he ever saw it.

I

Don Cirilo

SO ONE DAY I'M ABOUT TO ENJOY SOME TACOS THAT MY DAUGHTER JUST brought me from the house—still so hot that I have to let them cool off. I'm holding one taco in my hand, a napkin between my fingers and the tortilla—that's how hot it was—and I'm waiting for my opportunity to just bite into it—to bite into it and enjoy it because I deserved it, hard as I was working. Well, then the bus pulls up. I didn't hear the bus, being as my back was to it and I'm hard of hearing, but my burro, Don Jaspero, gave a start like he always does when the bus pulls up, and that's how I knew then and that's how I always know when the bus has come.

So I turn around, and instead of Doña Flor or Doña Eusebia or Don Pancho, or my compadre Don Gilberto, or even that old hag, Doña Hortensia, I see this chubby young man, a stranger yet not a stranger because I swear to God I'd seen his face around, but at the same time I also knew I'd never seen him before. He was carrying a huge suitcase. I say huge, and by the looks of it you could tell it was full and then some, and then some more after that.

He looked to be in his early twenties, though the truth is he looked younger. The baby fat was deceiving. I also remember the expression on his face. He was scared! That's how I knew—even before he told me, even before his suitcase burst open and revealed all the gifts from the North—that he was a foreigner. No one ever shows up scared to La Morada. No one. Now, La Piedad, that's a different story—plenty to inspire fear there, but in La Morada? Nothing, nothing, nothing, and even though a whole lot has happened since that day, things I couldn't ever have predicted then, I still maintain that La Morada is not a place you show up afraid. Well, he did. And being a friendly, helpful resident of La Morada, as we are all friendly and helpful, at least those of us who are left, I asked him, "Can I help you, young man?"

That was when the bus lurched forward—as if it needed to be in such a hurry!—before the kid was completely off the last step. He stumbled and the suitcase fell from his grasp, bursting open, and all the contents spilled out. I saw telephones and radios, alarm clocks, frying pans, several pairs of tennis shoes, several pairs of women's heels, blue jeans, baby clothes—the usual stuff northerners send to their families back home, as if what we most desired was a pair of white tennis shoes.

"So you're from the North?" I asked.

He scrambled about picking up the loose articles, dusting off the new pants and shoes and shoving them back into the suitcase, as if any minute a gang of thieves would emerge to steal his gifts. I told him not to worry, not to worry, that I'd get my daughter to help him cart his belongings to wherever he was headed. "Where are you headed, by the way?" I asked. "You look familiar? Do I know your family?"

Maybe I asked too many questions—I was only trying to be helpful—but after picking up and dusting off his treasured belongings, sweat pouring down his forehead, he just dragged his suitcase, which now wouldn't close, down the street. Who knows what direction he was heading in? I let him go. Why be helpful if he doesn't want help? I returned to my work, but first I ate my tacos, which were now almost cold.

I saw the young man again that evening. I was relaxing in my chair and watching the news, or what I could see of the news because some days it's fuzzy and some days it's not, and that day it was fuzzy, so mostly I was just listening. In the evening I can always tell when someone is at the door because his shadow appears first. The door faces west, and I always keep it open—no reason to shut it—so when someone approaches he blocks the sun. Well, that's what happened that evening when the young man came back. I knew it was him from his shadow. Don't ask me how, I just knew. I said to him before I actually saw his face, "So you're still lost, eh?" And he replied, "I was told this was my land. I was told you were living on my land."

At that moment I knew why his face was familiar: he was a Barraza if there ever was one. They all got the same round face and frog eyes, and why I didn't put two and two together, I don't know, but I sure did when he made that claim about my land being his. I told him, "Step in, son, and explain yourself."

I indicated that he should have a seat on the couch. He hesitated, but I insisted, and then I called my daughter to bring him some rice water. "Now, what are you talking about?" I asked him, even though I knew exactly what he was talking about.

"I was told that you took over my family's land," he said to me. "My dad's land. He showed me on a map the land that he purchased, and I've come down to grow stuff on it."

"Stuff?" I asked. "What kind of stuff?"

"Corn," he said.

Of course, I told him it was too late for corn planting, that I'd already planted, and he said, "So you admit this is my father's land? Well then, what are you doing on it?"

I just sat back on my couch and examined his pumpkin face and sleepy eyes. He was a Barraza, that's for sure. "It is your land," I told him as calm as can be, "so much as your father came down years ago and bought it. But he never came around, and no one grew anything on it, and times grew hard around here, for me, for my daughter, so I decided to ask Don Martín if I might grow some corn on his compadre's son's land, being as he wasn't using it."

Get this: the boy's face brightened and he said to me, "You know Don Martín? I was supposed to go to him first, but no one seemed to know who he was."

I told him, "That's because they don't want to get themselves wrapped up in any trouble." Then I added, "Of course I know Don Martín, or rather, I should say I knew him at one time. He's dead, God rest his soul."

"Dead?" he asked.

"Dead," I said again.

And he looked down at the floor as if unsure what to do now.

So I told him, "Look, do you want me to get off right this minute? Because I will. I'll leave tonight. I'll take out every single stock of corn, too, and then what would you be left with? Do you understand what I'm getting at? This may be your land, or your father's land, but its fruits are a result of my labor, and if you've come down here to push me off, well, then, that's what this world has come to, I accept that, but I can strike back as well—" And then I had to stop because my daughter entered the room with the rice water. She handed it to him and he thanked her, smiling. It was a kind smile, and then I remembered the scared look on his face when he got off the bus, and I realized maybe he hadn't come with bad intentions, and that maybe I was overreacting. So I composed myself and asked, "Why did you come?"

His reaction relieved me as much as it surprised me. He shrugged. All he did was shrug! Here he comes with a suitcase the size of my living room, all the way out to this little rancho, where everyone his age and every age except for my age and older has left, and when asked the purpose of his visit he can only shrug! So I asked, "How long do you intend to stay?" And all he did was shrug again and make a funny face that with his chubby cheeks and frog eyes made him look like he'd as soon croak as mumble an answer to my questions. Satisfied that I wouldn't have to vacate my land, or rather his land, but my crops, I returned to watching the television.

He didn't get up to leave.

Finally, he asked, "Is this my house, too?"

I was waiting for him to ask that. "No, I built the house myself, several years ago," I told him. Then I pointed outside. "Your house is the little one about fifty yards from here," I explained. "The tile floors have held up, but the walls are crumbling—need to be scraped and plastered again. The furniture is mine, I put there what I don't have use for here. You're free to use it. I'll have my daughter bring you some blankets and sheets."

And he said, "I have those already."

So I said, "Fine. Then I'll have her bring you dinner because the little shop is closed and you won't be able to go into La Piedad until morning."

He nodded and left my house, dragging the huge suitcase behind him. I returned to watching my program, and then the fuzziness, as it sometimes does, for whatever reason, disappeared, and because I was enjoying the picture so much I forgot to tell my daughter to bring him dinner. I only remembered two hours later as I was preparing for bed. I cursed my poor manners and immediately had her cook up a meal and bring it to him. When she returned soon after, I asked if the Barraza boy was okay. She told me that she left the food at the door because she'd heard him crying and didn't want to disturb him. "Crying?" I asked. "Sobbing," she said.

I didn't see him for over a week. Maybe he went to La Piedad, or maybe he never left his room. But every night I had my daughter check on him and bring him a meal, and every night she returned to tell me, "He's still crying." "Crying?" I'd ask. And she'd tell me, "Sobbing, poor thing." So one night I told her, "Well, don't feel sorry for him, he's come and he doesn't know why. If he's so unhappy he might as well return where he came from." And my daughter, bless her, said to me, "Maybe he had to escape bad memories."

I remember the day he first stepped out of his little home, pale as a ghost, his face about half the size it was when he arrived. He looked as though the only meal he'd been eating was the one my daughter brought him every evening. He was carrying a broom and making a show of sweeping leaves, performing woman's work while I was digging a fifty-meter ditch. I was glad when he went back inside, but the next day he came out again. It was ten o'clock and I'd already been working since sunrise. He watched me for a while, and I was aware of him, but I continued working, not paying him any mind. I worked and he stood watching. Finally the feeling of being watched bothered me, so I stopped and said, "What do you want, young man?" And he said, "Can I help?"

It was then that I should have realized he and my daughter had struck up more of a relationship than she'd let on. For one, my daughter was always trying to convince me to hire another

33

worker—"You'll wear yourself out, Father," she was always saying. "I worry about you, get some help"—and now, here was that worker. I could hear her telling him, "You can't keep eating free meals. You're going to have to work for your keep sometime soon." What's strange—or at least what I thought was strange at the time—was why this spoiled, lazy northerner, who had clearly not worked a day in life, decided to listen.

"Do you have a hat?" I asked him.

"I'll be all right," he told me.

So I put him to work, and an hour later he'd collapsed with exhaustion. I had to lug him onto my cart, and my burro Don Jaspero pulled him to his house, where I had to lug him off the cart and into bed. I called my daughter to bring some water. When he was asleep I chewed her out and told her she shouldn't have tried to get him to work. She told me that she never said anything to him about work and that he'd decided on his own. The next day he came out to help again. This time he didn't try to do too much nor move at too fast a pace. He also wore a hat that looked a hell of a lot like my old one, and I figured my daughter had given it to him. It made me feel strange, having another man wear my hat. But as a result he lasted until lunchtime, which was about three hours of work, being as he joined me at nine. Then he went to his house and slept for the rest of the afternoon. Each day he worked more and more. He may have been a softy before, but he hardened quickly. Every day he put in more work, and every day he came out earlier and earlier, until one morning I came out of my house, the sun not yet up, and there he was feeding Don Jaspero. I laughed. I don't know why, but I laughed. I shouldn't have laughed. I should have realized that a man doesn't go from fat and soft to thin and hard for no reason at all. He must have a reason, some force guiding him, and what that was, I should have been aware of. It wasn't to earn his meals, that's for sure. It wasn't to make life easier for this old man, that I was sure of too. I soon found out.

One Saturday I gave him the day off. I gave him some money and told him to take a trip to La Piedad. He'd been working too hard; he was too young to waste all his time slaving away. He had to enjoy life some. I told him where to go. I said, *This bar is good, This restaurant has decent food*, and *This clothing store sells quality merchandise*. I told him, "Enjoy yourself for the day, rest on Sunday, then on Monday we start the grain harvest." That night he returned. A taxi brought him. I heard him say something to the driver, and then I heard someone else's voice. A girl's voice. I heard them giggling, laughing, talking loudly—I was sure he was drunk. I sighed and said to myself, "Well, I told him to have fun. He was too young to be slaving away." That's what I said and I meant it, and I was about to fall back to sleep when I heard my daughter emit a small cry and rise from her bed. I asked her, "Mija, are you okay?" Without responding, without putting on a coat, she left the house in her nightgown, barefoot. I called after her, but she ignored me. I could hear shouts and cries. I jumped out of bed, put on a coat, and walked out to see what was happening.

There was my daughter—my sweet daughter who always makes my atole just right, who is always concerned about my well-being, bringing me rice water when I need it most—there she was yelling at this other girl, pushing her, telling her she'd better not ever show her trashy whore face in La Morada ever again. The other girl stumbled in her high heels and almost fell, and my daughter helped finish the fall with a shove. The girl's face hit the dirt. "Mija!" I called to her, my voice hoarse, "Calm down! What's going on! Leave that poor girl alone." But she ignored me. She ran that girl off our property. Then she came after me! "You! Encouraging him to go after whores," she yelled. "Giving him money to go to La Piedad, is that right? This is your fault! You brought filth into our lives!"

"I did no such thing," I told her. "I gave him the day off. Mija, what's come over you? I don't understand—tell me."

She didn't tell me a thing. She entered the house, then a moment later she left holding clothes and a blanket. Then she took off toward *his* little house! I crawled back into bed. I thought I heard more shouting, so I was about to get up and go settle things, but then there was silence, and I decided that whatever was going on could be figured out in the morning when there was more clarity. I for sure had no clarity at that moment. I kept waiting for my daughter to return home, but she never did. She spent the night at the Barraza boy's place, and every night after that she spent there as well. These are the things fathers must face at one time or another.

II

Lucio Barraza

My morning routine goes like this: I feed the chickens and the family dogs, Porfas, Chispas, and Dany, and then I take our horse, Don Paisano, who may look like a skeleton but he's fourteen years old after all, down to the reservoir for exercise and water. When I return home, my mother usually has breakfast waiting for me. Either huevos rancheros, chilaquiles, tamales with atole, or, if she's tired, corn-flakes and a banana. The rest of my day is free. Usually I'll mess about with my four-wheeler or read magazines or watch television with my father. Sometimes I'll play pinball at the corner store with two brothers, Marcos and Evelio, who've been left in their grand-parents' care. They're always asking me—as though my answer might change—how come I don't go north like their parents? And I tell them, "Why, when I'm used to living here?" And that's the honest truth. Oh, and two weekends a month I help a friend at a car wash in La Piedad. Why do I mention all this? Well, because people make it out like all I do is hang out at Doña Berenice's grocery store. Which isn't true. Just sometimes.

But this one time I did happen to be hanging out at Doña Berenice's store. I was just minding my own business when Doña Berenice tells me, "You might as well tell me, Fatty, why you're looking so glum and sighing every ten seconds!"

"I don't know what you're talking about," I said. "And don't call me Fatty." She rolled her eyes, and then immediately, as if she had a separate set of eyes solely for this purpose, she slammed her pink fly swatter onto the counter. "Aha!" she said. Then she flicked the dead fly to the floor.

Ten minutes must have passed, Doña Berenice swatting flies unfortunate enough to land on her counter and slapping mosquitoes unfortunate enough to land on her fat arms, and me staring at my four-wheeler and thinking it would look good with a new black leather seat, when she cried out, "I know what's troubling you!"

"Why are you yelling? It's just me here," I told her.

"It's my store and I'll talk how I want to," she said, but she lowered her voice anyway. "It's the kid from the North who has got you down, isn't that the truth? Well, I tell you, just forget it and count yourself among the lucky."

"I don't know what or who you're talking about," I said.

But she continued. She wouldn't let it go. "Of course you know what I'm talking about. You act as if it's possible not to notice. I see him every time I travel into La Piedad. There he is by Don Cirilo's side, like a hardworking son-in-law sent from the heavens."

I stood up at that point and turned in her direction. "You're really pushing it now, Doña Berenice," I said. "Do you want to see me in the hospital again, or what?"

She started laughing, her fat chest shaking along with her fat cheeks. "Aye, Fatty! I'm just teasing," she said. "I thought you were all good and recovered by now."

"Yeah, well, just forget it," I said.

Another ten minutes went by and I thought she had let it be, preoccupied as she was with swatting the flies and mosquitoes. I stared at my four-wheeler and realized that before a new seat it probably could use some new grips for the handles. I was thinking how much they would run me, when Doña Berenice says out of the blue, as if she were merely letting out a deep sigh, "Aye, Fatty, I thought you were all good and recovered by now. . . . I really did."

That's when I got up and left. I didn't even say, "Good afternoon," or, "See you later." I just took off, and I swore to myself I'd never go back to her shop again. Too bad her store is the only one on my street.

Later, back at home, lying in bed, I could hear my parents talking. They were whispering to prevent me from hearing, but one is deafer than the other, so whenever they whisper it's the same as if they were yelling.

"Does he know yet?" my mom whispered.

"Of course he knows!" my dad whispered back. "The whole rancho knows! They're living together now!"

"My poor boy!" my mom said, her voice unable to remain a whisper. "First Don Martín, then our Lucio! What will we do if he is unwell again?" she asked, now back to a loud whisper.

I couldn't hear exactly what my father said, but I'm sure it had something to do with sending me to live with my aunt in Penjamo, which was always his answer. He thought threatening me helped calm my nerves.

"Oh, my poor boy!" my mom said again.

Finally, unable to take it anymore, I turned on the television and watched an old cowboy movie, but then I changed it because all the actresses looked like Don Cirilo's daughter and the main actor reminded me of the kid from the North, even though he looked nothing like the kid from the North. They were both mysterious figures who had arrived out of nowhere.

The first story I heard about the kid was that he was the grandson of one of Don Martín's compadres. The father made it rich in the United States, but before handing his son a penny of his inheritance, he sent him down here in order to learn what it's like to grow up with nothing except his own labor to make it in this cruel world. To me it sounded like a soap opera I used to watch with my parents. I asked my mom if she remembered the soap opera, and she said she did, or at least that it sounded familiar, but we spent all evening trying to remember the name, and we still don't know it.

CHAPTER THREE

I

FOR WEEKS SHE WAS MERELY THE DAUGHTER OF THE MAN SQUATTING ON his father's land. He hardly thought about her. She brought him dinner and left, and that was it. His misery was such that all he could think about was his own misery. How he missed home, how he missed his parents and Lara, how he would do anything to be back in Woodland, to have his life as it once was. He wanted to be seated on the pink lumpy sofa, his father to his right, clicker in hand, watching television. He wanted to hear his mother in the other room, talking on the phone with a comadre, opening and closing cupboards and drawers. He wanted to visit Lara, even just to see her front door as he rounded the corner of her street. In his most desperate moments, he swore all he wanted was to see his front lawn, the driveway full of oil slicks, and the broken picket fence. Day after day he spent pacing the light blue tile floor of his one-bedroom shack as if it were a jail cell, a cell of crumbling plaster walls, nothing hanging, not even a wooden cross or an old calendar.

Sometimes he looked out his front door and saw the dirt path leading through the cornfields. In the distance, beyond the reservoir, he could see patchwork plots of blue-green agave, where occasionally he would see a lone donkey or an old man with a long white beard riding a horse. Out his bedroom window caked with dust, he could see the rest of La Morada: more brick structures like

39

his own, but the façades at least were plastered and painted bright colors—yellows, pinks, and greens, seemingly the brighter the better. The largest ones were empty, boarded up, some northerner's dream home rarely visited. He hardly ever saw people walking around. Occasionally he heard the bus's diesel growl, or dogs barking, or the passing sound of norteño and banda music from a car stereo. Nothing that he heard or saw made him feel like leaving the safety of his shack. Nothing beckoned him. He wasn't curious to explore La Morada, and even less so La Piedad, which seemed to him when he passed through as just a loud, polluted mess of traffic, taco stands, and tarp-covered street vendors. His father had told him that there were beautiful churches and plazas, but he didn't care to find them. He didn't have the energy.

The suitcase remained unopened, the gifts undelivered. On his first day in La Morada he'd gone to every place on his father's makeshift map, but everyone his father had instructed him to visit was gone or, like Don Martín, dead. He knew nobody except the old man and his daughter, and he didn't want to know anybody else. At night the same thoughts consumed him as during the day, but everything seemed even bleaker because making it through one day only meant that another day lay ahead. Plus, it was colder. The days were warm, even hot, but as soon as the sun disappeared the temperature dropped forty degrees. He wore five layers of clothes—a t-shirt, two sweatshirts, a hoodie, and a jacket—rather than ask for another blanket. He allowed his misery to dominate him, to render him useless. He imagined himself crossing the border, living illegally in Woodland for the rest of his life, and the idea brought him solace, and he told himself in his darkest moments that if it got any darker he would go home, whatever the consequences. It felt as if he spent his days crying or trying to cry, or, even more pitiful, thinking about how he felt like crying. He tried to remember the last time he had cried, after a locker room fight in the seventh grade. Those were a child's blubbering sobs. In his embarrassment he had decided that he was too old for it. But now it was as though he couldn't stop.

He didn't even care that the girl saw his bloodshot eyes and damp cheeks whenever she brought his meals. He made no effort to compose himself. So what if she thought he was a baby? Did her opinion of him have any bearing on anything? Did it change his situation? He couldn't even find it within himself to be grateful for the food or the plastic jug of water that was brought to him every evening, brought to him without question, as if part of some unspoken arrangement he and the old man had made in exchange for use of the land. He just waited for her to leave and then hungrily devoured whatever she left for him on a wobbly metal table that stood between the bedroom and kitchen area.

Then one evening she set the tray of food down and stayed. She didn't even talk to him; she just placed her back against the wall and in one motion slid down so that she sat with her legs crossed. Soon after she rested her chin in her hands and stared at the tile floor covered in dust. She was dark-skinned, her jet black hair pulled back in a bun, and she had small, almond-shaped black eyes. She wore a red-checkered apron over a flowery cotton dress that was much too big for her. He rose from the floor and sat at the table to eat the beans, rice, and carne asada tacos, watching her out of the corners of his eyes. He was conscious, finally, of her as a presence, as someone to acknowledge and communicate with. He made an effort to eat more slowly, more quietly. He wiped his face with the back of his hand. His mouth was full of food, his cheeks felt hot, and his eyes burned: he felt like a toddler recovering from a tantrum, the cause of which had already been forgotten. He tried pressing down his bristly hair, which had started to grow out; for the first time in years he didn't have a cleanly faded buzz cut. He tried to remember the last time he had showered. Lighting the gas heater always seemed too great an effort. He wondered if she could smell him. Maybe his whole place stunk. He wanted to say something, but he didn't know what, and she made no attempt to talk to him. She seemed merely to want to be in the room. When he finished eating and she took his tray of dishes and left, he wished he had at least asked her name.

The following evening she returned and followed the same routine. She set the tray down, picked a wall to lean against, slid down to a cross-legged position, and then rested her chin in her hands. They didn't speak, and when he finished eating she took his tray and left. He thought their silence strange, yet all he could manage himself was an awkward nod of his head, which he intended as thanks.

Several days passed like this before she asked him, casually, as if they'd been talking all along, "Do you like my cooking?"

"Yeah," he said, his mouth full of food. He set down his fork and finished chewing. "Yeah, I do."

She continued. "Which of my meals that I make is your favorite?"

He thought for a moment. All this time he had scarfed his meals without caring what the food tasted like. "I like all of them," he said.

"Really?" she said.

He nodded enthusiastically and then asked, "Do you know to make menudo?"

Her eyes brightened. "Of course!" she said. "I can make that tomorrow."

And as simple as that they began to talk. Soon she brought over more blankets, a few decorative pillows, and pictures from old calendars of saints and country landscapes for him to hang on the wall. She placed a glass vase with a bouquet of purple plastic flowers on the kitchen table.

He found out that she was twenty-nine years old, which surprised him. She looked barely eighteen. He thought of all the times she saw him crying. "She must think I'm a little kid," he said to himself. He wondered why she wasn't married, but he didn't dare ask.

II

Wopper couldn't explain why one day he decided to work, or at least attempt to. For almost a week, bored, not knowing what to do with himself, he had tried to clean his place, but all he found was an old broom made of twigs, which did a better job of leaving debris than collecting the abundant amounts of dirt that seemed to emerge from the walls themselves. Dirt was everywhere—on the sink counter, the wobbly table, the dresser whose drawers barely functioned; even his canary yellow bedspread and paper-thin sheets felt gritty no matter how often he shook them out. He became so frustrated with the twig broom that he threw it across the room. Then he grabbed it again and tried to break the handle in two, but he only succeeded in hurting his thigh. "Why would they make such a piece of shit?" he cried out. He decided to tear up one of his t-shirts and make rags. With a bucket of water he went around the room and tried wiping everything clean, but this only left muddy streaks. By the next day more dust had accumulated, and he started again, this time trying to gather as much dust as possible by first wiping the floor with a dry rag.

She found him busy at his task: on his knees, rag in hand, a bucket full of dirty brown water beside him. She started to laugh. He looked up, expecting to see someone else. He hadn't heard her laugh before; he had just seen a smile at times, and even then it just barely crept across her mouth. He didn't expect her laugh to be so playful.

"What?" he asked.

"What would you men do without us women!" she exclaimed. Then she left and returned several minutes later with a standard broom, a mop, and a bucket full of water and bleach.

"Why didn't you just ask me?" she said upon entering his place.

He was still sitting on the floor. He tossed his dirty wet rag into the bucket, feeling stupid. She grabbed the broom she'd brought with her and said, "It'll be hard to sweep with you in the way."

He looked at the twig broom lying where he last tossed it. He pointed to it and asked, "So then what's that one for?"

"Did you try and use that?" she asked, the playful expression still on her face.

He shrugged.

She laughed and shook her head. "That one is for outside. If you want to clear the leaves from the path you can. Try it." Then she added, "Go ahead, so that you're not in my way."

He got the hint. He rose from the floor, picked up the twig broom, and went outside, leaving her alone in his house. There wasn't much to sweep, but he kept sweeping anyway, without purpose, just to have something to do. Wopper looked around at his surroundings.

He realized he hadn't been outside in weeks. In the distance he noticed Don Cirilo's thin wiry frame digging a ditch. He watched him for several minutes, noting to himself that the old man didn't work fast, but rather kept a slow, steady motion, never once stopping to rest. Wopper looked at all the plots of corn growing, all the way to the edge of the reservoir, extending to the road that passed through town. It dawned on him that Don Cirilo had planted it all himself. Everything he saw growing was a result of one man's labor. For some reason, this impressed him greatly, if only because he hadn't thought about it before. Don Cirilo finally stopped digging and looked in his direction, his face lost in the shadow of his cowboy hat. They stared at each other for a moment, or at least Wopper assumed the old man was also staring, and Wopper wondered if Don Cirilo had seen his daughter enter his place carrying cleaning supplies. He now felt guilty for letting her. He decided he would pay the girl from the money his parents had given him.

After a while he heard her call out, "I'm done, you can come back inside!"

He opened the screen door and peered in. He could hardly believe the transformation. He knew it had been dirty, but he hadn't realized the squalor he'd endured until then. She looked at him, smiling proudly.

"Thank you," he said, a little embarrassed.

Her smile remained as she dumped the bucket of dirty water in the basin. He rushed over to his suitcase, felt for his wad of money, and pulled out a twenty-dollar bill. He held it out for her. "Here," he said. She set the bucket down, the smile now gone. He was confused. "If you want I can exchange it for pesos," he said, extending the bill farther, as though she didn't understand he was trying to give it to her.

"No, I don't want that," she said, then she quickly gathered the broom, the mop, and the empty bucket and headed toward the door, opening the screen with her foot. He called after her, "I'm sorry, it's just that—" but she was already halfway down the path toward her house.

When she brought dinner that evening, instead of staying to talk as she had done the last several weeks, she set the tray down and headed toward the door. "Wait!" he cried, somewhat exasperated. He didn't understand what he'd done that was so wrong. She stopped at the door, her back toward him, waiting for him to say something else.

"I'm sorry," he said, "I just don't feel right that you do all this work for nothing."

"I don't do it for nothing," she said, her voice unwavering. "I do it for you. So that you're happy." Then she opened the screen door and walked outside before he could respond.

Later that night he couldn't sleep. He kept replaying the events of the day over and over in his mind. He thought about her laughter and the playful expression on her face. He thought of what she had said, that she cooked and cleaned for him so that he would be happy. He wondered if she had developed feelings for him. Is that what she meant? How was that possible? Somehow it was easier to believe that she merely pitied him. Up until that moment, he hadn't thought about his feelings for her. He just knew that he liked having her around. Somehow she made his existence in La Morada bearable. Nevertheless, he couldn't expect this arrangement to continue. So what if it was his father's land? If he couldn't pay her, he at least had to do something. Maybe he would insist on helping her clean. Maybe he would help the old man out for a few hours each day. That would at least cover his meals.

He had a wristwatch with an alarm. Weeks before, he'd taken it off and placed it in his suitcase. The hours passed so slowly and so miserably that he finally had to force himself to stop checking it. He found the watch in one of the pockets and set the alarm for seven o'clock. He'd rarely used the alarm. In fact, he couldn't remember if he ever had. Usually, his mom or dad would knock on his bedroom door until he called out, "I'm up!" He experienced a sinking feeling in his stomach when he recalled that his court date was the last time he needed to wake up early. Before shutting off the light, he checked and rechecked the alarm function, hoping that it would work. He fell asleep thinking about the date, which he'd glanced at when setting the alarm. January 16. He left Woodland at the end of November. He had already been here a month and a half.

When the beeper went off the next morning, he felt as if he'd just fallen asleep. It was pitch dark. He felt for his watch on the plastic chair that served as his night table. He pressed the buttons until the beeping stopped. He told himself, *Let me keep my eyes closed for one more minute, just one more minute.* When he awoke again it was light outside. He jumped up from bed, panicked. Then he realized he had no reason to be. The old man didn't expect him anyway. He almost convinced himself to wait until the next morning, but when he walked to the doorway and peered out the screen, he saw Don Cirilo's daughter hanging sheets on the clothesline. He pushed open the screen door and immediately she looked up as if she'd been waiting for it to open. She saw him and waved, and like her laughter the day before, the joyfulness of the wave surprised him. He felt a rush of relief come over him. He awkwardly waved back and said to himself, *Come on, Wopper, what else are you gonna do?*

Her name was actually Mija, my daughter. Wopper thought for a while that she must've told him her name and he'd forgotten it, and after enough time passed, he didn't want to admit it. He kept hoping Don Cirilo would say it in a conversation, but he only referred to her as "my daughter" or as "the daughter." Surprisingly, not knowing her name wasn't much of an issue. It was usually just the two of them in the room and there was never a need for him to call out to her. Mostly he just said, "Hey," and she responded. In his mind, he thought of her as "Don Cirilo's daughter." At first, when she asked him his name (and when he forgot to ask her hers, or he did and didn't pay attention to her answer), he told her, "Wopper." But she made such a mess of the pronunciation—she actually kind of gagged on the W—that he took pity on her and told her his real name. She seemed relieved.

After weeks of daily interactions, Wopper came up with an idea to learn her name without letting on that he didn't know it. She was at the sink scrubbing his clothes and he was at the kitchen table drinking lemon water that she had made that morning. He told her how he'd been given the nickname Wopper. It was one of the few stories either of them had shared about their pasts. Then he asked

46

if there was a story behind her name. She shrugged and said, "No, I'm just the daughter of Don Cirilo."

"No, I mean, how did your parents choose your name? Did they ever tell you?"

"My mom died when I was a baby, and what would my dad tell me about my name? It's obvious that I'm his daughter."

Wopper was still confused. Also, he was surprised that he hadn't known about her mother dying. He hadn't even thought to ask what had happened to her. He imagined Don Cirilo taking care of a baby girl all by himself. It was then that it occurred to him that maybe her name was actually Mija.

The next day he tested it. "Mija," he said. It felt strange to say it. She was older than him, after all. But she turned around from the sink and smiled, gently swinging her head to remove the hair from her face and shoulders. He liked when she did this.

"Mija," he said again.

"Yes? What do you want?" she asked.

"Mija," he repeated.

Then she said, "I like it when you say my name. I have no idea why you're always saying, 'Jey,' 'Jey, you,' 'Jey, I'm talking to you,' 'Jey.'"

III

Everything changed the night Wopper returned with the girl he met in La Piedad. It was the end of March and he had worked every day for two months straight. He had made it through the corn harvest, and despite the difficulty of the first week—blisters on his hands and feet, symptoms of heat stroke, his back so sore he could hardly rise from bed—the work became, if not exactly easy, then automatic. When Don Cirilo told him to enjoy himself for the night, he expected to have just a few beers and then come home. But the first beer tasted so good that a few beers turned into six, not to mention three tequila shots purchased by men he didn't know but who seemed to know him. He assumed they mistook him for someone else. He couldn't remember how he met the girl, except that in his drunkenness he felt as though she had come on to him. He vaguely recalled that he kept trying to speak to her in English and all she would do was giggle in response. Somehow they ended up in a taxi heading back to La Morada. What he remembered most clearly was the mayhem that ensued, the swiftness of the confrontation: Mija appeared on their path, insults were screamed, and suddenly the girl was on the ground. All he could do was watch, stunned, as the girl disappeared, stumbling down the dirt path toward the main road.

Don Cirilo emerged from his house in his pajamas and cowboy hat and cried out, "What's going on?" Mija walked straight toward her father with such aggression that the old man actually flinched. She shook her finger inches from his face and began scolding him in a deep throaty voice that seemed incongruous with her petite frame. Wopper, feeling dizzy and unable to hear what was said, turned to walk away, but she yelled after him, "Where are you going? I want to talk to you!" He stopped, turning only to watch as she marched to confront him. She grabbed his arm and yanked him toward his house.

She began yelling at him: "Do you not think I have feelings? Do you think you can just do whatever you please and treat me like I'm nothing? What have I ever done to deserve this? I've been nothing but good to you!"

He couldn't respond.

"What am I, your maid? Do I clean your bedroom just so you can screw some girl in comfort?"

They arrived at his door and she ordered him to go inside. Then she abruptly turned and headed back to her house. He wondered if that was it. Was she coming back? He entered his bedroom and stood in front of his bed, not knowing what to do. He felt too drunk to make sense of anything. He just wanted to sleep. But before he could collapse onto the bed fully clothed, he heard the screen door squeak open, and Mija entered carrying clothes and a frilly white blanket. She looked around the room, the place she had cleaned and mopped and even started to decorate, and threw down her belongings, as if finally and definitively laying claim to it.

She stared at Wopper, her eyes wide, her jaw jutting forward so that her teeth were bared, and she spoke to him in a low, hoarse tone, almost a whisper. He had no idea what she said. He couldn't hear. Or he heard, but he was too alarmed by the wide-eyed, teeth-baring expression to register what was said. Later she told him, "Oh, it was just a woman being jealous." But he didn't believe her. It was more than that. He'd seen Lara jealous before, so mad at him for staring at another girl that she could've ripped his eyes out. That was nothing in comparison. Mija would never be as angry with him again, as least not in the same way, but he never forgot the expression on her face, the tone of her voice, or her eyes, all belonging to a different person, some creature within.

But then she changed. Her face softened and her expression became sad more than anything else. Remorseful maybe. And she walked toward him slowly. He was too shocked to move. But she reached for him and touched his cheek first, gently. Then she ran the back of her hand lightly against his neck, and his alarm began to subside. Then she pulled him close and directed his arms around her waist. She kissed his neck. She whispered, "You're with me now, yes?"

He nodded numbly, his mouth and throat too parched to speak.

"Yes?" she said again.

"Yes," he managed to say.

She took off his shirt. "You won't go out with anyone else again?" she said.

He shook his head, realizing what was happening, or what was about to happen. He didn't feel drunk anymore, but his legs felt weak, and his heart was pounding.

She undid his belt and fumbled with his zipper, unable to locate the top. She found it, and then she pulled down his pants and underwear so that he stood in the middle of the room with his pants and underwear around his ankles. She stepped away and looked at him, as if all this time she'd been curious to see how he looked naked. Or maybe she was curious to see how he looked after having lost so much weight, the long days in the fields transforming his body so that he barely recognized it himself. She then removed her nightgown and then her underwear. Wopper now stared at her naked body, and she kept a distance as if to let him. He didn't realize until then how much larger he was than her. He could see her ribs and hipbones, her small breasts. She turned around and walked toward the bed. His eyes followed her, and he felt his erection beginning to grow. Then she did something that surprised him. He expected her to climb underneath the covers, conceal herself in some way, but she seemed unabashed of her nakedness. She lay down on her stomach, her head against the pillow, her face turned toward him. They stared at each other for what felt like minutes. Finally, she said, "What are you waiting for?" He tried not to fall as he removed his shoes and stepped out of his pants.

They climaxed together, something Wopper had never even remotely experienced. Her orgasm was long and intense, and she kept saying, *Roberto, Roberto, Roberto,* repeating it over and over and over, each syllable emerging from deep within and reverberating throughout her body, until finally the sound of his name, the feeling of her on top of him, the lingering effects of the alcohol—all of it overwhelmed him and he just couldn't take it anymore. He burst into tears. He couldn't believe it. He tried to hide it, turning his face into the pillow, but he didn't do such a good job, because he wasn't so much crying as sobbing. Her cheek rested on his chest as she caught her breath and lifted her head to see what was wrong.

"Are you okay?" she asked, placing her hand on his cheek and turning his face toward her so that she looked directly into his eyes.

"I don't know what happened," he told her. He tried to stop himself. "I'm not always like this. I'm sorry. It's just that—"

She quietly shushed him. "You don't have to be sorry about anything," she said, gently caressing his face. "You don't have to explain yourself either."

Later that night, unable to sleep, replaying everything over in his mind, he contemplated only briefly the evening's strange turn of events. What he thought about most were Mija's cries and moans. At first he worried that he was hurting her and that she was crying out in pain rather than pleasure. He almost stopped to ask if she was okay, but then she started to scream his name, and he could think of nothing else. He heard *Roberto* as if for the first time. Something about the way she said it transformed his name into the saddest, most painful, most heart-wrenching word he could imagine. He stared into the darkness, his hands collapsed across his bare chest. He felt satisfied and whole in a way that he hadn't ever experienced before. He felt then and there that he never wanted to be called Wopper again. He was Roberto and that was it. For him, the stupid nickname just disappeared.

He had a generous thought. He wished that everyone he knew could hear their own name as she had said his. It seemed unfair to him that he should be the only one baptized like this. He wanted Raul to hear his name, and Rudy, and Manny, and Pete, and Frankie, and Ruben, and Oscar, and Arty—all the kids he had grown up with—he wanted each to hear his name as if it were the saddest, most painful, most heart-wrenching word he could imagine. Then suddenly his generosity turned on him as he realized that in order for them to hear their names like that, they'd have to be having sex with Mija, and the thought of her with anyone else enraged him, and he felt the rage so deep in his gut that he actually clenched his fists. He had never been jealous before, at least not like this. But then he relaxed. He recognized that he had created this jealousy out of nowhere. Wasn't she there in his arms? Hadn't she come to him? And plus, there was no one in La Morada except for old men. It was all the assurance he needed. He held her in his arms and kissed her forehead. He kissed her lips, waking her.

IV

He tried not to think about Lara. Every now and then an image of her pregnant would enter into his mind out of the blue—as he worked, as he filled a glass of water, as he brushed his teeth—and suddenly he would see her, sitting on her parents' floral-patterned couch, her hand gently cupped around a perfectly round stomach. And immediately he would push the image from his head. He would find a way to distract himself, because imagining made him wonder, and wondering only made him want to know for certain. How was she doing? When was the baby due? Was it a boy or a girl? Did she still think about him? Did she miss him? He didn't want to ask himself these questions. These questions tore him up inside. They made him feel guilty and helpless. *Things are good now*, he would say to himself. *I'm happier. I'm the one who had to face this, and I did, and it sucked, and I'm still facing it, but at least now it's better. I'm getting by. That's what matters. Plus, she broke up with me.* And he would always remind himself of this last part. He would repeat it until he almost convinced himself that he had asked her to come and she had rejected him. Her rejection meant that he was free to do whatever necessary to move on.

But sometimes at the corner market on an errand to pick up milk or soda or eggs, he would stare at the international phone cards wrapped in plastic and emblazoned with stars and stripes, and he would think about calling Lara. He would imagine the conversation, imagine all that they had to tell one another, and he would talk himself out of it. He called home once, only able to half-listen to his father's ramblings and his mother's scolding. Afterward, he plunged into a depression that he didn't emerge from for several days. He was reminded of the misery he felt the first few weeks in La Morada, when he was unable and unwilling to accept a life that was irrevocably changed. He never wanted to feel that way again. He would do anything for it not to return. And if that meant pushing his family and Lara and the baby from his mind, then that's what he needed to do. It wasn't easy, but it was easier than he expected. He worked himself to exhaustion. If he wasn't working he never strayed far from Mija's side. With time, his life in Woodland grew further and further away. There were days when it felt as if he had been gone for years.

CHAPTER FOUR

Jorge Barraza

I MISSED MY SON TERRIBLY, I REALLY DID. WHAT FATHER WOULDN'T? EVERY day I woke up and walked to the kitchen to make coffee and passed the door to the room where he used to sleep. I imagined opening it and finding him there, sleeping, snoring loud like he used to do. He would sleep until ten, eleven, the coffee long gone, breakfast made, everybody out of the house, but he'd still be there, the shades closed. When he left, the room stayed empty. A guest room, my wife said. If only we had guests!

Wopper never wrote. I wished he would. I checked the mail, always hoping to find a letter. I even asked my wife about buying a computer and signing up for the e-mail, but she only laughed and told me I wouldn't in a million years be able to figure it out. And plus, she said, Wopper wouldn't have a computer out there in the middle of nowhere. "You never know," I said. "Oh, I know," she responded. So no computer. He called once. My wife did most of the talking, and at that, all she did was scold him and tell him what not to do. Then she handed me the phone and I was too excited at hearing his voice to remember all that we talked about. He did tell me that he and this man Don Cirilo had been working our land. I didn't remember a Don Cirilo, but I was happy to know he was working. I held that image in my mind for months afterward. I imagined him cultivating the land I'd labored and saved so many years to buy. How I wished I had the strength and youth to go join him, so we could work that land together!

I left my own mother and father at the age of twenty-four. I came to the United States to join my cousin Beto, who lived in a place called *Burlan*. That's how Woodland sounded to me: *Burlan, Gurlan*. The cousin had come home during the annual fiestas, and he wore the finest clothes and bought everyone drinks and placed the highest bets on the roosters. But it wasn't the promise of money that made me want to follow him. I just wanted out of La Morada. I wanted an adventure! Something different from my life in that little rancho where all there was to do was farm. So guess what I did? I left a life of farming to find a thousand miles away another life of farming, picking tomatoes and fruit. There was even less to do in Woodland back then, so the workers, all of us lonely and missing home, missing the ranchos that at one time we thought we'd never think about again after our success in the North, would sit around outside of our apartments and drink and talk about what kind of houses we'd build back home, and the horses we'd buy, and the land we'd own. I always told my friends, "I want property overlooking the reservoir," and they all told me how stupid that was because that was the first land to flood. But I didn't care, because I never imagined working it. I just wanted to have it as my own and to look out on the water as if it were my own private lake. It took me fifteen years to buy that land and I had only seen it once. So it gave me pleasure to imagine my son working it, waking in the morning to the sun rising over the water. Was he living the life I wanted for myself?

When I left my parents in La Morada I never wrote, because my parents couldn't read. And I didn't call, either, because they didn't have a phone. Every couple years I'd return home and surprise them, but I would never stay for long. As much as I missed my rancho, I saw quickly that it wasn't the place of my imagination, where I went to at night when I dreamt of home. It was small. Too small! And I would feel claustrophobic as soon as I arrived and already begin preparations to return to the North, until finally I realized that it was too much effort to make the trip. So for years I didn't return. Not until my father died and I traveled home for his funeral. My mother was in bad shape, and I didn't feel right leaving her, so I stayed for a while. I missed an entire season and went through all my savings. But it was during this time that I met my wife. I danced with Raquel at a quinceañera, and afterward I asked her to walk with me, and the rest becomes a blur except that we became boyfriend and girlfriend, and soon I asked her to marry me, and she said yes, and I was happy in a way that I'd never been before or since.

For a long time Raquel stayed in La Morada and I left for the North to work. I'd return at the end of the harvest and stay for a few months, though the trips grew shorter and shorter, because even with a wife and a family—first Isabel then Rosa then Roberto—La Morada was too small. I'd feel the claustrophobia and need to move on. I had become a man in the North, and returning to La Morada made me into a boy again, and this was too difficult to square in my mind. Then I got my papers and decided to send for my wife and children. Raquel had complained and begged enough over the years, but I hadn't wanted to bring her, I don't know why, maybe because I knew that once I did I would lose my independence and cease to be the man I'd become, returning again to the boy from La Morada, only now in Woodland. This is what I feared, and in a way this is exactly what happened. Suddenly Woodland was no longer mine. It became small, too. As small as La Morada, even though it was many times larger. I felt the claustrophobia all over again, but this time I had nowhere to return to. I had nowhere to escape. My family was here, and my children soon went to school, so I had to support them, and not just with the couple hundred that I used to send to La Morada, but with everything I earned. Everything! Well, everything except for the little I set aside each month, hidden from my wife: the money that I was saving to buy property.

So maybe in my head I imagined that once I bought the land overlooking the reservoir, I would return and La Morada would be my sanctuary. But the years passed and the only escape I had was in my daydreams, when I went to La Morada and imagined it early in the morning, the sun rising over my lake, my own land underneath my feet. But maybe it wasn't all in vain, because now I was able to live through my son. And wouldn't it be strange if Wopper went there to become a man, just as I had to come here? But if that's true, I often thought, then he should never come back. He should never return to Woodland, because then he would have to live with the boy he left behind, just as I used to when I returned to La Morada. And believe me, it's too difficult to square in your mind. It's difficult enough to be in one place, always dreaming of another. You can live with your past selves as long as they remain there, but to be both at the same time, to be both yourself and your past selves . . . No, it is too difficult.

Several months after Wopper left, an old compadre came to the house and told me something very troubling that I thought about much afterward. He had visited La Morada the year before and had news about everyone I remembered. There was not much news to report. Everyone had been old when I last saw them, and now they were even older. But my friend was a talker and managed to extend the information about each person for a good long time, so long that I started to become impatient because I wanted to hear more about the people I knew best rather than just some neighbor I hadn't thought about in thirty years. I asked about my aunts and a few cousins, but he could only tell me that they'd moved to La Piedad or to the North. This was very possible as it had been a long time since I'd had contact with anyone. I asked about a few of the people whose names I'd given to Wopper. Again, my compadre told me either they'd moved to La Piedad or the North. "Don't you remember, compadre," he said, "La Morada is disappearing."

Finally, I asked about Don Martín. Surely the unofficial mayor of La Morada was still around handling business. He would never abandon his rancho! But as soon as I said my father's compadre's name, my friend's face darkened and became serious, which was rare for him. He was always happy; nothing ever fazed him. "What happened?" I asked. And he said to me, "You really haven't heard, compadre?" "Heard what?" I asked. "What is it that could've happened?"

"He's dead," my compadre said.

The words jolted me, sending a tingle through my spine. Not because I found it hard to believe—Don Martín was old, and he had already outlived most of his compadres, including my father—but it was the way my friend said it, as if it were a curse merely to repeat the news. I asked my compadre how the old man had died, but my compadre just shook his head and told me that he didn't know. He had asked around, but everyone seemed to avoid his questions or found ways of ignoring him altogether. I asked my compadre what reason people could have to ignore such a simple and basic question. But he couldn't exactly say. All he could gather was that Don Martín didn't die from old age. That it was something painful and drawn out, and that it had left a scar on all those who remained in La Morada.

The news truly shocked me. "What could it be?" I kept saying. "Nothing bad happens in our ranchito!" But then I stopped, remembering the death of my uncle years ago. He'd been stabbed over a property dispute. But nothing like that had happened in recent memory. I continued to imagine different possibilities, still in disbelief, when my compadre began talking. He told me about his last exchange with Don Martín.

He had met him on the street, and Don Martín invited him for a shot of homemade ponche. My compadre walked with him the couple of blocks to his home, and he was surprised to find the place in impeccable condition, as ordered and spotless as Don Martín's wife must have kept it before she died. He also admired the old man's good shape. Tall and broad shouldered, he looked as ready to take down a stallion as he'd been famed for years ago. Don Martín found glasses, and he and my compadre went outside to the patio, which Don Martín had built the year before, complete with a running fountain and plenty of potted plants. "My projects," he told my compadre. "Those are what keep me young. Once I run out of things to do and just sit in my house watching television, that's when I'd rather die." My compadre asked Don Martín about the old days, and once he got the old man going it was hard to stop him. He held the entire history of the rancho in his head. He'd seen everything, knew everyone. My compadre said that he felt then, listening to the stories, that when Don Martín died, the entirety of La Morada's past would die with him. But he wasn't worried about it then; the old man seemed to have years and years ahead of him.

They were silent for a moment, and my compadre was about to leave when Don Martín said to him, "I'm happy, young man, you know that?" And my compadre told him that he could see this, and he only wished it for himself one day. Don Martín nodded his head and said that he wished it for everyone. Happiness like his inspired generosity. He wanted to share it with my compadre. "Let me explain," he said. He had worked all his life, worked and worried and tried to bend the forces of his life so that he always felt exhausted. But finally he had reached a point where he no longer felt like he had to bend or force anything. He woke up every morning like a child whose only wish was to go out and play. "I've achieved all that I set out to," he told my compadre. "I have raised my children right, I provided for my family, my friends and neighbors respect me, I have stories to tell. . . . I am allowed to rest, isn't that right, young man?"

Before my compadre could answer, a young girl, just a skinny dark girl from the rancho, entered through the front gate. She closed it gently behind her, went inside the house, and then emerged through the side door and greeted them on the patio. She began watering plants, and my compadre didn't give the girl a second thought. She was just a maid, a washerwoman, someone to help out around the house. But he noticed a change in Don Martín. The old man suddenly became antsy, more animated in his talk, and my compadre couldn't tell whether he wanted him to stay longer or leave immediately. My compadre decided he'd stayed long enough and rose from the table. Don Martín rose too, anxiously, almost knocking over the two shot glasses on the table. The old man had turned around and was staring into the house. My compadre followed the old man's gaze, and through the screen door he could see the girl as she washed dishes. That was it, nothing more: just a girl from the rancho washing dishes, slowly, in no rush to finish her chore. Later, when he learned that Don Martín had died, this image flashed in my compadre's mind, and he couldn't understand why. My compadre kept thinking about the girl and about Don Martín's happiness. The old man was almost giddy, which, in looking back, was almost strange and unbecoming of a patriarch, of a man who commanded respect from everyone who knew him.

PART II

CHAPTER FIVE

I

AFTER THEY HAD BEEN LIVING TOGETHER FOR ALMOST TWO MONTHS, Wopper asked Mija if her father minded their relationship. He didn't care whether or not Don Cirilo approved, but he thought it strange that the old man had never, not once, said anything to him about it. He waited for a fatherly lecture, but Don Cirilo never acknowledged it, as if somehow the relationship didn't exist. But maybe he didn't mention it because there was, in fact, nothing to talk about. Wopper still awoke at dawn and met the old man for work. Mija cooked for the two of them and took care of both houses. Don Cirilo wanted for nothing; Wopper wanted for nothing. What did it matter where she lived? Maybe he thought Wopper and his daughter would soon marry and this was just how things were done nowadays. Wopper didn't know. He spent more waking hours with Don Cirilo than he did with anybody else, but he knew little about what went on inside the old man's mind. He knew as much about Don Jaspero the donkey. They helped each other in their work, grunting and sweating alongside one another; they took breaks, passing each other a canteen of water. "This tastes good," Don Cirilo would say, always the first to drink. They ate their tacos in silence, crumbs of tortilla forever collecting on the stubble of Don Cirilo's chin.

If they ever talked about anything, it was related to work. And they worked plenty. They began planting corn in May. In a month they expanded the crop to the edge of Wopper's father's property. On Don Cirilo's urging, they expanded onto the adjacent property. "There's no fence," Don Cirilo explained, more to himself than to Wopper. "And I haven't seen the man in fifteen years. If he comes back we'll deal with him." This seemed reasonable. He had dealt with Wopper easily enough. La Morada was so empty it felt as if you could take over any property or work any land and go undisturbed for years.

One early morning, walking through the rows of corn with shovels in hand, Don Cirilo stopped suddenly and pointed at the large reservoir. The sun was rising and the water was as pink as the sky. They could hear a tree full of birds chirping and squawking. Wopper couldn't tell what Don Cirilo was pointing at, and the old man didn't say. Wopper squinted his eyes and looked out over the water, thinking something would emerge, but nothing did. It was just the black hills in the distance and the pink sky reflected in the water. They continued walking, and Wopper didn't think of it again until that night. He and Mija were having sex, and all of a sudden the old man pointing across the pink water popped into his mind, causing him to lose his momentum. He had to struggle to regain focus. Afterward they lay in the dark, both of them staring at the ceiling and catching their breath, and he told her about the strange thing her father had done. Then, as if they were somehow correlated, he asked what her father thought of their relationship.

She laughed gently. "He's a simple man," she said.

Wopper remembered that his own dad would say the exact same thing. "What does that even mean, though?" he asked.

"He makes sense of his life as it comes to him. He's already made sense of this."

"I come from simple men," Wopper said. He didn't know if this was necessarily true. His father was simple, he knew that, and his mother had once told him, "You're just like your father. You go through life pretending that nothing matters. You're happy as long as you can eat, use the bathroom in peace, and watch television on that very couch." She had been lecturing him about something.

Mija was silent for a long time. He couldn't tell what she was thinking. He rarely could, especially when she was serious.

Finally, she said, "You're not simple."

"You don't know me," Wopper said.

"I do know you."

"How? I've never told you anything about my life, about where I come from. Nothing."

She laughed. "Roberto, that doesn't mean I don't know you. You're not simple in the same way my father is. He's a farmer, always has been, always will be until the day he dies, and he's never thought of anything beyond that. But you're capable of more."

Now it was Wopper's turn to laugh. "I'm not capable of shit! Just ask anyone who's ever known me. My favorite thing to do back home was play racquetball, and I'm not even good at it."

"What's racquetball?" she asked.

"I don't know. . . . It's like handball but with a racquet. I used to play handball but I got tired of it."

"What's handball?"

"What's handball? Uh, well, basically you hit a rubber ball with your hand against a wall."

She didn't seem to understand. She rose from bed, found her underwear on the floor and put them on, and then went to the kitchen and brought back two glasses of water. She handed him a glass and then set her own on the floor before crawling back into bed next to him.

Wopper thought about his life before coming to La Morada. The years had passed so quickly. One day he was in junior high, then he was in high school, and then he started dating Lara. Even their relationship seemed routine: they were friends first, he remembered, and then it just gradually became more serious. One year became seven. He finished high school, barely graduating, then he took classes at the community college, and then after a semester (or maybe it was two, he couldn't remember) he dropped out. Sometimes he worked, mainly side jobs in construction, roofing, or house painting, helping out friends. He didn't feel the need for a full-time job. He lived at home, his mother fed him, and he and Lara rarely went out. His only real expenditure was his gym membership, but his parents helped with that too. At one point, he started drinking a lot—every other day, sometimes every day. All the side-job money went toward his bar bill. The years blurred together. The only memory that kept coming back to him was the time he ate all those hamburgers and scored the winning goal and got his nickname. He was ten years old then, eleven maybe. As if every time someone called him Wopper he was supposed to be reminded of the one moment in his life that mattered, and all because his dad called every hamburger *un gwopper.*

She nudged him. "What are you thinking about?" she asked.

"Nothing," he muttered.

After a long silence, she said, "You know, you've never had me."

"What's that supposed to mean?"

"Maybe you didn't do much before," she said. "But you also never had me at your side. Now you do."

Wopper almost cracked up. It sounded strange. But there was something in her voice that told him he shouldn't laugh. She was serious. So he said, "Well, just tell me what to do. That's what everyone else has always done, and where has it led me?"

"But I'm not everyone else," she said.

"No, I guess you're not," he said, chuckling. He had no idea what she was talking about.

II

Not too long after that conversation, Mija told Wopper that he had been nominated for the municipal board of representatives. At first he thought she was joking, but in a very matter of fact tone she explained that each rancho sent a representative to attend weekly meetings in La Piedad. As the only man in town he was the right choice.

"That's ridiculous. How can I be the right choice?" he asked. "What about your father?"

"He's too old for politics," she replied.

Wopper threw out the names of younger men he'd seen around, the fathers of the children constantly playing pinball at the corner grocery store. She explained that they didn't own land or property, and plus, they were gone for most of the year. Racking his brain for other possible candidates, he half-jokingly asked about Lucio Barraza, who was always around and whose family owned a plot of land.

"He was the representative before," she said, "but then he went crazy."

Wopper had met Lucio several times, always in the presence of Don Cirilo. He had a patchy mustache and a potbelly and wore grease-stained tank tops and tight t-shirts. He seemed nervous and overly polite. He shook their hands and held on for too long. Wopper's impression of him was that he seemed slow, a little sneaky, but harmless. At first, he had wondered if they were related, but Mija told him that they merely shared the same last name.

"How did he go crazy?" Wopper asked.

She shook her head and sighed deeply, as if not caring to go into detail, and then said, "It's too long to explain. It had nothing to do with being a representative, though."

Wopper thought for a moment. He knew that if Lucio could do it then anyone could. Still, he was unsure. "But what's the point of it?" he asked.

"Someone has to be on the council," she said, looking at him as though this should be obvious. "If no one is there at the meetings then we have no idea what's going on—" then she stopped. She lightened her tone. "Don't worry, it'll be easy. You just have to trust me. I'll help."

"How do you know about it?"

"Everybody knows about it. At least if you've lived in La Morada all your life."

"Everybody?" he asked.

She shrugged. "Those who pay attention."

"Why don't you do it then?" he asked.

She laughed. "No one would take me seriously."

"And they will me?"

She nodded and then abruptly changed the subject as if it had already been decided. He wondered what he would have to do. Would there be a campaign and an election? He didn't ask. He hoped the conversation would be forgotten.

But a week later, she told him that he was now La Morada's municipal representative. "That's it? Just like that?" he asked.

"No one else was nominated," she said.

Wopper felt sick to his stomach. He was already imagining himself speaking at a podium in front of a large group of people. Who those people would be, he had no idea. "I don't know about this," he said. "You don't understand. I was never good at school, I barely passed my classes—and that was in high school. When I took classes at the junior college I couldn't even follow what they were saying. What makes you think I can do this?"

"This isn't school," she said. "Just go and you'll see that it's not that hard."

Before the first meeting, Mija bought him a new denim work shirt, ironed out the wrinkles, and then ironed perfect creases into his jeans. She even cleaned and shined his boots. After he was out of the shower, she helped comb his hair, parting it to the side. He felt like a little boy on the first day of school. As if to add to this idea, when he was all dressed and ready to go, she gave him a spiral notebook and a blue pen.

"What am I supposed to do with this?" he asked.

"Throughout the meeting," she explained, "no matter what nonsense they're talking about, I want you to keep writing in this notebook. You can draw smiley faces and hearts, but just make sure it looks like you're taking notes."

His stomach was in too many knots to ask what this would accomplish. He took the faded green bus into La Piedad, sputtering and lurching all the way until it dropped him off behind the government building. He decided to sit in the plaza for a while and collect his thoughts, but he found that the more time he spent thinking about it, the more he kept imagining himself fucking up and looking like an idiot. The wet season had started and the sunny day had given way to clouds. It would soon rain. People were still walking around the plaza and sitting in cafés. The merchant carts and food stands were still open, but at the first raindrop they would pack up and disappear. He looked at his watch and saw that he was already a few minutes late. He followed the signs directing him to the municipal offices and asked a secretary with dyed red hair and bright red lipstick where the meeting was to be held. His throat felt tight and he could barely say the words. He had to repeat himself because she didn't hear him.

"May I ask your business, please?" she asked.

"I'm Roberto Barraza, the new representative from La Morada," he said.

"Licenciado!" she said, blushing. "I'm so sorry, please excuse me. You look younger than I imagined. With all that you've accomplished! La Morada, I know, is honored to have you represent them."

Wopper knit his brow and was about to ask what he'd accomplished, but she rose from behind her desk and said, "Follow me, I'll show you." She wore three-inch heels and a tight skirt that seemed to restrict her movements, but she walked rapidly. She kept turning around to make sure he was behind her. They walked down a dimly lit corridor and then down two flights of stairs into a windowless basement area. Boxes were stacked everywhere, and yellowed newspaper clippings were pinned to a bulletin board. She pointed to an open door at the far end of the hallway. It was sweltering in the basement, and Wopper was already sweating.

"Just introduce yourself," she said, smiling. "They'll know who you are." Then she walked back up the stairs, the sound of her heels against the cement drowning out his own footsteps.

He heard them before he saw them, several voices talking at once, mixed with laughter and a few whistles. When he arrived at the doorway he found a group of men who all looked like slightly younger versions of Don Cirilo: cowboy hats tipped back to reveal leather-skinned faces, all of them dressed in starched and pressed versions of the clothes they wore every day to work. He peered down at his own clothes and realized that he was, too. They sat around a long rectangular conference table that dwarfed them. They looked as if they'd have been more comfortable seated on buckets and crates, with nothing separating them except a fire pit. They were debating something, but Wopper couldn't deduce the topic, because men on each side of the table were crying, "No, no, no! You got it all wrong!" Others were laughing boisterously. They stopped abruptly when they noticed Wopper's presence at the door, peering up at him like schoolchildren caught roughhousing by their teacher. They seemed unsure of what to do. Again, Wopper found it difficult to speak. Finally, one of them said, "You must be the new representative from La Morada."

There was silence as they waited for him to confirm this. Mija had instructed him to say something specific, but at that moment he couldn't remember what it was. She told him, *Say this*, and he had said, "What? Why?"

"Just say it," she said, "trust me."

"You're talking about Lucio going crazy, right?" he asked. "Why won't you tell me what happened to him?"

"They'll know what you're talking about," she said. "Just say it as soon as you walk into the room."

And he promised her he would, but it had completely slipped his mind. The men were still waiting for him to respond. Then it came to him.

"My last name is Barraza," he said. After a pause, he added, "But don't worry, there's no relation. Or let's hope, right?"

After a second of silence, which to Wopper felt like an hour, all eight of them burst out laughing. They rose one by one to shake his hand, welcoming him to the municipal council.

"If you are like that idiot, I'm sure as hell not going to wrestle you off the roof like I had to do last time!" said a man with puffy eyes and a speckled gray mustache, as he vigorously shook Wopper's hand.

"Ah, we already know he's not another Lucio!" said another man with a deep gravelly voice. "This guy is not another one of *us* either, thank God! We finally have someone with education on the council!"

"That's right, *Licenciado*, we must call you that!" said another man as he placed one hand on Wopper's shoulder and pounded his back with the other. "Don't mind us, we're just a bunch of farmers. So are you, but *we* had no choice. You had a choice and still chose farming, at least for now, and I can admire that. It means you're one of us. But you have the education behind you, and that's the most important thing!"

Wopper just shook their hands and said, "A pleasure to meet you," as he felt drops of sweat trickling down his spine. There were other references to his "high-level of education" and to "what he'd accomplished in the North," and all he could do was smile broadly and nod his head in response. He wondered where they'd received this information. Shortly after he arrived, a large imposing man who introduced himself as Pilimón showed up, and the jovial, comfortable air of the meeting dissipated somewhat. Later, he was told that they all met a half hour earlier so that they didn't have to suffer Pilimón's presence the entire time. "He's Don Elpidio's right-hand man," one representative said. "He just comes to intimidate us." Wopper didn't ask who Don Elpidio was, but he made sure to write the name down in his notebook.

They didn't meet for long, and nothing important was discussed, at least in Wopper's mind, but he diligently jotted down notes anyway—not smiley faces and hearts, but real notes. He was afraid he'd forget everything upon leaving. The other representatives were aware of his note-taking, and whereas it made them curious and they nodded to each other approvingly, as if they assumed he would be so diligent, it seemed to make Pilimón suspicious. Even though he sat at the far end of the table, he kept peering over as if he could actually make out what Wopper was writing.

Following the meeting, Wopper shook hands with each of the representatives. They invited him to have a drink with them at El Capitán. Mija had told him they would ask but that he should refuse. "Tell them you have to work early tomorrow morning," she said. So he did, and all the representatives looked down at their boots or removed their cowboy hats and wiped their brows. They mumbled words of understanding, as if he had just reminded them that they too should go home and rest. An awkward silence followed, as if they weren't quite ready to let him go and were hoping he would change his mind. Finally, the representative from Sana Ana said, "We'll toast to you, all the same!"

Wopper rode the bus home, amazed that it had been so easy. The other municipal representatives were country farmers, humble and unassuming. They didn't intimidate him. In fact, he felt at ease. He'd grown up with men like this—his own father, his father's friends—and they could have been any one of those men at the table. He didn't yet know his role, or even the purpose of the meetings, but that didn't matter. It didn't yet, anyway. He was merely relieved that everything had gone as planned. He had performed well, and he couldn't wait to tell Mija how everything had gone.

When the bus arrived in La Morada, he jumped off before it came to a full stop. He had to keep himself from running the rest of the way. He felt as if he should contain his excitement even though no one was around to see him. The rain hadn't started yet, but the clouds still threatened. He could smell the dampness in the air, and in the distance he heard thunder. As he came down the dirt path, the dust already settling on his once shiny boots, he saw Mija waiting for him at the door. She was sitting in a white plastic chair, her bare legs crossed, her hands folded in her lap. She was staring out at the reservoir. She looked serious, worried even. Wopper's pace slowed as he approached. But then she turned and saw him, and immediately her face broke into a smile and she stood up and waved.

Later that night, lying in bed, they heard the rain begin to fall. They listened to its patter against the roof. He held Mija in his arms, and he could feel her warm breath against his neck becoming heavier. He could tell she was about to fall asleep. He didn't want to disturb her, but something kept nagging him about that afternoon. "You know what's strange is that they all assumed I had gone to college," he said quietly, trying not to startle her. "They kept calling me the most educated member of the council, and they insisted on calling me Licenciado."

Mija was quiet for a while before responding. "Well, didn't you go to college?"

"I took a few classes."

"Well, then you did go."

"Yeah, but—"

"And most of them probably didn't go past primary or secondary school, so you *are* the most educated member of the council."

Wopper considered this for a moment and realized it was probably true. "But they mentioned other stuff, though. 'My accomplishments in the North,' they kept talking about. It was strange. I didn't say anything different, though."

"People always talk," she said, yawning. "You never know how something gets started. All you know is that it's probably traveled fast. That's how people are in these ranchos."

He was about to push further, but then she placed her hand on his thigh and inched closer to him. "Let's go to sleep," she whispered. He let it be.

CHAPTER SIX

Arnulfo "Arnie" Beas

I WROTE MY MASTERS IN EDUCATIONAL LEADERSHIP THESIS ON THE LATINO EDU-cation crisis. For the most part it was a straightforward analysis of the many texts documenting the Latino student population's overall underperformance, as well as the future ramifications if drastic policy measures were not implemented. When I arrived at the last chapter, which was framed basically as a summary of the previous three chapters, I found myself unable to continue. For weeks, I couldn't write one word, despite almost daily pressure from my advisor. Well, the night before the deadline, my writer's block finally broke. It was ten thirty at night when I started typing. I wrote until nine the next morning. First I wrote the required summary, ten pages, but then I continued, unable to stop myself. I had no idea where all the words were suddenly coming from.

I talked about my own experience with students as a counselor at the junior college and high school level. I described my frustration at seeing students with so much potential, students who wanted to be astronauts and presidents and soccer stars, become slowly anesthetized, numbed to a point that they couldn't move forward, so that by the time they were fifteen, sixteen, seventeen, they could no longer even understand the concept of envisioning a future for themselves. They couldn't see past Woodland. They couldn't see past tomorrow. I spoke about my parents' generation, how they had left everything behind, risked everything, sacrificed everything, all for one thing: an imagined future. Somehow the next generation had lost this ability. In total I wrote thirty-four pages that night, the latter twenty-four without sources, with sentences running together and ideas repeated—embarrassing when I think about it—but I submitted it as is.

Later, I received an e-mail from my advisor congratulating me on finishing the final chapter but also instructing me to please remove the delirious ramblings. I complied and simply deleted the entire section without bothering to save it. I did have one hard copy, which earlier I had placed in my file cabinet, but I didn't want to look at it again. Not even to throw it away. As I remember them, the contents of those pages were naïve, overly idealistic, mostly irrational, and above all strange. What was I, a philosopher? I tried to never think about the inspired torrent again. I wished to erase the passages from my memory. But they were always with me, and I didn't understand the extent until Wopper Barraza reentered my life.

Believe me when I say that I was not a willing partner. Yes, it's my own fault for accepting the task, but what could I say? I went to visit my aunt before taking off and there was Lara sitting on the couch, holding her baby, a little frog-eyed fat thing, and she's reading a letter and crying. Do I not ask what's wrong? Do I not ask if everything's okay? Do I not ask what the letter contains? In retrospect, of course I don't. I say my hellos, my good-byes, and leave on my trip, my long awaited and deserved vacation.

Believe it or not I used to counsel Wopper, but I used to call him by his real name, Roberto. At seventeen it was funny to call him Wopper; at twenty, less funny; at twenty-four or however old he was, no job, dating my cousin, spending all his time playing racquetball, it became pathetic. Well, at nineteen or twenty, whenever it was he was taking classes at Woodland Community College, I was one of the only people to insist on calling him by his given name. I'm sure he thought I was trying to maintain a "professional" relationship, or being "the square," or maybe even that I was "trying to be white," as my family always says. But I didn't care—his name in my records was Roberto.

I used to ask him what his life plans were, as I ask all my students, since I'm a counselor, and he told me, "I don't know," which is common enough. So I asked him his interests. He had none, he said. "Well, what do you do all day?" I asked. He couldn't exactly say. Believe it or not, most of my counseling sessions go like this. I blame it on our educational system, for one, but also on the numbing effects of television, video games, and our society's overall obsession with material wants. The guys know what their next tattoo is going to be and what kind of muscle car they'd like to buy, and the girls know they want to have a good enough job to buy clothes and shoes and have a house in the new section of town. But as far as vocations, they haven't given it much thought. The girls sometimes do, but usually it doesn't extend much beyond beautician. At most, a career in fashion. I don't necessarily discourage them, but it's hard to be enthusiastic when your most intelligent and creative students envision the exact same career path over and over. I guess that's where I come in, but whereas I began my job thinking I'd inspire future lawyers, doctors, educators, and businessman, I now just help them select classes that won't bore them to the point of dropping out. If they finish with their associate's degree, I've been a successful counselor. They even come up and thank me at graduation. Guys shake my hand, girls give me hugs; they introduce me to their parents and say, "I couldn't have done it without Mr. Beas!" And I smile. I smile so wide my face hurts. Yes, you couldn't have done it without me. You couldn't have gotten your AA without my invaluable assistance. I've churned out at least seventeen hundred AAs. Wopper Barraza wasn't one of them.

So it came as a surprise when I read the letter my cousin Lara handed me. I knew Wopper had been deported after his fourth DUI, which is about what I expected of him (though I always assumed he was a citizen). Honestly, I never gave much thought to what he'd actually do in Mexico. To do so would have meant caring, and I have more pressing concerns: paying my mortgage, tending to the winter garden, various picture-framing projects, finding a wife, etc., etc. The list is long, and, frankly, charting the course of Wopper Barraza's failings does not rank very high. But even if I'd given his predicament more thought, I probably never could've guessed what happened to him. A year had already passed since he left, and from the sound of it, Wopper was my most successful student. Associate's degree or not, he was a citizen of influence. Only not in this country. This is what he wrote:

Lara,

A little while ago I was asked to be the municipal representative from La Morada porque soy como la unica persona in this rancho under 70. No sabia que hacer, but I followed along and I had to go to all these meetings and porque todos saben que I'm from the United States y alguien I guess told everybody that I had a lot of connections or whatever in the North so por supuesto la gente empezo a preguntarme cosas like my opinion on stuff. I thought soon they'd know que no sabia nada de what I was talking about pero la cosa es que they continued listening to me. And what I voted for everyone else voted for. I know all this sounds crazy pero es la verdad. Only once things started happening I found myself over my head y ahora no se como I pissed off some corrupt official and I've started receiving threats. I need to get out of here y pronto sabes. I have to get a coyote and I don't have that kind of money. Can you send me $2000? No quiero preguntar a mis papas because they'll freak out. I'll pay you back, I promise, te lo juro. Sorry that I have to put you out like this.

Believe it or not aqui me llaman el Licenciado. Espero que estes bien y todo.

Wopper

When I finished reading the letter, I looked up at Lara. I was unsure what to say, so I merely remarked on the stationery. "It looks like official letterhead," I said. She started crying more and rocking the baby in her arms. "Arnie, he forgot his own son!" she sobbed. "I haven't heard from him since the day he left. Not a phone call, nothing. If he forgot about me, fine, but here he writes the longest letter of his life, and he doesn't even ask about the birth of his own son!" I scanned the letter again and saw that this was true. So impressed by his new life as a politico (not to mention, distracted by his inability to stick to one language), I hadn't noticed either, and now that I noticed, I didn't attach much significance to the fact. To console her, however, I said, "He's probably under a lot of stress." She said, "Well fuck him then!" A typical response from my father's side of the family.

When my aunt came into the room, she asked Lara to switch the laundry. Lara handed her mother the baby and walked out, leaving me with the letter, which I would've wished to return to her. My aunt set the baby down in its crib. The room reeked of baby wipes, and it was giving me a headache. I was preparing to say good-bye, but my aunt was eyeing me strangely. She wouldn't take her eyes off me. I was fumbling with the letter in my hands, not sure what to do with it, when she asked me, "What do you think of that?"

I said, "Interesting," or something along those lines. The smell of baby wipes was really getting to me now. My eyes were watering and I needed to sneeze.

"Strange is more like it," she said.

"Yes, strange as well," I said, just to agree with her.

Then my aunt said, "You know what we'd like you to do, right, Arnie?"

I looked at her strangely. I had no such idea. "What would you like me to do?" I asked. My aunt looked at me as if I was purpose-fully trying to make things difficult.

"Well, you're going down there," she said. "So . . ."

Suddenly, I was clued in to her intent. I told her, "I'm going on vacation—*vacation*."

My aunt replied, "Yes, but you'll be in the area, and what would it hurt to take a trip out to La Morada, just to check on him?"

"And do what?" I cried. "Check on him and do what?"

"We're giving you money to bring to him," she explained. "So that he can cross back over, but we're not just going to give it away and never hear from him again."

I couldn't believe it. "What do you mean never again?" I asked. "Don't his parents live close by?"

My aunt's voice rose. "Just check on him," she said. "I don't know about this whole *municipal representative* thing, but I'm not going to give my hard-earned money to some lowlife deadbeat father—in that letter he didn't even *ask* about his own son!"

I felt like saying, *What'd you expect, it's Wopper Barraza!* Instead, I repeated my earlier conclusion: "It sounds like he's under a lot of stress."

"Yes, it seems like it," she said. "Things are bad down there now. It's not like it used to be. . . . Better that he kept to himself and stayed out of people's way. He better be careful."

There was silence after that, and then my aunt began asking me about work and my family, and as I was answering she rose from the couch, walked into the kitchen—"I'm still listening," she told me—opened a cabinet, and emerged holding an envelope. She handed it to me, saying nothing about its contents, and then asked after cousins she hadn't heard from in a while. I placed the envelope in my jacket pocket. It had the distinctive feel of an envelope full of bills. I imagined myself getting beat up and robbed in some dark alley. But what does one expect when his family is full of degenerates? I kept repeating that to myself as I packed for my trip. I repeated it on the drive to the airport. I repeated it on the entire flight to Guadalajara. When I landed, however, I had ceased belaboring my mission. Curiosity had gotten the best of me.

When I arrived in La Morada, I went to look for Don Martín. My aunt Lupe, whose husband was from there, told me that Don Martín knew everything there was to know in town, and that if I needed to find out what Wopper Barraza was up to, he was the man to ask. Only later did I recall that they hadn't visited in six years. After a few hours walking the crumbling cobblestone streets, knocking on empty doors, peering through windows to find sheets draped over furniture, all I encountered were a few mangy dogs, some manic-eyed kids playing pinball, and three old ladies wearing black shawls. When I asked them the whereabouts of Don Martín, they turned away from me and refused to look back. I said, "Excuse me, have I said something wrong?" But I was ignored as if I'd uttered some magic words and vanished from the face of the earth.

Near the town's pink stucco church I came across a man having little success trying to start a four-wheeler motorcycle. The man's mustache was thick and black, and he wore a paper-thin white t-shirt covered in grease. I noticed it doubled as a hand rag. I loudly cleared my throat, but he didn't look up. He was too focused on his task. He repeatedly jumped on the pedal and then revved the engine. It would begin to putter, then he'd jump on the seat and kick one of the gears, but the engine died each time. Finally, after seven failed attempts (I kept track, waiting for him to stop), I asked loudly, "I'm looking for Don Martín; do you know where he lives?"

The man looked up, his eyes wide. He shook his head and brought his finger to his lips. "That's not a name you go around just throwing about!" he exclaimed.

"I don't understand," I said. "I was told Don Martín—"

The man immediately kicked the petal and exaggeratedly revved the engine so as to drown me out. Once again he brought his finger to his lips. "*Shhh*! Please don't say that name in front of me," he exclaimed. "I have a mother and father who depend on me. I don't want trouble, you hear?"

"Okay, okay," I said, flustered. I was sweating and felt covered from head to toe in dust. "I'm looking for someone to help me. I'm looking for Roberto Barraza. Do you know him by any chance?"

The man's face broke into a smile, and he said to me, "Do you mean my compadre, my friend of friends, Licenciado Roberto? Of course, why didn't you say so at once? I'll bring you to him right now. Right now, immediately! Here, hop on. I'll take you right to his office at the municipal building—he's sure to be there today. Aye, so the Licenciado, he is a friend of yours?"

I hesitated, unsure what to say. "Yes, he's actually my—"

"Well, a friend of Roberto Barraza is a friend of mine," the man blurted out. "Hop on, I tell you!"

I stared at the bike, the man already straddling the seat. "I thought it didn't work," I said.

"What? This?" he asked, looking at me incredulously. "Oh, it works. I was just messing about." Then he added, "But you'll have to push me for a good ten meters. Once it starts I'll circle about the block and pick you up."

I set down my rolling suitcase and began pushing the motorcycle while the man kicked the pedal over and over. Finally the engine popped and the bike leaped forward. When the man circled around, I had to grab hold of my suitcase in one hand, grab the seat with the other, and pull myself onto the four-wheeler, the bike increasing speed all the while.

Once on our way, the man introduced himself as Lucio Barraza. I asked him if he was related to Roberto. He shrugged and said, "We're all sons of Adam and Eve, so I guess we're related somehow, no? Why do you ask?" I thought he was joking. When I realized he wasn't, I explained that they had the same last name. Lucio laughed. "Half the town are Barrazas, a quarter are Barajas, and the rest are Velorios," he said. "I know that at least for a couple of generations I'm not related to the one and only Licenciado Roberto Barraza." Then, as if inspired by the mention of his name, for the rest of the bumpy ride into La Piedad he listed off all the good deeds that Wopper had achieved in his term as municipal representative. In addition to the new bus stop, the more frequent bus routes, and the paved roads, he'd also made sure the highway turnoff was paved, replacing the potholed dirt path that had existed before. He also had the primary school grounds paved so the students didn't get muddy every time they went out to play. He was also able to save the La Morada Soccer Club, which was in severe need of players as so many had left for the North or jumped to other clubs, by getting much needed sponsorship. The sponsorship attracted players from surrounding ranchos and even a few from La Piedad. Now the team competed with the best in the league.

"Who's the sponsor?" I asked. Lucio said it was a concrete company from La Piedad. I found this interesting, especially because it seemed that all the projects Wopper had secured for La Morada involved pavement. I mentioned this fact just as Lucio was merging onto the highway, dangerously cutting off cars coming from both directions. From one end I saw a rapidly approaching semitruck and from the other a beat-up Volkswagen Bug. I almost lost hold of my suitcase; I thought for sure we were both dead, and I quickly imagined the ingloriousness of such an end. Lucio was unfazed. He moved the bike to the side of the road and let the impatient cars pass. In response to the annoyed and drawn-out honks, he waved his hand dismissively.

I completely forgot my question about the concrete company. Lucio asked me my occupation. I told him I was a college counselor. My heart was pounding and I was squeezing my suitcase with all my might. We rode in silence until we reached the center of town.

The four-wheeler died right in front of the plaza. Lucio attempted to restart the engine, but it was even less cooperative than it had been in La Morada. A couple of older men all in white cowboy hats sat at an outdoor café and stared in annoyance as Lucio performed his kicking and revving routine, disturbing the otherwise tranquil late afternoon air. I looked around. I always forgot how beautiful the plazas in Mexico were. White iron benches and perfectly groomed trees surrounded a bandstand. At the far end of the triangular-shaped plaza an ornate nineteenth-century church with an impressive yellow-tiled dome towered over the rest of the buildings. I tried to remember the location of a restaurant my parents once brought me to for my birthday. I thought maybe I'd go there for dinner once I was through with Wopper. I turned my attention back to Lucio, who was still struggling with the four-wheeler. One of the seated old men said, "Give it up, Lucio!" Lucio waved him off. Another man said, "Maybe it's time La Morada began buying cars for all its paved roads, eh? Eh?" The other men laughed heartily.

Lucio stopped trying to start the bike. He looked at the men and pointed at me, breathing heavily because of the effort to start the bike. He continued pointing in my direction, waiting for his breath to return, leaving me to wonder what he was on the verge of saying. "You know who this is?" Lucio said finally. "He's a representative from the North, a councillor! He's here to see our representative, Licenciado Roberto Barraza, and why? Why? Because La Morada knows the importance of its connections in the United States, and those connections will take La Morada into the future."

The men stared at me suspiciously. I felt as though they were sizing me up. Two of them nodded their heads in greeting, but the other three glared, stone-faced. I wanted to explain that I was a college counselor. The way Lucio said it made it seem like I was a consulate of some sort. One of the men stood up from the table and walked toward me. For lack of anything else to do, I held out my hand in greeting. The man shook it firmly and used the contact to pull me close. He smelled strongly of the same Brut aftershave my father used. He leaned in and whispered, "What do you think you're doing?"

"I don't know what you're talking about," I said.

"Don't you know who you're with?" he asked.

I hesitated, wishing to admit my ignorance. "Yes, I do," I heard myself say.

The man stepped back, letting go his grip on my hand. He stared into my eyes as if trying to divine my thoughts. I would have happily told him: my thoughts are to see Wopper as soon as possible, get him his money, visit family members, and then take off for the coast. But the man's distrustful stare made me feel as though I was already deeper into a situation than I would've wished.

"At your service," the man said.

"Arnulfo Beas," I said.

The man stared quizzically as if trying place the name. "Do you have family here?" he asked.

I nodded.

The man laughed and said, "Who doesn't? Hah!"

I laughed too, but I didn't know what was so funny.

Lucio parked the four-wheeler on a side street, and the two of us walked through the plaza, empty except for more old men and a few groups of teenagers in school uniforms. I asked Lucio about the men in the café, and he looked at me as if he didn't know what I was talking about. "You didn't see the way they stared at me?" I asked. Lucio shrugged. "That's how we are," he said. "We stare at strangers. Curiosity, that's it."

"Yes, but the man who came up to me, what was that about?" I asked.

"Who knows," Lucio said. "I didn't hear what he said to you."

I didn't push further. As we approached the brick façade of the municipal building, the church bells rang loudly, and Lucio started slightly.

"Are you all right?" I asked.

Lucio nodded, but it wasn't too reassuring, especially as he almost tripped on the steps leading to the building's entrance. We walked down a flight of stairs and passed several heavily made-up women wearing business attire. They stared at Lucio then at me. I smiled and wished them a good afternoon. They responded in kind but glanced warily at Lucio, examining the man's dust and grease-covered clothes, which I realized were now out of place in the stately building. Lucio was silent. He held the handrail as he descended the stairs to the lower level. "This is where the municipal representatives and all the party officials have their offices," he said.

We sat in a dimly lit waiting area. Several other men and women, all humbly attired, sat patiently. The men held their hats in hand, taking turns flipping them around or spinning them on their fingers. Men and women in suits passed hurriedly in and out of offices, carrying documents and folders. They spoke to one another in murmurs. A young girl with a clipboard approached us and asked the purpose of our visit. Lucio answered, "We're here to see Licenciado Roberto Barraza." The girl looked at her watch, jotted down Lucio's name, and said that there were two appointments ahead of us. She then mumbled that we were welcome to water from the dispenser.

I unzipped my suitcase and felt for the envelope my aunt had given me. I wanted to be done with this business. I had already wasted an entire day trying to find him, and now I was waiting around the municipal building as Wopper Barraza met with constituents. Of course I was curious to hear how he had ended up in this position, but not enough to forgo precious days of vacation. I was supposed to be relaxing, and instead I was exhausted. An attractive young woman with dyed blonde hair walked out of one of the offices, and my eyes followed her. I thought I saw a slight smile on her lips. I entertained the idea that maybe the smile was for me. Whenever I travel down to Mexico my parents tell me to bring back a wife. I haven't had much luck. I almost rose from my chair to get some water and maybe cross paths with her if she walked back into the room, but then the door to Wopper's office opened.

A tall man emerged, laughing. He wore a cowboy hat, a maroon polyester suit, and an impressive ornate belt that matched his yellowish tan boots. Still laughing, he turned around and said, "Friend, I thank you. Always a pleasure," and he reached out and shook another man's hand. I couldn't see whom the hand belonged to. The secretary waiting near the door with her clipboard followed the tall man out. A moment later another secretary entered the office. She emerged again and walked straight toward Lucio.

"Lucio Barraza?" she said.

"At your service, yes I am," he said.

"You've been asked to leave," she said nervously.

Lucio started to speak but wasn't able to begin what he intended to say. "Uh," he stammered, "Um, uh."

"Licenciado Roberto Barraza has asked that you leave the building," she repeated.

Lucio overcame his shock and cried, "I am a citizen of this municipality, and I can remain here as long as I want!"

The woman sighed. "Well, you won't be allowed to see the Licenciado," she said.

"I can see him!" Lucio exclaimed. He was on the verge of shouting. "He's my representative! And what's more, I've brought him an important visitor. A councillor from the North."

She glanced at me disapprovingly. "What's the problem?" I asked her. "Tell Roberto—the Licenciado—that he's with me. He helped me; it's okay."

"And your name?" she asked.

"Please explain to Roberto that it's someone he's asked to see," I said. "I'm family, a cousin, Arnulfo Beas."

The woman abruptly turned, knocked lightly on the door, and, without waiting for an answer, reentered the office. When the door closed I turned to Lucio and said, "What's going on? I thought you said you were compadres."

Lucio shook his head desperately and then placed his hands together as if in prayer. He brought his hands to his lips, seeming to look for the words to explain the predicament. He breathed in deeply, closing his eyes, and then reopened them when he began talking. "Look, the thing is this: we've had a misunderstanding," he said. "All my fault, all my fault, I tell you, but the Licenciado is not a forgiving man. No matter how much I apologized, he refused to accept it. It's all been a horrible misunderstanding. I've been nothing but supportive of his work, his important efforts in La Morada! You heard me on the way here—who is his biggest supporter? Me, of course. He could do no wrong by me, but apparently I can do wrong by him."

The door opened and the secretary emerged, followed by the man and woman who'd entered previously. They followed the secretary out. I looked up expectantly, waiting to see if Wopper would emerge.

It took me a moment to realize that the man standing at the door *was* Wopper. He had lost weight, but his hair is what really threw me. For as long as I knew him he wore a razor-cut, practically a 0 faded up to a 0.5, but now his thick, black hair was long enough to part to the side. He was about to call the next visitors when he glanced over and recognized me. He froze for a moment as if trying to place my face. Then his demeanor changed. If before he was stern and official, instantly—but only for a brief moment— he became the kid I used to counsel at the junior college. The same kid who answered questions about his career goals with hardly a shrug, too lazy to give a full one. Wopper's eyes brightened and he said, "Mr. Beas?"

I rose from the chair, almost jumping up. "Roberto, yes, it's me," I said. I don't know what kind of greeting I expected. Maybe a handshake and one of those half embraces. Instead, he merely said, "Good to see you," and then indicated that he first had to see the man and woman sitting next to me. I told him that was fine, of course I understood: he was a busy man. I sat back down awkwardly, my feelings slightly hurt, as if I assumed I'd be treated differently, like an old friend, like family. Suddenly, I realized that I coveted Wopper Barraza's approval! I almost began laughing, but then I looked over at Lucio's glum face and felt bad for him. He too wished to be in Wopper's good graces. At least the secretary hadn't asked me to leave.

Another ten minutes passed, then finally the man and woman emerged from the office followed by Wopper. Both Lucio and I rose from our chairs.

"You need to leave," Wopper said as soon as the man and woman left the waiting area. He was staring at Lucio.

"But I've brought him to you," Lucio said shrilly. "See that as a gesture of my support."

"If you hadn't brought him, someone else would have," Wopper said.

I was struck by Wopper's assertive tone. This was a side of him I hadn't seen before. Lucio continued to plead. "Just let me talk for five minutes. Let's sit down and chat like we used to, like compadres. We need each other, we do! I know things about La Morada that you don't. I've been there all my life. We can help one another. Let's just talk, that's all I ask—"

Wopper ignored him. He indicated that I should walk past him into the office, and I obeyed, expecting Wopper to follow. I felt bad that Lucio was to be excluded, but then again, there were clearly goings-on of which I wasn't aware. It wasn't my business to get involved. I turned around to say something, but Wopper had remained in the waiting room and had shut the office door, presumably to prevent me from hearing what he had to say to Lucio. I strained my ears, but to no avail. All I could hear was Lucio's pleading. "Just five minutes," he said. "Is it because of her? Because of her? Don't judge me because of that!"

My ears perked up at this. Whom was he talking about? I glanced at my surroundings. A dingy office, old furniture, and a few framed certificates on the wall. As I scanned the room I heard Lucio say, his voice even shriller, "All I tried telling you was that she's controlling you just like she controlled me. And for that you can't forgive me. Well, see what happens when you try to do your own thing, Licenciado. Tell me that she hasn't had her hand in everything! Is she in there? Is that why you won't see me?"

That was when I realized I wasn't alone in the office. A girl was sitting in the corner, half-hidden in the shadow of an empty bookshelf, thumbing through a magazine. She was small, scrawny even. She wore an outdated woman's suit much too large for her. It had shoulder pads, lumpy but stiff, that extended well beyond her thin frame.

I was about to say hello when the door opened. She looked up and her dark eyes met mine. She wore thick eyeliner, her eyebrows partially drawn in. Her black hair was pulled back in a bun. It had an unnatural shine, like it was dirty or she'd used cheap hairspray. Wopper closed the door behind him and sighed. "So, Mr. Beas, what brings you here?" he asked in Spanish.

I chuckled. "You don't know?" I asked.

He indicated that I should sit down, and he walked around the desk and sat in a rolling office chair that had seen better days.

The blank expression on his face told me that he really had no idea why I was there to see him.

I looked at the girl in the corner. Her legs were now crossed, the magazine resting on her lap. I could see the lower half of her legs, her dark skin covered in scars from bug bites scratched raw. She wore heels that didn't match her suit. I smiled inwardly and said to myself, *A country girl from La Morada if I've ever seen one.* Except my smile must have crept outward, because Wopper asked me, "Why are you smiling, Mr. Beas?" Caught off guard, I stammered out a question to the question. "Does she speak English?" I asked.

Wopper frowned and said, "What do you think?"

I assumed she didn't and proceeded, aware of my nervousness, or rather, that I was on edge. Why did I feel the need to explain myself? Wopper was the one who needed to provide answers, not the other way around. I could just as soon pick up and leave, head to the rental car place, take off for Ixtapa, and never think about Wopper Barraza again.

"Who's she?" I asked him.

"I live with her," Wopper said.

"What about Lara?" I said.

"What about her?" he muttered. "She broke up with me."

"Really?" I said.

Wopper nodded.

"Well," I said, unsure what to do with this new piece of information. I never thought to ask about the status of their relationship. "Lara and my aunt showed me the letter you sent," I began. "They wanted me to come down and see what had happened to you. They didn't want to send money and never hear from you again."

"Then you have the money?" Wopper asked, shifting in his seat.

I hesitated. I've never been a good liar, at least not on the spot, so it wouldn't have done me any good to invent a different story. I hadn't been prepared for such a straightforward conversation. This was all business apparently.

"Yes—yes, I do," I said.

Wopper stared at me, saying nothing, and yet his silence was far from quiet. With each wordless moment, I felt the room filling with tension. I wondered if Wopper was waiting for me to just hand him the money right then and there. Discomfort made me chuckle. I looked around the office, wanting to avoid Wopper's eyes. "So you've done well," I said, probably a hint of sarcasm in my voice. "Why would you want to . . . to . . . ." I hesitated, still unsure whether or not the girl spoke English. Wopper seemed unconcerned with anything I might say, so I continued. "Why do you want to go home?" I asked. "You've flourished here."

"Flourished?" Wopper repeated.

Again I found myself chuckling. "Well, Roberto, let's remember you weren't exactly political material back home," I said. "On the way over here, Lucio told me about all your renewal projects in La Morada. How have you managed such a turnaround?"

"It wasn't so hard," he said, unsmiling.

"Oh?" I said.

"Once I got used to how things worked," he said.

"And how did you do that, exactly?" I asked.

"What's that?" he said.

"How did you get used to how things worked?" I replied. "I mean, politics isn't the easiest field to enter."

"I just figured it out," he said, as though it were so simple.

"Just like that?" I said.

"I guess," he said, shrugging.

"Roberto," I said, trying not to chuckle, "if I recall correctly, back home you didn't have a job, and you always struggled in school. You don't find it odd that all of a sudden you're involved in local government and apparently doing quite well?"

He shrugged again and said, "I don't know, I guess."

I felt as though we were back in my office at the community college. Why is it so damn hard for my students to speak abstractly about their experience? I wanted to shake him and scream, "Step out of yourself for one moment and think about it! How did you go from here to *here*?" But I guess that would've only served to satisfy my curiosity. I momentarily thought to ask him if I should encourage more of my students to consider this path. Not drunkenness and deportation, but living abroad for a period of time.

I veered back to the practical: "So you do plan on coming back?"

"Yes," he said slowly, nodding his head even more slowly.

I waited for more, but he didn't elaborate. Later I realized that I should have picked up on his hesitancy, but I was distracted. I was aware of the girl's eyes on me. I met them but had to turn away. She made me uncomfortable. Her heavily made-up eyes, her dirty hair, her scrawny little face, her ridiculous outfit . . . I had initially dismissed her role in Wopper's life, but there was something I couldn't quite place about her. For one, she was older than her appearance first suggested.

"What's your deal with Lucio?" I asked.

"I don't want to talk about it," Wopper said.

"Oh, and why not?" I responded.

"Will you accompany me somewhere?" Wopper asked, clearly changing the subject.

"Sure," I said, but then I thought better of it. "Wait, Roberto. I have to get going. This was just supposed to be a brief visit and then I'd be off. It's my vacation."

But Wopper had already risen from his chair, and the girl followed him, rising from her corner and placing the magazine in her cheap leather purse. I repeated what I said about my vacation, but Wopper said something to the girl about being home late and pretended not to have heard me. Then he looked at me as if awaiting an answer. "So?" he said.

"What?" I asked.

"Ready? Let's go," he said.

And as simple as that I was following him out of the office. I had no idea where we were going or for what reason, but once again my curiosity intervened, preventing me from getting this business over and done with. I followed Wopper up the stairs and out of the municipal building; all the while he stayed about five steps ahead of me and expected that I be closely behind. I had to lug my suitcase, which made it difficult to keep up, but Wopper didn't seem to notice, not even when we stepped onto the cobblestone walkway and the click-clack of my suitcase wheels echoed loudly in the empty afternoon streets. *Click-clack, click-clack, click-clack*—I felt as if people could hear me approaching from blocks away. Finally, I decided to lift the suitcase off the ground and carry it in my arms. Wopper was now an entire block ahead of me. "Hey!" I called out.

Wopper turned around.

"Where are we going?" I asked, feeling like an idiot peering over the suitcase in my arms.

Wopper waited for me to come closer. "I have to see someone," he said quietly. "Can you do me a favor?" He didn't wait for my answer. "I want you to just follow along with what I say," he instructed. "I'll explain everything afterward, okay? But right now it's good that you're here."

"Roberto, I need to go," I said. "Seriously, I can't. I just need to—" I stopped. Clearly he didn't care about my vacation, not to mention the fact that my insistence lacked conviction. Hadn't I followed along so far?

Wopper had already turned around and started walking away from me. Several doors down he stopped and rapped loudly on a metal curtain storefront. He looked back at me as if wondering why I was still standing in the same place. I set the suitcase down and walked toward him, the click-clack of the wheels drowned out by the rising metal curtain.

CHAPTER SEVEN

Don Elpidio

IN BUSINESS, IN POLITICS, IN EVERY FIELD, I IMAGINE, A MAN IS CONFRONTED by sons of bitches. And by sons of bitches I specifically mean those whom at first you underestimate, but then later you pay for that underestimation. That's my advice to any youngster entering the field of business or politics, but like I said, I'm sure it applies to any field: beware of the man that you underestimate, because it's usually him who will deal you the hardest blow. It's the sucker punch, the unseen left hook that hurts most. I can't exactly describe Roberto Barraza as one of these sons of bitches, but I still underestimated him and paid for it, not dearly and not for long, but I'll get to that.

I began hearing about him before I actually met him. First, I assumed he was older. The last municipal representative from La Morada was Lucio Barraza, no relation I believe, and he was going on forty and considered a youngster by La Morada standards. Before him was Don Martín, may God rest his soul; he didn't deserve the end he met, and Don Martín was one of the rancho's patriarchs, at least in his seventies. These ranchos are full of empty homes, boarded up, the furniture all covered in sheets, cockroaches their only visitors. Northerners build their dream houses, thinking they'll return when they retire, but they rarely do. They come for a few weeks a year, but the rest of the time the rancho is empty except for old people with nothing to do except gossip about events that happened a half century ago. So when I heard that La Morada's new municipal representative was recently arrived from the United States, I thought for sure he was one of these rare old retirees who actually come back to live in the shithole rancho they'd left years ago. "Let's see how long he stays," I said to my right-hand man, Pilimón.

And you know what Pilimón tells me? "Oh, he'll stay longer than you think, Don Elpidio. He's with Don Cirilo's girl."

Another poor sucker! Another poor sucker! That's what I said to Pilimón. She'd already been through two municipal representatives, and now she was onto her third. I couldn't make heads or tails of her angle, I really couldn't. Daughter of a poor farmer, lives in the shittiest of shitty ranchos, yet she wants something and believes that something can be found in local government. I've been in business for forty-three years, politics for half that, and I can usually guess someone's angle the minute they enter the room. But this little slut was a puzzle I couldn't piece together. No one could. My right-hand man, Pilimón, told me, "Don Elpidio, that slut is like all the sluts I've ever known—crazy. What's to figure out? She's crazy. All sluts are crazy." I didn't used to use the word slut, I found it offensive and disrespectful to the gender of which my mother and grandmother and sister are a part, but Pilimón refers to women exclusively as such, so it's found its way into my vocabulary. I don't call all women this, as Pilimón does, but Don Cirilo's daughter deserves the name, she really does, if not for what she did to Lucio, then for what she did to Don Martín, the poor old bastard.

Well, when I heard that he was with her, I assumed right away that he was another Lucio Barraza, another country idiot I'd have to deal with at the municipal meetings. The meetings are a sham. I'll tell you that right away. One of those democratic façades Mexico is known for. The idea is that each rancho and pueblo in the greater area of La Piedad should have a say in municipal affairs, but the point is these little backward villages are just that, backward, and I can't tell you how many meetings are wasted just talking about weather and what can be done about the rain, and if it'd be helpful to bring in a weatherman to make predictions. They're obsessed with meteorologists, seem to think they're what every village needs. After the weather they're obsessed with pavement. They want everything paved. Life would be easier, they tell me, if only they could pave their front walkway. Needless to say, as the head of the municipal council of representatives (the official in charge of these meetings), I get plenty tired of hearing about the weather and pavement, especially because all I have to do is tell them at the end of every session, "I'll report your suggestions to the municipal president," and of course the municipal president doesn't care to hear what these little ranchos want, so I keep the minutes to myself. I'm a figurehead, nothing else. I was appointed to this office, but mainly just to be close to what's happening, to protect my business interests and whatever else I feel needs protection. I have direct access to all my associates, the officials needed to issue permits and block permits from competitors, so I put up with the rancho representatives and their pointless demands. But still, I can get away with not attending a few meetings here and there. Actually, before Roberto Barraza entered the picture, I had stopped attending meetings altogether. My right-hand man, Pilimón, went in my place and reported back to me. "Same old, same old, Don Elpidio," he always said.

Then one day Pilimón tells me, "I think you should attend the next municipal representative meeting." And of course I told him I was all tied up, which I guess I was, but I don't remember doing what. Anything was more important than those meetings. So I missed the next one, but then again Pilimón tells me, "I really think you should attend the next meeting." I told him that's why I sent *him* in my place: to fill me in on what happened. Well, he begins to tell me about the new representative from La Morada, and how he's from the United States, and how he has an astounding—Pilimón's word, I'd never heard him use the word before, but that was his description—astounding influence over the other members. Everything he votes for they vote for. Everybody waits to hear what he has to say, and then they follow accordingly. In just a handful of meetings he's become the most influential member. I asked Pilimón to tell me exactly what this son of a bitch had to say that the other sons of bitches found so necessary to follow along with. That's when Pilimón put his hands to his head and cried, "Boss, he says the same thing as they all do! He talks about the weather and pavement!" That's when

I raised my voice and scolded Pilimón—he was really taking this too far—and I said, "Pilimón, what is there to be upset about? You've been to how many meetings, and all they ever talk about is the pavement and the weather! I told you that before you started going. The municipal representative council means nothing, nothing at all. So what are you worried about?" That's when he reminded me again about Roberto Barraza being with Don Cirilo's slut daughter. This made me think twice, but that was it. Only later, when I heard that my competitor Valentín Moreno, of Moreno Concrete, had agreed to pave La Morada's primary school, did I think that maybe Pilimón wasn't exaggerating after all. In more than forty years of business, never has any son of a bitch moved in on a contract, large or small or entirely insignificant, without me knowing about it. In more than forty years of business, I've never heard of the Valentín Morenos of the world doing anything for free. Petty unsophisticated backward bastards don't know the meaning of pro bono. They take all the money they can get. They don't know that in order to make loads you have to invest loads, to sacrifice a job here and there for the long run, but here all of a sudden Moreno Concrete is paving a primary school. Next thing I know my other competitor, Ernesto Maya, of Maya Brothers Concrete, has agreed to sponsor the La Morada Soccer Club. Now players from other ranchos are jumping ship to play for them. Two players from La Piedad's best club team, F. C. Atlas, agreed to sign for the season—a season with La Morada, a second division team! Then Ernesto Maya pours the foundation for a locker room. Then he constructs concrete bleachers. That may seem like a lot in a short period of time, but believe me, my competitors will drive their workforces to death if they can avoid me breathing down their back.

I decided I would attend the next meeting.

As I said, I expected someone much older. A man, a presence, tall and broad shouldered with a man's mustache, like mine for instance. But there he was, not older than twenty-five years old, fuzz on his lip. This, the man stirring things up! He was a baby! I welcomed him to the meeting, shook his hand, and apologized for not being able to attend the previous sessions. I prepared my notes, gave my introductory remarks, informed them about some new projects that were developing, and then turned the floor over to the representative from Santa Clarita to discuss his housing initiative (of course all he discussed was the flood zone, and then it was onto concrete foundations). As the man spoke I scanned the table and found Roberto Barraza staring at me. Staring like I was some slut at the end of the bar. I met his gaze.

I'm not one of those excuses for men made uncomfortable by a stare down. The expression on my face made this clear. I've returned a stare many a time before, and it's always the son of a bitch who looks away first. Not Roberto Barraza, however. His big, bulging, heavy-lidded eyes continued to stare. This was a challenge. So I smiled and pointed at him. Why did I point? Those who know me understand its significance. Those idiots at the table, they may have known too. I know the representative from Santa Clarita understood, because he was so distracted that he stopped talking. *I'm after you*, the gesture said. *I don't waste time. I go for the jugular.* The table was quiet, the smile still on my face, my finger still pointed at him, his eyes still meeting mine. That was when I realized he wasn't actually looking at me. He was staring past me, at my ear, maybe. I suddenly felt the presence of someone behind me. I didn't want to look, because doing so would mean dropping my gaze. Without moving my eyes I told the rep from Santa Clarita to continue. He did and then we moved onto other issues.

When the meeting adjourned I was finally able to turn around and confront the son of a bitch behind me. There she was. The skinny little slut, sitting against the far wall, thumbing through a magazine. He wasn't staring at me; he was staring at her! I walked in her direction. She didn't raise her head from the magazine, not even when I stood in front of her with my hands on my hips, waiting for her to look up. Finally I said, "Since when has the general public attended our humble meetings?"

She still didn't look up. She turned the page and stared at a photo spread of some Mexican actress.

"Excuse me, I asked you a question," I said.

"I heard you," she mumbled. "The meetings are open to everyone."

"Yes, yes, I guess you're right," I said. "Just so strange to me that you care to be here. You used to be content to let Lucio run his mouth off. I guess that plan backfired, didn't it?"

"I don't know what you're talking about," she said, turning another page, as though she were actually reading the stupid soap opera rag.

"Look, I don't know what you're after," I said, "but I'll find out soon enough. This fellow you've latched onto isn't going to last long. I can tell you that much."

Still without looking up from her magazine, she mumbled something I didn't hear. "What was that?" I asked. She looked up coolly, cocking her head to remove the strands of hair from her face. Her painted cheeks, those beady eyes caked in mascara, burned in my memory. Smirking, she said, "Don Martín told me everything. He told me what you're all about."

What she meant by this I don't know. But the way she said it made me want to take the back of my hand and break her jaw, and I'm not a hitter of women, never have been. I may be known for a firm hand, but with women I'm as gentle as a lamb. She stared at me, still smirking, her eyes squinting, awaiting my response. I wasn't about to tell her I didn't know what she was talking about. I knew she had nothing on me. So I told her, "One day, when you want a real man, you come to me and I'll give you what you want. Until then, I'll be watching you and your representative. You think we're playing the same game, but we're not. I'm on a completely different level." Know what she did? She started laughing. She laughed as if I'd told her a fucking joke. She laughed like I'd tickled her underarms.

By that time Roberto Barraza was at my side, and she directed her smile toward him. She closed her magazine, placed it in her ridiculously oversized purse, and rose from her chair. I glared at him, expecting a glare in return, but he wasn't looking at me. He didn't even so much as glance in my direction. His eyes were fixed on her. An adoring gaze, as if she were the goddamned princess of La Morada.

"Ready?" he said, holding out his arm for her to hold.

"What a gentleman," I said. "Nothing quite like young love. Young man, young woman, as it should be."

Now they both looked at me strangely, as though I were some lecherous old man about to beat off as I imagined their union. Of course, what I was referring to was her history with Don Martín.

"Remember what I told you," I said to her as they walked away. She didn't even turn around.

The next day I wrote up some documents, had the municipal president sign them, and then had my right-hand man, Pilimón, drive out to La Morada and inform Licenciado Roberto Barraza that each construction project—the primary school paving as well as the soccer bleachers and locker room—required a thousand dollars in permit fees. La Morada had two months to pay the money or else, as municipal representative, Roberto would be held responsible.

CHAPTER EIGHT

I

Arnulfo "Arnie" Beas

WE TOOK A SHOT OF TEQUILA THAT BURNED MY THROAT AND CHEST SO badly that I couldn't even reach for the lime before I burst into a coughing fit. My face was inflamed and I had tears in my eyes. I wiped them before taking the second shot. This one went down easier.

I stared at Wopper Barraza across from me. He was looking at his empty shot glass. He drank his tequila like a sip of purified water. I had just seen him confront a man who with a mere glance almost had me pissing my pants. As it was, I could barely keep my knees from shaking. I cursed myself. Why couldn't I just leave, go to the beach, start my vacation? Five books I brought with me, an assortment of titles that I'd been meaning to read for some time. I pictured myself sitting on a deck, an umbrella providing shade, the sounds of waves accompanying my reading, a Corona in one hand—yes, straight from the commercial, but it's what I wanted. Instead, there I was drinking tequila, which I don't even like, still in La Piedad, waiting for Don Elpidio's right-hand man to show up and deliver documents! Official documents for what? Another concrete permit? Land titles for Licenciado Roberto Barraza, the man in front of me, my enigmatic former counselee, the one who'd played me like a fool just a half hour before? The shots reached my head, a dizziness replacing the nervousness that had descended upon me the moment that metal curtain rose.

"What'd you do that for?" I asked.

Wopper looked at me as if he'd just now become aware of my presence. He had become quiet after we left Don Elpidio's office, a pensive expression on his face. "I had to," he said after a long pause.

"Was this your plan from the beginning?" I asked. "Just a way of getting several thousand dollars!"

He shrugged. Shrugged as if I was supposed to take that as a suitable answer. I could have thrown something at him.

"Don't shrug!" I said, my voice more shrill than I intended. "You realize you're digging yourself deeper? Just because you used me to get by this time doesn't mean that it's going to end. You can't deal with people like that and expect to come out on top."

He looked me squarely in the eyes. "What makes you think that?" he asked, not as a challenge but as if the thought had never occurred to him.

"Why?" I cried. "Did you look at him? He's the spitting image of every Mexican gangster lowlife corrupt politician surrounded by his cronies who'll shoot you on the street and face no repercussions. This isn't Woodland! If I were you, I'd watch my back, or else you'll end up bound and gagged and left to suffocate in some trunk."

He shushed me and looked around. I hadn't realized how much my voice had risen.

"That's right," he said. "It's not Woodland. But I'm doing fine here."

I slammed my hand on the table, once again not intending such an emphatic gesture, but the tequila was hitting me hard. "That's what I want to know!" I told him. "You are doing fine here. Absolutely fine!" I started to laugh. "And it's throwing me for a friggin' loop. I can't make sense of it. Here you did nothing back home, and all of a sudden I show up and you're playing me for some pawn in your intricate scheme. What happened to you? I want to know. I seriously want to know. And they call you Licenciado, as if you had a degree, huh? How did that happen?"

He shrugged.

"Stop shrugging!" I cried, then I caught myself and lowered my voice. "Tell me what is going on so I can leave and enjoy what's left of my vacation."

"You can leave whenever you want, Mr. Beas," he said.

"No, you see, that's not the case," I spoke slowly. "I was supposed to come down, check on you, make sure that you were really going to use the money to cross the border, and then, if all checked out, give you the money. But that's not what happened, is it?"

To my annoyance he shrugged again, then he called for two more shots. I continued, "Now what am I supposed to tell my aunt and Lara?" I asked. "And don't shrug at this question, because it's your problem to deal with!"

He looked at me with those languid frog eyes as if I was the one in error, and then suddenly I realized I was. This wasn't his problem to deal with. I'm the one who gave him the money. I'm the one who didn't follow my directions. I leaned back against the wall. The tequila arrived and immediately, without thinking, I took the shot.

"Calm down, Mr. Beas," he said, smiling. "We might have a long wait."

I scoffed, but I don't know at what. Maybe the fact that he kept calling me Mr. Beas. I was still thinking about what I was going to say to my aunt when she learned I'd given away her hard-earned money and that her grandson's father was most certainly *not* using it to come home.

As if reading my mind he took his shot and said, "I have a son."

I turned my head toward him, my face feeling flushed, the third shot not wasting any time in taking effect. "You do," I said.

"What's his name?" he asked.

I raised my head from the wall. I couldn't remember. Instead of admitting that, my drunkenness provided an edge. "What does it matter?" I said. "He'll never know his father. You know, you didn't even mention him in your letter to Lara. Here she is waiting for any news from you, and all you tell her is that you're involved in municipal politics—real nice letter! No mention of the child she just brought into being."

"She broke up with me," he informed me again, his voice trailing off into a murmur. He was silent for some time. He took his shot and said, "She was there watching me write it—I thought she'd ask what I was writing, and I didn't want to lie. I didn't want her to know I had a son."

"Who was there?" I said. "The girl you live with?"

He nodded.

"Was it *her* idea to ask for the money to cross?" I asked. I didn't feel as drunk anymore. Or maybe I was drunker but more accustomed to the feeling. Either way I felt as if I finally had some focus. I was getting somewhere. "Why would she have done that?" I asked.

"It was just an idea that came up," he said, shrugging.

"An idea to embezzle money?" I exclaimed. "Was that it? Develop elaborate schemes to get your ex-girlfriend's cousin to come down to Mexico and deliver money at your doorstep—"

He interrupted me. "I didn't know you'd be involved, Mr. Beas, I swear," he said. "I thought Lara would send the money, no questions asked. I'm going to pay her back, with interest. But we were desperate. These projects, we—"

Now I cut him off. "It's a cruel trick, if you ask me," I said. "It can't be easy for Lara, you know that, and this'll only make it harder."

"It wasn't easy for me, either," he muttered. "But I've tried to make the most of it. Plus, what do you expect? Do I actually try to go back, live there illegally? Is that what she wants me to do?"

"I don't know what she wants," I replied. "All I know is that you asked her for money to cross back over, and clearly that's not the case. Now I have to explain that to her."

"I'm sorry," he said.

I allowed his apology to settle in, not sure what he was apologizing for. For inconveniencing me or for lying to Lara and my aunt?

"What's my son's name?" he asked again.

I sighed. "I don't remember," I said. It was true. All I'd heard was Precioso and Corazón.

We were both silent for a long while. Wopper kept looking behind him, expecting Don Elpidio's right-hand man to walk in at any moment. We switched to beer.

"So you aren't going back?" I asked.

"Back where?" he said.

"Where else?" I said.

Once again he shrugged.

II

Don Elpidio

The bastard was digging himself a hole. He really was. He may have had that slut behind him, but now he'd brought associates from the North, and that was where it got complicated. I had heard about all his so-called "connections" in California, but who doesn't have connections in California? I have aunts and uncles, two brothers, and at least fifteen cousins in Sacramento alone, so does my right-hand man, Pilimón, and so does the fucking shoeshine boy in the plaza. We live in Michoacán; there are michoacanos in Detroit for God's sake, in New York, in New Jersey. I wouldn't doubt the presence of michoacanos in Russia, but no one's claiming connections to the Russians. Connections!

So that's why I didn't pay any mind when everyone started talking about Licenciado Roberto Barraza's northern "associates." I even told the representative from Santa Clarita about Pilimón's ten cousins in Denver. "And what does that mean?" he asked. *What does that mean, you numbskulled idiot? It means even my right-hand man has connections, but a right-hand man is a right-hand man, in the background following my every order.* "And what does that mean?" he asked again. *It means that Roberto Barraza is just like you and me, except that unlike you and me, he's from the shittiest rancho in the municipality, and everybody who left La Morada is probably still working as a dishwasher or field hand. So if you're impressed by those connections, then be my guest.* "Your guest to what?" he asked. I gave up at that point. Backward municipal representatives— you'd think these towns would have more qualified individuals, but they don't, they really don't. These are the most capable numbskulled idiots they have, and I'm their appointed leader.

To get to the bottom of this issue, however, I asked the representative from Santa Clarita where he'd heard about Licenciado Barraza's northern connections. He told me that he'd heard about it from the rep from Pardo, so I went to the rep from Pardo and asked the same question. He told me that he'd heard about it from the rep from Agosto. I went to the rep from Agosto and was directed to the rep from San Formio, and so on until I'd gone through all the reps except one, Don Humberto from Aguilar, the most respected rep on the council. He told me he'd heard about it from Lucio Barraza. "The former representative from La Morada?" I asked. "The one we kicked off the council because he was going insane? The one who threatened to throw himself off the municipal building if we didn't pave the road to La Morada?" "Yes, him," Don Humberto said. "Since when do we listen to him?" I asked. He shrugged. The most capable of my reps, and he shrugs! Here they've been following the directives of Licenciado Roberto Barraza for weeks, months, all because they were sure he was well connected, and they never even thought to question the source. This is the kind of nonsense I have to deal with.

I went and found Lucio and confronted him about lying to people about Roberto Barraza's connections in the North, and he denied everything. So I informed him that Pilimón would be visiting shortly. That's when he began talking. He told me that Don Cirilo's daughter had made him go tell Don Humberto. She'd also instructed him how to present the connections, and he told me how she had everything so well planned out that he didn't even have to do much before Don Humberto went and told the representative from Rosio, as if he himself had discovered the information. "Lucio, this slut made you go insane," I said. "Why would you be doing her favors for her new man?" He smiled. I asked him, "What the fuck are you smiling about?" And he shrugged. I swear to God there's a language between backward idiots based on shrugging, and only inarticulate idiots can decipher it.

So then I knew that Licenciado Roberto Barraza was a sham and that he had no connections in the North, and that he was down here for some reason, but whatever that reason was didn't matter. The point was he was here alone. And that's what I needed to find out, because now he was at my disposal. Even with connections I could've handled him, but a chump like him, just a young kid—I could finish off what that slut propped up. I began my own campaign against him. Those connections he was supposed to have, well, I made them seem a bit more sinister. I asked the rep from Pardo, "Do you know anything about the presence of marijuana farms in La Morada?" And I mentioned to the rep from Agosto, within hearing range of the rep from Rosio, "Don't tell anyone, but they intercepted a reputed dealer from Los Angeles, and guess where he was headed? To La Morada of all places. Can't figure for the life of me why." That's all that was required to cast suspicion. The backward municipal ranchito types love to gossip, and the higher a man rises and the juicier the gossip, the quicker it spreads. I was sure Licenciado Roberto Barraza's influence would lessen considerably. No one wanted to be involved with those kinds of connections.

But then he confused me, and I hate being confused. Two months I gave him to pay the permit money for the foundation and concrete projects he pushed through without my consent. Two months before I sent Pilimón to collect in whatever form he saw fit. Well, then I heard the metal curtain rolling up in front, and I instructed Pilimón to find out who it was. But before my right-hand man could leave the office, in walked the Licenciado Roberto Barraza as if he owned the place, followed closely behind by a man in a white dress shirt that looked like it had been in crisp clean shape when he left the house that morning but had since undergone a day of sweat and La Morada dust. He looked to be in his thirties, still young looking but with a more mature bearing than the Licenciado, who still looked like a kid to me. The man rolled a suitcase behind him, which I noted by glancing at Pilimón, who noted the suitcase as well and nodded back. Suitcases are always causes for suspicion.

"What do I owe the honor?" I said, leaning back in my chair. I was still trying to figure out what was about to happen. Usually when men have fallen in my disfavor they don't come to me, I go to them, or rather, Pilimón goes to them and asks that they set up an appointment. I thought for a second that maybe I'd forgotten the appointment, so I leaned forward and peered at my desk calendar, which, I realize, seems the kind of thing a secretary or clerk would have, but in my business—of which politics is a large part—the meetings and appointments add up. I can trust Pilimón with the muscle, but not with keeping a schedule.

"I'd like to present an associate from Woodland, California," the Licenciado said without taking his eyes off me. "He's a highly respected councillor with influence in many sectors. Licenciado Arnulfo Beas."

I stared at the man. He nodded his head in greeting. He looked nervous, or not so much nervous as confused. That made two of us. He avoided my eyes.

"Pleased to meet you," I said. "I hope you're enjoying your stay in La Piedad. You're a councillor, is that right? In what capacity, might I ask?'

"Mostly education," Roberto Barraza answered for him.

"Education, huh?" I said, trying to make sense of this detail. What business did the education councillor from Woodland, California, have with La Morada?

"He's appointed, much like here," the Licenciado continued. "Education, you know, but just like *you're* the head of the municipal council of representatives."

What was that supposed to mean? Before I could fully size the man up, the Licenciado said to me, "The councillor has brought your money. We've struck a partnership with our associates in the North. As you know, most of the residents of La Morada are in California, but they continue to have an interest in their hometown."

"First of all," I said, "it's not my money. It's for the city permits, as you yourself agreed to pay in accordance with the contract."

"That's right," he said, "the contracts. So then I'm supposed to receive the permit documents once I've given you the money."

I nodded, not remembering the specifics of the documents I had drawn up. I never thought he'd be able to pull together the money. Not with his occupation as a corn farmer and La Morada empty of all moneymaking men. And I was sure his relationship with my concrete competitors would sour the moment he began asking for funds to be handed over to me.

I looked at the councillor. Roberto looked at him as well and said something in English. The man's face paled. He leaned down and unzipped the suitcase. I glanced at Pilimón, who had his hand within reach of his gun in the back of his belt. He looked to me for instructions. I squinted my eyes, which he'd recognized to mean, "Calm down, this isn't one of those situations."

The man produced an envelope that he then handed to the Licenciado. Roberto peeked inside and made an empty gesture of counting its contents. It was at that moment I noticed the slight grin creep onto the corner of his mouth. A giddy smirk, as if he'd just read a love note. When he looked at me the smile was gone. His frog-eyed countenance was serious. He stepped forward and placed the money on my desk. I picked it up and looked inside. All American dollars. I counted it, knowing already that the funds were there. I cursed myself for not making it a larger sum.

"I thank you, Licenciado. Sorry I hadn't let you know beforehand," I said. "These construction projects always have these kinds of hidden bureaucratic measures—"

"I know," he said, cutting me off. "But, in this case," he went on, hesitating, as if having rehearsed this line before but unsure whether he wanted to deliver it, "the fees were developed later. Developed by you. I already checked through the municipal projects records, and no other municipality of La Piedad has had to pay this kind of permit fee, and definitely not for projects on government property."

I laughed. It was all I could do in response to the kid's nerve. No one had talked to me like that in years. It was almost refreshing. I peered over at Pilimón, whose face had flushed red at hearing such words directed at his boss. He was not reassured by my laughter. "Okay, okay," I said. "But now you understand that what you do behind my back is not behind my back at all. I have my ways, and maybe you have this . . . this official from the North to bail you out this time, but he won't always be able to. So be careful in your dealings, son. You don't want to get in over your head."

You know what the kid said to me?

Nothing. He just shrugged.

Son of a bitch pissed me off. Made me lose my cool. As he left I couldn't help but call out to him, "*Oye,* have you asked your girl about Don Martín?"

He stopped. I knew I'd struck a nerve. But all he did was turn halfway around and say, "We'll be waiting at El Castillo for the receipt documents. Otherwise you'll have all the northerners from

La Morada calling the municipal president about the permit funds. The councillor will make sure of that."

Then the two men left. And I had to admit I was impressed. He was no Lucio Barraza. I said to Pilimón, "That slut may have actually found the man to get what she wants." Now I had to find out what that was.

CHAPTER NINE

NOT TOO LONG AFTER, DON ELPIDIO CALLED TOGETHER HIS COMPETITORS for a rare meeting. He sent Pilimón and Pilimón's cousin Marcos to extend the invitation. First they went to Valentín Moreno of Moreno Concrete. He was so suspicious of any emissary from Don Elpidio that he spoke to Pilimón only through the gate intercom.

"What does he want this meeting for?" he asked.

"Don Elpidio just wants a general assessment of the situation," Pilimón answered.

"What situation are we talking about?" Valentín asked.

"He wants to discuss the new representative from La Morada," Pilimón replied.

"What is there to discuss?"

Pilimón sighed and said, "Don Elpidio asked me to stress the fact that this meeting is not to be an inquiry, but more like a meeting of minds." These were the exact words his boss had instructed him to say, and he'd committed them to memory.

There was silence on the other end of the intercom. Finally, Valentín Moreno told the men to leave the details with his secretary.

Valentín Moreno had inherited the concrete company from his father, whose business skill far outmatched his son's. In appearance they were the same, pale and slight, but the elder Moreno had flair, a winning personality. As intense as the competition for contracts grew, he never lost a friend or a competitor's respect. Valentín, however, found the cutthroat nature of the business crippling. He never figured out how to maintain friendly relations, especially after losing a contract to two-faced backroom dealings. His ever fewer subordinates reassured him that the concrete business had become dirtier and dirtier over the years. His father never had to deal with this level of trickery and backstabbing. Moreno Concrete had slipped far behind Maya Brothers Concrete and was in danger of being pushed out completely when Valentín and his advisors decided a desperate change of tactics was required. They needed to branch out. They couldn't go head-to-head with the now larger companies, because they'd lose every time.

It was around this period of strategizing that Licenciado Roberto Barraza, the new municipal representative from La Morada, approached Valentín Moreno about a business deal. Valentín didn't question the representative's youth. Instead, he saw it as a refreshing change; he considered himself young, or at least of a younger generation than his competitors, and he preferred to deal with someone open and willing to offer new ideas. Licenciado Roberto Barraza had just that. He explained that the residents of La Morada had asked that he make paving the primary school his utmost priority. This was not the new idea Valentín Moreno had in mind. He almost laughed out loud at the notion that his company would bid on such an insignificant contract. Had his company fallen that far? But the young representative told him straight-faced that there was to be no bid. This job would be done for free.

Again Valentín almost laughed out loud, but Roberto was quick to explain that residents of La Morada in the North eventually (very soon, in fact) desired to have all the streets repaved, and that once the money was raised the contract would go to Moreno Concrete. "Those who immigrated have done well for themselves," the representative explained. "They want to turn La Morada into their vacation spot, and they have money to build. It is a good investment. You can't just keep thinking about the money that's here in La Piedad. More and more those who left to the North are going to have money to bring back, and not just to spend at las fiestas, but for big projects like I described. They are better organized than you imagine." It was this idea of an organized body of northerners who would one day invest in their hometowns that sold Valentín Moreno. His company began paving the primary school almost immediately.

The same line was delivered to Ernesto Maya at Maya Brothers Concrete, a misnomer as Ernesto had bought out, or rather, as everyone knew, run his two brothers out of the business. A short, stocky man with a pug nose, he was a businessman in the same mold as Don Elpidio, the kind that needs a right-hand man like Pilimón to do his negotiating. Ernesto Maya's right-hand man was a tall and wiry bruiser named Rooster, who had once been the best goalie in La Piedad. In fact, several professional teams had recruited him, but before his tryout in Morelia he'd broken his leg in a car accident and had limped ever since. His career was over, but in subsequent years he'd become a successful local trainer and coach. He was not as much Ernesto Maya's muscle as Pilimón was Don Elpidio's, though he did his fair share of intimidating. He was more of an assistant, and Ernesto respected the man's advice. Rooster's family had originally been from La Morada, and he had aunts and uncles and cousins who lived in Woodland. In fact, the new representative, Roberto Barraza, knew a cousin of his from high school— Victor Ochoa—who'd also been a great soccer player. They discovered this over a round of beers and shots at El Castillo, where Rooster was known to frequent. After they were sufficiently drunk, Roberto Barraza asked Rooster if he would do his family's hometown the honor of training the local club. Rooster said that he would if only there was a team left to train! Every player had jumped ship. Although this was true, the Licenciado explained that if Rooster were on board, players would return. He also had another idea for recruiting players, but for that idea he needed to speak to Ernesto Maya. It was Rooster who introduced the representative to his boss.

After the night at El Castillo, Rooster spoke so much about reviving the La Morada Soccer Club and how it was just the challenge he was looking for that Ernesto Maya actually grew curious to hear the representative's idea, if only as a new diversion. Don Elpidio's concrete company sponsored the best club team in La

Piedad. Maya's company sponsored the second best, but the team had been demoted to the second division for two years because of a betting scandal. Licenciado Roberto Barraza explained that if Ernesto Maya threw his weight behind La Morada's club, they'd be sure to rise out of the second division, and they would be competing for the regional title long before the scandal-ridden premier division team. Maya liked the idea, but he wanted to know why Roberto chose him and his company specifically. The Licenciado told him that in order to attract better players, they needed new stands and a locker room.

"And La Morada has the funds to support such a project?" Ernesto Maya asked.

The young rep shook his head and clarified that the project would be done for free.

"For free!" Ernesto Maya said, laughing. And that was when it was explained that this was an investment in further projects. Roberto Barraza went on to describe the impact of the increasing number of northerners with dual citizenship, and how more and more of them were willing and anxious to invest in their home-towns. La Morada was going to be a model for all the other municipal ranchos. Ernesto Maya heard him out, but he was already thinking about next season's league standings.

By the time Don Elpidio called the meeting with his competitors, both Valentín Moreno and Ernesto Maya were beginning to doubt Licenciado Roberto Barraza's claim that northerners would be investing in future projects. Moreno Concrete paved the primary school and Valentín Moreno had to answer more than he cared the question: "What the hell are you guys doing pouring a blacktop for a rancho primary school?" His doubt was furthered when he heard that Maya Brothers Concrete had begun construction just down the road on stadium stands and a locker room. That would have at least been a respectable job. When he spoke to Roberto Barraza about his concerns, he was merely told that there'd be "plenty" to go around. When discussion of any further projects was dropped, Valentín Moreno felt as if he'd been swindled. But still he held out hope that this venture would pay off.

As far as Ernesto Maya was concerned, he may not have believed that northerners would be knocking down his door, but when Rooster told him that he'd convinced two premier division caliber players in La Piedad to transfer to La Morada's team, his pet project took further shape.

"How'd you convince them?" he asked.

"I just made it in their best interests," Rooster said.

That was enough for Ernesto Maya.

Don Elpidio sat behind his desk, Pilimón behind him. Only Valentín Moreno was alone, but he prided himself on this fact. He didn't need muscle. Both Don Elpidio and Ernesto Maya thought to themselves that he was too insignificant to need it. They were sure Moreno Concrete would be out of business within three years, but they needed to maintain relations if they wanted to absorb his company. Don Elpidio wasted no time stating his business.

"Please tell me, my friends, what you fuckers are doing bidding on contracts behind my back?"

"I'll save you the mystery," Ernesto Maya replied. "I don't know about Valentín, here, but on my end there was no bidding."

The two men turned to Valentín Moreno. "Same for us," he said. "No bids."

"So then are you telling me that you actually did these projects for free?" Don Elpidio asked.

The two men glanced at one another before answering. Ernesto Maya nodded his head first. Valentín Moreno followed his lead.

Don Elpidio grimaced and clasped his hands together. "And please, explain to this old man why you would take on these projects for no foreseeable profit? We're dealing with the shittiest rancho in the municipality here. You must have long-term plans, and I want to know them."

Valentín Moreno squirmed in his seat and nervously combed his mustache with his finger. He didn't want to explain Licenciado Roberto Barraza's promise of future northern investment for two reasons: if true, he didn't want Don Elpidio to gobble up those contracts; if not true, he didn't want to reveal that he'd fallen for empty promises. He also wanted to wait and see what Ernesto Maya had to say. He'd been wondering why he accepted the project as well. To his relief, Maya began speaking first.

"I want to tell you, Don Elpidio, that it was a great disappointment to me that my team was demoted to the second division; a harsh penalty, harsher than need be. I also know that the judicial board was in your pocket, which is fine, such is the game we play, but I've found a way around it." He said the last part in a jocular manner, and both he and Don Elpidio began to laugh heartily. Valentín Moreno knew the laugh well. It was a laugh his father had but that he hadn't yet mastered, if he ever would. It was a laugh that cleared the air and at the same said, *I'm going to fuck you over before I'm through.*

Then Don Elpidio turned to Valentín Moreno and said to him, "So tell me, son, has the company fallen on such hard times that you're forced to accept jobs from primary schools?"

Valentín again shifted in his chair. "Well, yes, as you both know," he said, feeling as though his voice were quavering. "It is no secret that my company has struggled in recent years, and I just had too many employees in need of work. So I had to come up with something. The La Morada primary school job at least kept my labor force happy, if only for a short while."

Valentín didn't expect Don Elpidio to feel compassion for his plight. He did want the old man to at least hear him out. But Don Elpidio abruptly cut him off and said, "Okay, well then, all right. What we're dealing with is this: I decided to call this meeting because just the other day the representative from La Morada, the Licenciado Roberto Barraza, came to my office accompanied by a councillor from Woodland, California. I'm sure you're all familiar with our sister city. This councillor provided funds for—well, let me just put it this way—provided permit fees for the jobs you two completed. Do you know what this means?"

Valentín Moreno suddenly sat up in his chair. So the representative did have connections in the North. Maybe the promises weren't empty.

Don Elpidio continued, "What this means is that the slut who did in Don Martín Solorio and Lucio Barraza has found the man she needs to get the job done. Now I want to find out what you guys know about her angle. What does she want? What is she aiming for?"

Both Valentín Moreno and Ernesto Maya had no idea what Don Elpidio was talking about.

"With all due respect, Don Elpidio," Ernesto Maya said, "I've only been in touch with the Licenciado."

Valentín Moreno nodded his head in agreement.

Don Elpidio was silent for a moment before resuming. He spoke slowly. "I know we're competitors, and there's no reason we need to share information, but this is one instance where I believe we all have something to lose. I want to get to the bottom of this. Now Don Martín, may God rest his soul, was heavily involved with municipal politics, and many said that—"

"What does Don Martín have to do with our separate projects?" Ernesto Maya interrupted.

"It has to do with the girl that . . . that . . ." Don Elpidio seemed to find it difficult to say.

"The girl he died fucking," Ernesto Maya finished for him. "Yes, so what? Wouldn't we all wish ourselves that death? I don't believe the other details, I really don't. That's just rancho gossip. But still, what does that have to do with my company's sponsorship of the La Morada Soccer Club?"

"It's not rancho gossip!" Don Elpidio exclaimed, slapping the table for emphasis. But then he withdrew, visibly calming and lowering his voice. "Look, she sent Don Martín to his grave, and she made Lucio Barraza, the last representative, go insane—I saw it myself. But this new rep isn't an old man ready to keel over, nor is he a simpleton like Lucio. As I now know, he's connected. I don't have an idea *how* connected, but enough that he's not on his own. But I do know he's not pulling the strings. She is."

"Who is, Don Elpidio?" Valentín Moreno asked, confused, as he didn't know any of the circumstances surrounding Don Martín's death.

"A corn farmer's daughter from La Morada."

"We're worried about a corn farmer's daughter?"

"Look, I have intuition about these kinds of things. I usually know someone's angle, what they want, what they're driving at, and when I don't, I grow suspicious and it's cause for worry. In this girl's case, I don't know what she wants. And that's fine as long as she stays in La Morada—the slut can kill every old fucker there—but when I heard that my competitors were brought in, understand, I began to worry a little bit more. And I don't like to worry, you know that. I'm going to let him enjoy his run a little longer, but understand that at some point I'm going to shut his operation down."

"But that's not fair!" Valentín Moreno blurted out.

Both Don Elpidio and Ernesto Maya raised their eyebrows in amused surprise.

"We're working with him," Valentín Moreno continued, controlling his voice. "You shut him down, you shut us down." He turned to Ernesto Maya for support, but he didn't seem the least bit alarmed.

"Well, you should've thought about that before you went behind my back," Don Elpidio said. "The way you save yourself now is to keep your eyes and ears open and keep me informed of what she's after. We're going to let them fall into their own trap." Then he glanced in Valentín Moreno's direction and added, "And please, Valentín, watch that you don't get fucked."

Both Don Elpidio and Ernesto Maya began to laugh.

Valentín Moreno left Don Elpidio's office frustrated and confused. The meeting was seemingly called for no other purpose than to let him and Maya know that Don Elpidio had his eye on them. It was a waste of his time, but both Ernesto Maya and Don Epildio seemed to think the meeting had gone extraordinarily well, and that great pieces of information had been exchanged. To Valentín, all that seemed to have been exchanged were rumors, threats, and rancho gossip. He kept thinking about Don Elpidio's comments about the girl. He thought it strange that the old man was giving her so much thought and worry. He decided to drive out to La Morada and address the matter directly.

When he arrived at Roberto Barraza's home, he found the young man sitting on a stack of bricks and removing mud caked on the soles of his boots. The sun was beating down on him, and perspiration made his face glisten. He looked up, held his hand over his brow, and said, "I thought that was you, Señor Moreno. What brings you around here? You want something cold to drink? I can have Mija get—"

"Actually, Roberto, I was wondering if you wouldn't mind taking a drive with me around La Morada."

Roberto eyed him strangely but then said, "Sure, just give me a minute." He ducked inside the house and emerged a minute later in a fresh white t-shirt.

Once in the car, Valentín told Roberto about that afternoon's meeting. At first, Roberto's only response was that he was surprised it hadn't occurred earlier. He was quiet for a while before he said, "Of course he's going to threaten to shut it down, but Don Elpidio only *thinks* he knows everything. If he could have shut us down so easily, don't you think he would have done it earlier? It's his own fault that he stopped attending the meetings."

"Well, that's the thing. He's letting it go on because he's curious to find out what we're after. Actually, he's curious to—" Valentín stopped, suddenly feeling awkward. He feared offending Roberto. On the way over he had rationalized it by saying it was his money, his company, his investment, and he needed to be kept informed. But in person the question was much more difficult to ask. He liked the kid and had no wish to stir things up in his home life. So instead he asked about the progress of the street-paving project. Roberto explained that letters had been sent out, and they were just waiting to hear back. He reassured him that everything was going smoothly. They were already on the outskirts of La Morada, surrounded by corn and agave fields, and the roads were getting narrower and bumpier, clouds of dust enveloping the gray Chevy truck. Valentín found a driveway to turn around in and then headed back toward the center of town, their dust trail now settling before them.

They drove in silence, and Roberto stared out the window. His mouth hung open and he had an exhausted look in his eyes. Valentín thought it must be obvious that he'd come out there for a more significant purpose, but he couldn't expect Roberto to ask him what that was. They drove past a small store, where a group of kids stood outside playing pinball. The kids turned to stare at the truck, waiting until it passed before returning to their game.

When the truck turned down the dirt path toward the Licenciado's home, Valentín finally found the nerve to voice his concern. "Don Elpidio seems very suspicious of your girlfriend. Do you have any idea why?"

Roberto gave Valentín a brief puzzled look and then turned to stare out the window. "No," he said.

Valentín pushed further. "At the meeting, he kept on talking about her involvement not only with you, but also with previous representatives, including some old man, Martín Solorio. Do you know anything about her relationship with him?"

"Relationship? What are you talking about?"

"I don't know. I really don't, honestly. Just that Don Elpidio, today at the meeting, he kept bringing her up."

Roberto's brow furrowed, and he stared fixedly at the plastic gold Chevy emblem on the dashboard. He didn't respond for a long time, and Valentín worried he had overstepped his bounds. Finally Roberto said, "I don't know what you're talking about, but I wouldn't trust anything that Don Elpidio says. I mean, did your father ever trust Don Elpidio?"

"No, but . . . I mean," Valentín stammered. "He didn't. You're right, you're absolutely right. I'm sorry. Like I said, I just felt I should ask. I didn't mean to offend you."

"You didn't offend me."

Valentín Moreno left it that. He saw that the young man didn't know anything more than he did. He could've asked him to confront his girlfriend's odd involvement with successive municipal representatives, but that would've only served to stoke his confusion. No more information would've been gathered. He remembered that the Licenciado had only arrived in the area recently. There was probably plenty he didn't know, and maybe that was for the best. He dropped the Licenciado off in front of his house, just a humble brick shack surrounded by dirt and weeds, and he compared it to his own expansive home. He had no doubt that Ernesto Maya's home and Don Elpidio's especially were many times the size. The Licenciado's shack wouldn't have served as a potting shed on their property. The whole rancho was full of potting sheds—just a collection of brightly colored shacks—and they called it a town. This was the place on which he had staked the future of Moreno Concrete? Maybe it had come to that. This wasn't the first time his thoughts had gone in this direction. But more than ever he wondered why Don Elpidio was so worried. Why couldn't he just let it be?

As he was driving away, he noticed someone hanging towels from a clothesline. He assumed it was the girl, though all he could see was the bottom of a red-checkered apron and two skinny brown legs. He wondered what would now ensue between the young couple. What would they say to one another? Would she ask Roberto why Valentín had driven all that way to see him? Would Roberto tell her? Would he ask her about Don Martín? Or would he just let it silently smolder inside of him, wondering what the hell it was that Valentín Moreno was talking about?

Chapter Ten

Lucio Barraza

I WOULD WATCH THEM GET ON THE BUS, THE WEEKLY AGENDA TUCKED underneath the Licenciado's arm. He would be freshly showered, dressed in a nice shirt, starched and ironed, his hair parted just right, his boots shined. He looked happy. Mija looked happy. Only I looked on miserably. I would imagine the two of them reviewing the agenda together at the kitchen table, just as Mija and I used to do in happier days. Happier days for me, anyway, if only because I was in her presence. At least then I could smell her, which might sound strange, but I would give up my four-wheeler for the chance to just smell her from time to time. For Mija I know those review sessions caused nothing but frustration. I couldn't ever understand a damn thing in those binders! Not one damn thing. She tried to explain things in so many different ways, even boiled down the whole municipality to cows, sheep, donkeys, and wolves (Don Elpidio was the top wolf, of course), but still I didn't understand. I didn't even really try, to be honest. Because it didn't matter, you know. No one else on the council read the agenda either. So why did I have to? I just wanted to look at her, to hold her, to kiss her, and all she ever wanted to do was talk about building contracts and zoning.

She learned it all from Don Martín, she said. Why Don Martín thought it important to pass along his knowledge of municipal affairs to his washerwoman I have no idea. So what if she's good at reading and learning things? Seems to me if you have a washerwoman, you just let her clean and cook and run errands. But Don Martín probably didn't have anything better to do, old as he was. I never believed the rumors about the two of them. They started after Don Martín died and decided to leave Mija a good chunk of money in his will, without warning or explanation. Why should he give an explanation? It was his money. But when his children came to gobble up their inheritance and learned that the washerwoman was to share, and then when they heard from gossipy neighbors that the two of them spent hours and hours together every single day doing who knows what—well, then, that was all they needed. They decided to accuse her of all sorts of nasty things: seducing an old man, luring him into her web of witchcraft; they even went so far as to invent details about the circumstances of his death, which out of respect for Mija I won't repeat for the rest of my days. She didn't deserve that kind of treatment. The whole rancho turned against her. If Don Cirilo had known, I'm sure he would've defended her, but somehow, against all odds, that man manages to preserve his ignorance. The day Don Jaspero the donkey learns to talk is the day gossip will finally reach Don Cirilo! But I heard what was being said—whispered from one old batty woman to another, my mother among them—and I didn't stand for it. I came to her defense because that is the kind of man I am. In the short run it worked out for me. But in the long run, not so much. She appreciated my gallantry, yes, she did. We became friends, then lovers, and if only I hadn't followed her suggestion to join the municipal council . . . I had no business pursuing politics.

There's the issue of my nerves, of course, but my main problem was basically this: Mija never understood that a man needs to feel in control. Never mind that she's calling the shots; she has to loosen the reigns a little bit, let the man make his own mistakes if need be. But there she was, constantly telling me to do this and to do that, without question, without debate, and I did it, I did everything she told me to do, but occasionally I did something she didn't tell me to do, and it blew up in my face. Like the time I accepted money from the Pork Manufacturers Association in exchange for allowing them to dump their waste on the outskirts of La Morada. It was on the outskirts! It was good money! You'd have thought they were dumping it on her mother's grave. She made me take the money back, and I did, except for the money I spent on new tires for my four-wheeler. That's why I work at Poncho's car wash twice a month—I'm still paying them off.

Anyway, maybe it wasn't my place, but I felt that I had to caution the Licenciado. He couldn't get swallowed up by her maneuverings and lose complete control. Because once that happened, well, then you were at her mercy. Believe me when I say that I would've done anything to remain at her mercy, but it wasn't good for my nerves, as the whole municipal council and staff and those in the plaza the day of my breakdown can attest. We are made of different material, the Licenciado and me. He was clearly a better man for the job than I was. But I felt as if I needed to at least give him fair warning. Can't everyone benefit from the advice of those who came before?

So early one evening I was out with our horse, Don Paisano, taking him for some exercise and water at the reservoir. It was the end of September, and the rainy season was just about over, meaning Don Paisano would no longer be able to just drink out of any old puddle or bucket of water. Well, I saw the Licenciado walking along the path by himself, hunched over, dirty from having worked all day, and I decided that now would be a good time to offer him some words of wisdom. One broken man in La Morada was enough. No reason for there to be two of us. I also thought I'd mention a few projects I'd lined up that had lain fallow ever since I resigned my position on the council. So I tied Don Paisano to a tree, not that the feeble old thing would ever go anywhere, and stepped out onto the path just as Roberto Barraza passed by. He must have been deep in thought, because I startled him.

"What are you up to around here?" he asked.

"Oh, you know, a little bit of this, a little bit of that!" I said, trying to be cheerful. "Do you mind if I join you?"

"I was actually heading home to eat," he said.

"Fine, fine, I won't keep you," I said. "I just wanted to pick your brain about the municipal council, offer some of my own thoughts. As you must know, I was the representative from our rancho before you. Of course, I didn't have quite as much success as you've had so far, but then again I warned Mija that I'm not cut out for politics! But she insisted I do it."

He looked at me as if I had sprouted another head. "Mija encouraged you to be the municipal representative?" he asked.

"Yes, and I made La Morada the laughing stock of the municipality," I said to him. "I'm a delicate soul and I snapped. I couldn't handle such heartache."

"Heartache? Because of the council?" he asked.

"No, of course not because of the council!" I said, laughing, thinking he was joking. I winked and slapped his shoulder to show him that I got it. Again, he looked at me oddly. Could he really not have known?

"Who was the municipal representative before you?" the Licenciado asked, seemingly out of nowhere.

"Why, Don Martín was," I said, not wanting to bring up the old man. It wasn't my place to do so. "God rest his soul," I continued. "There was a short gap after he died, but then when Mija and I started seeing each other, it wasn't long before I was nominated."

We had been walking rapidly, the Licenciado walking faster and faster, but now he stopped abruptly. "You and Mija saw each other?" he asked, a look of disbelief on his face. "As in, you were together?"

"Oh, you didn't know," I said, realizing at once that maybe the poor guy was as oblivious as Don Cirilo. "I just assumed," I said. "I assumed you knew, that she told you, or at the very least that the guys on the council told you. I'm sorry, my friend." And I was sorry. I didn't intend to spill the beans. But shouldn't he have known something like that?

As a result of his confusion, I myself was thrown off guard and wasn't thinking straight. So my attempt at encouraging him to maintain his independence instead became a long complaint about Mija's domineering ways. No man likes to hear that his woman has him by the balls (I knew firsthand), and that was basically what I was telling him. But what I meant to say was *avoid* letting her grab hold of them. He let me talk. I wish he had interrupted me immediately, but I went on and on, digging my hole even deeper. By the end Mija was an evil sorceress, I was a man under her spell, and he was her inevitable next victim. So of course he had every right to tell me to go screw myself.

If only we had been able to talk a little longer! I could've explained myself better. Instead, Mija emerged from the house (we were now on his property), saw the two us together, and said, "My love, dinner is ready." I saw him sigh heavily, as though he hadn't yet decided what to make of the news I'd just shared with him. But what was a heavy sigh compared with the blood pouring from the wound in my heart? She called him *my love*! She never called me anything but Lucio, which of course is my name, but who doesn't wish for affection from time to time? And not only that, she never made me dinner, not once.

In my defense, if I had truly desired to stir things up, there are many things I could've told him that day. For one, the distasteful gossip surrounding Mija and Don Martín. But I didn't. I could've told him how on occasion she still sought out my help. Especially when she needed word to spread quickly—I was always good at that—like when she asked me to tell Don Humberto, the loose-lipped representative from Agosto, about all of Roberto Barraza's connections in the North, his college degree, and his numerous accomplishments for a man so young. I willingly obliged because even after all that has happened, I still seek to please her. I was actually discreet considering all that I could have shared with the Licenciado.

Well, he was young, and he would've done better to have listened to a man maybe not smarter but at least older. I was trying to caution him, but I only pissed him off, and for that he never forgave me. For that he refused to see me the day the councillor came from the North and I accompanied him to the municipal offices. As if I hadn't suffered enough embarrassment in that building!

PART III

CHAPTER ELEVEN

Lara Gonzalez

WHEN THE BABY WAS BORN I GOT REALLY DEPRESSED. EVERY TIME I LOOKED at him, I couldn't help but think of Wopper; they looked just like each other. I think when I was pregnant I was able to stay pissed off at Wopper because it was still just me, and I was uncomfortable and felt shitty, and I didn't want to be cooped up with my parents all the time. So I just blamed Wopper and stayed mad. But when the baby came, I suddenly realized that my life had changed forever and that now I was really alone. We were alone, me and my son. My family was around, but they didn't change that feeling. In some ways, they made it worse.

At night I would think of Wopper and wish that he were sleeping next to me, even though we were hardly able to do that when he was here. I would wonder what his life was like, how he was living. I couldn't picture him in some rancho, living in a brick shack painted some ugly-ass color, dust everywhere, having to light the gas heater every time he wanted to take a shower. Sometimes I'd imagine the two of us in our own place, Wopper working, me at home waiting for him to arrive so I could fill him with meat and tortillas. This made me laugh. Somehow I just couldn't picture it. Wopper working! Me cooking! Hell no. I'd laugh, but then I'd get even sadder because I'd think of how we were before and how I never appreciated it, just grew used to it: me and Wopper seeing each other every day, eating together (my mom always complaining about having an extra mouth to feed), watching television, and even though we fought all the time over the stupidest shit and didn't say much else to one another, that all seemed not to matter anymore.

We were all expecting Arnie to come over right away. I was anxious to hear from him. I needed to hear from someone who had actually seen Wopper. I wanted to know when he was coming back. I never thought that he wouldn't. I just wondered how long it would take him once he had the money for the coyote. Weeks? Days? It was January and freezing outside. Was that a good time to cross? Would he wait until spring? Not that there was anything I could do except wait, but I needed to have something to hold onto, even if just to know what he looked like before I actually saw him again.

But Arnie never showed up. After a few weeks I couldn't take it any longer, and I called him and left message after message. In some of them I was so upset that all I could do to keep from telling him off was to hang up, I swear to God. But the asshole never returned my calls. Eventually my mom and I went to him directly. We left the baby with a cousin and just showed up at his office at the college. We could tell he was surprised to see us. He claimed he'd been nonstop busy since getting back from vacation and that he'd been *meaning* to come by, but we weren't buying his excuses, at least I wasn't, and finally he gave up giving them.

He asked to speak to me by myself. My mom said that she wanted to hear everything, being as it was her money. He was about to give in, but I told her to leave. When she complained, repeating the same thing about her money, I yelled, "And it's the father of *my* child!" Arnie shushed me and put his finger to his lips. We both glared at him. My mom was pissed, but she got up to leave anyway. Arnie asked that she close the door behind her, and she slammed it. Should've seen the look on Arnie's face! He mumbled something about the president's office being just down the hall.

I waited for him to start talking. Honestly, I'd never seen him so nervous.

"Lara, I gave him the money," he said. "But he didn't use it on a smuggler."

He sighed and stared at his hands resting on his desk. Without looking up, he began talking all fast. I could barely follow what he was saying. "You have to understand that Wopper is not coming back," he said. "Never. Why would he? He's become something there. People respect him, they seek his advice; he plays the game like he's been doing it for years."

Then Arnie stopped and shook his head as if he was remembering something. He told me that he had seen Wopper handle this one man, some gangster-politician-businessman. He had even used Arnie, worked him over before he even knew what was happening. He couldn't understand, but it seemed that all these people down there trusted Wopper completely. Trusted him, respected him, whatever. They thought Wopper was a man on the rise, and they wanted to rise with him.

He kept talking as if I wasn't even there in the room. I had to cut him off or else he wouldn't have shut up.

"How do you *know* he's never coming back?" I asked. "Is that what he said?"

Arnie didn't answer my question, at least not directly. He just kept going on about Wopper's political involvement, telling me all about Wopper's different projects, but I didn't hear any of that. The only part I heard was when he said that Wopper was living with someone. He just slipped it in there, like it wasn't anything. But it felt as if he'd reached across the table and grabbed hold of my throat. I don't know why, but I never pictured Wopper being with anyone else. I really didn't. He was mine and that was it. I think that the whole time Wopper had been gone, all those months, I had hoped that he'd come back, even though I told myself I didn't want him to. And now I learned that Wopper had become someone different, he'd become *someone*. And it sounded so unbelievable that I could've easily not believed it, but then it was coming from my cousin Arnie, who may be too uppity for his own good, but he wouldn't gain anything by lying to protect Wopper. He wouldn't have any reason to make up this story, and so I had to believe it was true. I had to imagine a different Wopper from the Wopper I knew, and the only way I was able to do that was to imagine the changes in his life. Was it Mexico? La Morada? Some rancho? If anything, that would drag him down and make him suffer. So I could only think of the girl he was with, the girl who took my place. With me he drank too much and hardly ever worked. We just fought and watched television. But her? What was she like? What did she give him that I wasn't able to? Was it me who was lacking something? Did I drag him down?

I didn't want to ask, but I did anyway. "Did you meet his new girl?"

He nodded.

"What was she like?" I said. I was clenching my jaw, and I felt my lip trembling, but I kept it in. I wasn't going to cry, not in front of Arnie.

He looked like he didn't want to tell me, like he was searching for a way to describe her without hurting me. I could see his mind racing. Fucking Arnie, he's such a horrible liar. "She's just some girl from the rancho," he said.

I didn't ask any more.

CHAPTER TWELVE

Raquel Barraza

I COULDN'T STAY ANGRY WITH MY SON FOREVER, BUT THERE WERE TIMES when I thought I would. No, there were times when I wished I could. I missed Wopper terribly, but missing has little to do with anger. You can miss someone and still want to slap him across the head the minute you see him again. I mean it. And that's what I told Jorge every time I was sulking on the couch as I watched my soap operas and he said to me: "If you're so depressed we should go and visit him!" Depressed? A mother suffers for her children! Agonizes. But it was his own fault, his own stupidity, his own laziness and thoughtlessness. Let him suffer too! Jorge called me heartless. I told him that heartless was the father who raised a son in his own mold: drank too much, worked too little, and let life make his decisions for him rather than making his own decisions for his life. And my husband's response was that Wopper was going to become a man in Mexico. A man! I didn't dare tell him that I didn't care whether our son was a man or always a boy. I just wanted him back in Woodland, back in our home.

When Wopper called for the first and only time, I shouldn't have been so hard on him. It's true. But I wanted him to know that I was still angry with him for messing up his life. God forgive me, how I regretted my rush to scold! It was just that he left so quickly. I didn't have enough time to get out all my anger. So when he called I couldn't help myself. He felt so close, as if he were just down the road, calling to let me know he'd be late for dinner or that he needed a ride home from the bar, which of course he would never do. Of course! Otherwise he wouldn't have been in this mess.

Every time the phone rang Jorge and I wanted it to be him. We'd look at one another as if to say, "Could it be?" But it never was. It was always our daughters or sisters and brothers, cousins, neighbors, compadres and comadres, but Wopper never again.

Jorge waited a couple of months to tell me that Lara was pregnant. I asked him, or screamed at him, "Why did you take so long to tell me?" and all he did was raise his hands in the air. I know he was afraid of my reaction, that my anger at Wopper would be directed at Lara, which would then be directed at the baby. And Lord knows he was right. It was just one more of Wopper's stupid mistakes. Now the baby would grow up without a father, because I knew for sure that Lara wouldn't ever follow Wopper to some nothing rancho in Michoacán.

When the baby was born I only got upset all over again. I couldn't bring myself to go. The birth was only a reminder of the time gone by and the difficulty of Wopper's absence. Plus, I never liked Lara. I always thought that she wasn't right for my son. She didn't treat him well. She didn't love him, and I knew it. How did I know? A mother knows. They were fine as long as they were in high school, but once high school ended and they continued together, both of them getting comfortable, seeing each other every day as if they were already married, doing nothing, going nowhere, I knew that they continued because they believed they had no other choice. But isn't that how it usually happens?

My daughters visited the baby, and so did my husband. My comadres also visited, and they told me I had to go, too. They said the boy was the spitting image of my son. *What son?* I asked. It was a joke. A half joke. No one laughed. They told me that a grandchild should know his grandmother. They told me that I shouldn't be so cruel. I was suffering, and they called me cruel? As if I had no right to be angry. That was another reason to continue my stubborn fight, if only because they didn't understand my side of things. So I would wait until they did.

There were nights when I dreamed of Wopper as a baby. I saw myself holding him, nursing him, rocking him to sleep. But then I would realize it's not me, and the baby is not Wopper, it's Lara. She looks up and the dream ends. She looks up as if in surprise, as if in horror or fear. Fear of me? Is it my face that she looks up and sees?

One day we received in the mail a letter from Licenciado Roberto Barraza, from the Office of the Municipal Representative of La Morada. At first the name didn't look familiar, it really didn't. The envelope was official, so was the stationary, the seal—even the signature looked like it'd been written in a fine pen. I didn't recognize his handwriting. Why would I? Had I ever seen Wopper sign his name? If I did it was never next to *Licenciado*, that's for sure. It was only when I looked at the bottom of the page and saw a little note in a different pen. *Mom and Dad*, it said. *Please help me out on this project. Thanks, Your Son, Roberto.*

Only then did I realize the Licenciado was my son. I read the letter, and then I reread it, again and again. I couldn't understand it. I understood it, but I kept looking for something else. I expected more about him, about his life—God knows there had to be more! No news from him in over a year, and now just an official business letter. I read the handwritten note again. He wanted our help? *Of course* he wanted our help, I wanted to say, as if I was still too angry to give it to him. But this was not the kind of help I wanted him to ask for. Why didn't he say, *Please come visit me here*? Why didn't he say, *Please help me cross back over*? One or the other. Instead, he writes three paragraphs, or someone wrote them—I realized then that I'd never read anything Wopper wrote—giving details about a fundraising project!

Jorge came home and read the letter. You should have seen the joy in his face. He recognized immediately that the Licenciado was his son, as if he had expected this from the beginning. That his drunken lazy son, who never had a job longer than a couple months, was destined for politics in Mexico! "What does this mean?" I asked him. And all he could say was, "That we must help him, as he asked us to do. We must help him!" And I yelled at him, frustrated at his excitement. Why was he not bothered? Did he not want to have his son home? Did he prefer him gone forever? I yelled and told him I didn't understand one thing in that letter, that it made no sense at all. "What's not to understand?" he asked. And he explained how the rancho had to raise a third of the money, and the municipality and the federal government would match the rest. I asked him who cared about paving the streets of some rancho. That was when my husband grew upset. "That's not just any rancho," he cried, "that's my hometown, your hometown, too, if you weren't so ashamed! And everybody knows that paved streets are necessary for anything and everything to progress. But what does it matter," he went on. "Your son is in charge of the project, and if you were any kind of mother you wouldn't ask whether anyone cared or not, you would just recognize that your son needs your help and give it without a second thought!" I fought him for a while, yelling at him that I'd sacrificed myself enough over the years, that I'd done much more than give money for a street-paving project in a rancho that I'd left and never cared to return to. I gave up exhausted. Jorge was too excited about the news to be affected by my yelling.

That night I couldn't sleep. You know what I kept thinking about? The handwritten note on the letter. A personal note from my son that couldn't have been less personal. *Please help me out on this project*, as if we were neighbors buying raffle tickets. But the more I thought about it, the more I considered the fact that Wopper had never shared his feelings much, never talked at all about his relationship with Lara, never told us what he wanted with his life. Why would I expect him to pour out his heart now? Maybe I always thought that he was too simple, like his father. That he didn't think much beyond the moment. What was the future except the day after right now? What was love except routine and comfort? But maybe, maybe he was trying to tell us something. Maybe he was trying to show us, *this* is what he'd done on his own—a municipal official, a politician—but now he was extending his hand, not completely, just enough to show he wanted us, needed us to be part of his life. And maybe my greatest fear was that he'd

left and would never return and had done so easily, without looking back. But no, he wrote to us. Over a year had passed, and he
gave us, gave me, an opportunity to enter back into his life. He
wanted help with his project. Right? That's what he asked for. I
would do everything in my power.

CHAPTER THIRTEEN

WOPPER NEVER THOUGHT IT WOULD WORK, BUT ONE DAY HE RECEIVED A money order from Elias and Francisca Solorio and a short letter telling him how excited they were to hear that La Morada would finally have decent streets. Then more money orders arrived and more letters, too. Most of the senders Wopper knew, those from Woodland at least, but he didn't know them well. From the sound of the letters, however, one would've thought they helped raise him. Roberto, you are making your family proud! All of La Morada thanks you! You will see La Morada into the future! Others, in addition to sending money for the paving project, included money asking him to take a look at their property and make sure everything was okay.

Many of the letters were personal, containing details about Wopper's past or his current situation that not everyone could've known. One woman even wrote, *You have turned your life around from drinking, and we have God to thank for that.* Soon he began to wonder how much his parents were involved with the fundraising success. They knew everyone from La Morada who lived in the area and could've easily paid a visit to encourage them. But when Wopper started receiving money from family friends who were from La Piedad, who hadn't received a letter and had no connection whatsoever to La Morada, he knew for sure his parents were involved. Which was fine, as long as the money was raised. What mattered first and foremost was that Valentín Moreno got his contract. When a third of the money was in hand, Moreno's company began leveling the roads almost immediately. Moreno knew that the municipal and federal funds would take longer to process, but he wanted to begin as soon as possible, before Don Elpidio invented any obstacles.

Ernesto Maya was upset when he heard about Moreno Concrete starting work, but Wopper was prepared for that. He went directly to Maya and presented the plan to build model homes overlooking the reservoir. Wopper and Mija's home would be the first. Wopper explained that they had raised enough funds to build a completely new road along the water—the perfect property for anyone looking for a vacation home. Ernesto Maya laughed at this notion. He said, "You talk like this is Puerto Vallarta or Zihuatanejo! Those that come down from the North just want a place to rest their heads without depending on family or friends. They're not going to want reservoir-front houses that they have to worry will be flooded year in and year out. What's good for irrigating crops isn't good for living rooms and kitchens!" That's when Wopper told him about the concrete embankment. He could see the wheels in Maya's head spinning: the houses would come first, then the flooding, then the municipal government funds for a concrete wall to prevent it. Ernesto Maya agreed to build Wopper's home first, for a significant reduction in price, if he threw future contracts his way. Wopper told him there were sure to be plenty: once one northerner does something, all the others follow suit—they don't want to be outdone.

The pieces of Mija's plan couldn't have fit together better. Wopper may have struggled to figure out what to say or do if things had gone awry or if anything unexpected had happened, but he never had to. There were times when he would ask her how she knew about Moreno Concrete's struggles and Valentín Moreno's desperation, or even how she knew about Moreno's touchiness when it came to mentioning his father (he became clay in your hands). Wopper questioned her about the federal and municipal fundraising initiative, which she knew about before anyone else. And all too often she would mention some idea or some bit of information—such as the name registry of all the La Morada families who lived in the North—along with Don Martín's name. *Don Martín told me this*, or *Don Martín told me that*, which made sense to Wopper because he knew that Don Martín had been the town leader, not only as the municipal representative, but also, as one of the oldest residents, he knew everyone and everything there was to know about La Morada. She never explained, though, how she came to know so much of Don Martín's information.

At first he worried that she'd learned it all from Lucio Barraza, who must have had some connection with Don Martín, but then as he began to doubt that, he started to wonder if there wasn't another Lucio Barraza before Lucio Barraza. At these moments he considered her age: she was five years older than him—in his mind, years unaccounted for. Had she been with someone else? He wanted to know, but at the same time he didn't. The thought alone created a sinking feeling in his stomach. It had been difficult, even painful, to learn about Lucio. It took him a long time to get past it, to not think of Lucio every time he and Mija kissed or had sex, to not imagine the two of them, she and that idiot, doing the same. He didn't even know for sure if she and Lucio had had sex. She hadn't been a virgin, right? So it had to be Lucio, right? The doubts fed on themselves.

The truth was, they never talked about the past. Nothing was ever fleshed out. Questions were asked, but subsequent questions rarely followed. They made no attempts to dig deeper so that an incident, a person, or a memory was understood from every angle and perspective. On the contrary, any answer, however inadequate, was sufficient.

Wopper thought this was his own doing. He didn't want to talk about Lara or confess that his ex-girlfriend was pregnant, and when enough time passed, he didn't want to acknowledge that he was now a father. Nor did he ever wish to explain why he was in La Morada or why he couldn't go home. So he avoided delving into Mija's past in order to avoid revealing his own, as though if he kept asking, she could rightfully do the same.

When Lucio first told him that he and Mija had been together, a sense of confusion came over Wopper that he'd never felt before, a physical pain, as if the wind had been knocked out of him. Until Lucio's confession, Wopper's relationship with Mija just *was*, and nothing had to exist before. He thought they were alone, just the two of them in their little world contained by the brick walls of their home, but suddenly the outside had entered in, in the form of Lucio Barraza. He discovered they weren't alone at all. She had a past just as he had a past, but her past had seemed so small before: she was Don Cirilo's daughter, she had lived in this nothing rancho all her life, and that was it. But now that he knew this wasn't the case, he couldn't control his doubts and suspicions. It seemed that anything was possible.

He remembered all too well when Don Elpidio called after him, "*Oye*, have you asked your girl about Don Martín?" At first he thought it was just Don Elpidio's way of getting under his skin, and he had dismissed it. But when Valentín Moreno came asking about Mija and her relationship with Don Martín, it became harder and harder to remove the uncertainties from his mind. He couldn't help but wonder how come everyone else was afraid to mention the dead man's name. If he was ever referred to, the speaker crossed himself as though warding off curses and evil spirits. "They are silly," was Mija's answer when Wopper asked. And when he asked her how Don Martín had died, she merely said, "He was old." Wopper left it at that. Clearly something must have happened, and somehow she was involved. Otherwise, he'd know more; she would be more forthright. The question was, to what extent? He couldn't even fathom what it could be, and yet he couldn't bring himself to ask, as though he preferred the not knowing and the doubt to the possibility of knowing and suffering. He tried not to think about it, but the doubts remained. So he waited for her to tell him, if there was anything to tell.

CHAPTER FOURTEEN

Mr. Gregory

I WAS IN THE REAL ESTATE BUSINESS FOR YEARS. REAL ESTATE AND DEVEL-opment. Mostly local projects. As Woodland grew bigger it out-grew me, outgrew my expertise, or should I say my capital, my finances, and my connections. I just couldn't compete with the big gun developers from elsewhere in the state. You'd think it'd only be Sacramento folks as it's just down the road, but no, they came from everywhere, and they weren't interested any longer in apartment buildings and redevelopment projects, but big shopping malls and megastores. Woodland is a good location, just off a few highways, the 5, the 113, close to the airport, to Sacramento, the last city in the North, really, before you head off into the middle of nowhere. Also, surrounded by farmland in every direction, it had plenty of room to grow.

I made a lot of money, and then I lost a lot of money. I lost most of it trying to make one last deal that would've set me up like I'd been before. I was like those gamblers up at Cache Creek who make a few thousand, then lose a few thousand, then get down to their last thousand and bet it all, hoping to get back to where they'd been earlier, only to lose it and then go into debt still trying for one last win before calling it quits. Well, I wanted to get back to my heyday, but deal after deal fell through. I kept trying and went into debt, wagering it all. I lost my wife over it—she couldn't take it anymore, and I guess I don't blame her. I used our house as collateral in one deal, and it looked like it was going to work out and I'd be saved, along with my company and my years of hard work, but then the deal collapsed and I lost everything. My wife left me. She told me the stress was too much, that she wasn't going to live in an apartment after all those years putting together a home. She lives in a retirement community now—an apartment, but I guess there's some respectability attached to it. She's close to my son and his wife. My son says she's happier now, which is good for her. I never meant her any harm. I just tried to set us up for retirement. Now it's just me I set up. Her loss.

My last deal was my biggest, and, without going into all the details, basically my success on this particular venture boiled down to my years of knowledge of Woodland and its residents, but it also came down to the business of local development, which those big players think they have mastered but actually don't. They just outmuscle the little guys, but that doesn't mean they know what they're doing. City politics is a funny business, and you have to know how to work it. Unlike bigger political arenas, the city arena still involves a good amount of neighborly front porch plain talk, and those big guns don't realize that one little guy, in this case me on my last dime, can cover a lot of ground if he really wants to get something done. Simply put, I talked to everybody who would listen. I told them my situation and explained that we had the same interest, which was to protect ourselves against the big guns taking over every single project. I managed to garner strong support for a proposal—boring project, really, but it involved a good deal of money and that's all that really mattered—but folks wouldn't truly commit until I could reassure them that they wouldn't lose on their investment or even lose political capital if they pledged their support. Well, I couldn't do that alone, especially because I had lost out on previous projects and most of them knew that already—gossip, especially business and political gossip, spreads quickly here—but I was able to convince an old friend of mine, maybe you heard of him, George Athanous, from Stockton, big real estate guy who owed me a favor, to simply back the project in name only. All I needed was his presence, and that'd be enough to reassure others. And he came on board. The project was mine. My last coup. Left the big players shaking their heads, not knowing why Athanous supported me, not knowing why the city council approved my bid when theirs were many times cheaper.

To make a long story short, this is why, when Arnie Beas came to my door with a message from Wopper Barraza asking me to go to Mexico and show my support for his development project, I knew exactly what he was asking of me. Exactly. What I didn't expect was to go down there and see the possibilities of the project. Now I never knew Wopper except as my racquetball partner, and I just figured him for a young kid who may or may not turn out to be something one day. He had time. I wasn't worried about him, just like I never worried much about my own children. The first one I did, the second one less so, but by the third and fourth, I realized that no matter how much I worried they were still going to have to find their own way. And they did, more or less. I guess they're still finding their way. Does one ever stop? Anyhow, I never took Wopper for a real estate man, but that just goes to show you how much you actually know about a racquetball partner. He was lazy on the court, so I figured he was lazy off it. I forgot to turn the standard on myself: I was slow and clunky on the court, but off it I'm a fast-talking self-starter. Arnie gave me the letter, and then he seemed embarrassed as he explained a little bit of the background, as if he expected me to laugh and slam the door in his face. Basically, he made it clear in so many words that what Wopper needed—or rather, Roberto Barraza—was a distinguished-looking gringo to come give the impression that his project was no small fry deal.

Surprised at my enthusiasm, Arnie confessed, "I was supposed to come to you earlier. Roberto was hoping I'd come to you about a month ago . . . but I got held up."

He said it in a way that made me think that more likely two or three months had passed. I told him, "Well, what matters is that you came. Now it's up to me to make it happen." Up until that moment, I don't think he understood the importance of the message he carried.

I was Wopper's Athanous. I understood. Immediately I went inside my apartment and turned off the television that had been giving me a headache the entire afternoon, as it did every afternoon, but which I couldn't bear to shut off because what else was there for a retired man without a wife, kids gone, to do? Other than drinking, that is. But now I had something. I packed my bags, placed my best suit in its carrier, and took off for the airport. I was in Guadalajara that night; stayed at a Best Western just like the one off Highway 5 except with a Mexican food buffet and a lounge singer playing a keyboard. Next morning I put on my suit, hired a driver for the weekend—the sleekest vehicle I could find—and we took off for La Piedad, Michoacán, straight to the government building, as instructed. I was supposed to make a big show of my entrance, ask as many people as possible for the office of the municipal representative. The city was bustling when I arrived. I expected something more quaint and tranquil. Quite the opposite: roads clogged, trucks puffing black smoke, pedestrians everywhere, honking horns, radios blaring. I honestly had expected to show up and have everyone turning around to see who'd arrived. I had to go more out of my way to make an entrance. So I told the driver to drive right up to the front of the building. He told me that wasn't allowed, that the plaza was only for pedestrians. I told him this one time wouldn't hurt, and I pulled a twenty from my billfold. He shrugged his shoulders and drove forward. Some menacing-looking guards started in our direction, but they must have assumed we had approval, because they saw me and waved us through, making sure pedestrians stayed out of our way.

I made it clear who I was looking for. I asked everyone who passed, "Licenciado Roberto Barraza?" They pointed me in his direction, and even if they didn't know who he was, they still seemed curious to know who I was and what I wanted. I turned around and saw secretaries whispering. "Who is he?" "What is he doing" "*He* wants to see Roberto Barraza?" I assumed that's what they said, not being much of a Spanish speaker. I smoothed down my suit and straightened my tie. I hadn't enjoyed myself so much in years. "I'm his Athanous," I kept telling myself, recalling everyone's willingness to join the project when they found out he was on board. And to think I'd helped George Athanous when he was fresh out of college. Now I'm helping another youngster. From experience, these things have a way of paying dividends. And it did, sooner than I expected.

Wopper had changed. He had lost weight, but it was more than that. He had a graveness I didn't remember him having. He looked like he'd lost a loved one, like he'd experienced something hard and, though weakened, had grown stronger for it. We made the same jokes about racquetball, and as soon as we'd exhausted those jokes we struggled for words to say to one another. But that was all right.

He showed me around the office, speaking in English loud enough so everyone could hear. He made sure to introduce me to everyone who passed. They asked if I was staying in La Piedad. Wopper was sure to tell them that I was there to check out La Morada. Soon we drove out to his small town. The entire way he described the projects he'd been working on. He told me how he'd gotten involved with politics as a representative and discovered that he had a knack for it. "For some reason, people listen to me," he said, laughing for the first time. "I'm still waiting for them to figure me out." I told him that they never had to. That everyone feels the same way. Even the most successful businessman, politician, whatever, feels like he got there by accident, that he's not talented enough, smart enough, crafty enough—even those who delude themselves into thinking they got there on their own merits—but the more you push forward the more you'll realize that momentum itself is enough to sustain you. Head in the right direction and you'll continue that way.

He told me, "But Mr. Gregory, I was a loser back home. I didn't have a job longer than three months before I got tired of it and quit or made them fire me."

I laughed at this. "Well," I said, "that proves my point exactly. You had bad momentum back home and couldn't reverse it. But it looks like you hit the ground running here."

And he had. I saw firsthand the projects going on in his town, all basically stemming from his playing the different concrete companies off one another. And to look at the homes and fences and roads, concrete was just about all that was required. Cinderblock structures and fences wherever you looked. After the bustle of La Piedad, the air full of diesel exhaust, it was a nice change to head to the outskirts. Everything was quiet now; the fields were an array of greens and blues and golden oranges. We passed donkeys and children playing soccer. We drove slowly, which gave me more time to take in the surroundings. I could hear buzzing dragonflies, at least that's what I thought they were. It felt good to be there. It'd been a while since I last traveled, since I'd left Woodland even. When Wopper showed me his land I was envious for some reason. Envious of his youth, of having land to work—all the land I ever had I built on. We left the driver and the car and walked along the fields. It was corn mostly, they had just planted it, all different varieties, some blue, some red, and he showed me how you could tell from the shoot with the pride of someone who's learned something new, carefully explaining in too much detail the differences of each one. We came to the edge of the corn and there was a blue-green field of agave, which he said he'd use someday to make tequila. The crop was still too young. At the end of the clearing I saw the reservoir. He pointed out where he was building his house, just up from the basin. He said he had a view of the distant mountains, his property, and the sun glistening on the water. He told me construction would be complete in a few months. He said that his house would be a model and hopefully others would want to build, too.

We walked up to the structure. It was only the shell, but I could tell it was going to be something special. Just about every room had a large window overlooking the water. When he finished showing me the inside, we walked out to a patio area and stood in silence, both of us staring out at the landscape before us. I felt a calm inspiration right then. Calm because it was a beautiful day and I was happy to be there and I had nowhere else to be, and inspired because I suddenly knew what was going to be my life for the next however many years. I broke the silence by saying, "I'd like to learn Spanish. Do you think it's too late?"

"Too late? How so?" he asked.

I laughed. "Too old to learn anything new."

He smiled.

I told him, "Wopper, I'm going to invest in your project."

He paused for a second before telling me that that wasn't neces-sary. He'd only needed me to come down so that others could see he had backing, if only the appearance of it. I cut him off and told him I knew that. I told him I wanted to invest for myself. You have the first model, I want the second. I explained that I had a good chunk of money left from my last big business deal, the deal that saved me from ignominy, and the way I was living now I would die with most of it in the bank. I just didn't know what to do with it. Nothing appealed to me anymore. That is, until now. "I'm going to come down here," I said, "and I'm gonna live part of the year as your neighbor whether you want me to or not. And others will follow. You'll have contracts coming out your ears."

I expected him to jump out of his socks with joy. It wasn't set in stone, I know that, but I was promising him a good deal. Promising him something he hadn't expected. That was worth at least a glim-mer of excitement, I thought. But he looked at me as though I'd placed something burdensome on him.

I said to him, "You'd like that, right?"

He smiled finally and said, "Of course."

So then I just assumed he was overwhelmed by the possibilities of what now lay before him, and I can understand that. As anyone who's achieved any measure of success knows, that measure only leads to more and greater expectations. This project of his was only the beginning. At least that's what I thought.

CHAPTER FIFTEEN

I

Jorge Barraza

ONE EVENING MY WIFE CAME HOME LATE FROM FUNDRAISING, HER FACE sad and tired. I was upset because I had to walk down the street to Tacos Jaliscense for dinner, but I didn't say anything. I stayed quiet because my wife is rarely sad. Tired sometimes, but usually her mood leans toward frustration or anger. Over the years I've learned to stay out of her way. I don't make any noise, I don't ask questions, and if I do, I take the answers with the insults. But when she's sad I don't know what to do. I never learned. Do I ask what's wrong? Do I try to distract her, cheer her up? The very truth is that I'm afraid of her when she's sad. Why? I can't exactly say, except maybe I feel it is my duty to be there, to do something for her. When she's angry, it's not my duty, I feel no obligation. But with sadness she needs something from me, and I've never been capable of providing whatever that is.

Well, she made me dinner without my asking for it. I'd purposely left the foil and paper bag from the taco truck on the counter so that she'd know I'd been inconvenienced, but she didn't pay attention. She was distracted. I didn't tell her I was full. I ate everything she put in front of me. I watched her. She moved as if lost in a fog.

After dinner I watched television. She cleaned up the kitchen, and I felt bad when she picked up the paper bag and foil and looked at it, realizing finally that I'd gone out to eat. She didn't say anything. She just came and sat down next to me. Not in her usual place, the recliner where she read magazines or folded clothes or filed her nails. No, she sat right next to me on the couch, as close as she could without sitting on my leg. Maybe she misjudged her drop. Maybe she thought there would be more room between us. Is it strange for a wife to sit so closely to her husband? Of course not, but I couldn't remember the last time we'd touched, except for maybe grazing fingers in passing plates or keys. I swear, it was as if a stranger had suddenly entered the room. It was my wife, but then it wasn't. She needed me, I can tell you that much. Her face sad and her body tense, she sat there next to me, waiting for me to do something. Like what? A pat on the shoulder? Should I have grabbed her hand? Well, I decided to ignore her and watch television, a variety show with dancers and singers. She tried to as well, but her body remained stiff and unnatural, and she kept sighing every few seconds as if struggling for breath. Out of the corner of my eye I could see that she wasn't watching the television. She was staring at photos on the shelf. Were her eyes watery? Was she crying? I couldn't tell.

"Raquel," I said cautiously, almost wishing I could ignore her and return to the program. "What's wrong?" I asked her.

She began to cry. Yes, *my* wife began to cry. My wife! She turned into me as if to hide. She pressed her face into my chest. She clutched my arms and pinned me against the back of the couch. I realized right then how much bigger than me she was. She had grown over the years while I had shrunk, and never was it more apparent than at that moment as I cradled her in my worthless arms.

"I went and saw him," she said to me.

"Who," I asked.

"The baby," she said.

She explained that she went to visit her friend, Nidia, to tell her about Wopper's project, but that she wasn't home. After waiting around for a while, she realized she was in Lara's neighborhood. She walked past her house several times, wondering whether she should go in or not. Lara must have spotted her through the window, because she came outside and invited her in, and Raquel accepted. And, of course, as soon as my wife saw the baby she regretted that she had already missed so much of his life. "He looked just like Roberto," she said. "Just like him."

It was what I had told her all along. My daughters had told her too. Everyone had encouraged her to go. We knew that as soon as she saw the baby she would forget all her anger, her stubbornness, all because of why? Because Wopper made one too many mistakes. But this wasn't a mistake, it was a blessing, this child, this baby. She knew this now.

So I said to her, "But this is a good thing. Why are you so sad? Only a small amount of time has been lost. Now you have nothing but time ahead of you."

At this she shook her head slowly. She looked me in the eyes and pulled away. She sat on the edge of the couch, staring, as if her mind had gone blank, as if I was only a mirror, a reflection; she stared at anything but my presence.

"What is it?" I asked.

"He's sick," she said.

"Who is?" I said.

"The baby," she said. "There is something wrong with his breathing."

"But what do you know?" I said.

"I know!" she cried. Then she quieted and said, "They need to take him to the hospital. There is something wrong with his heart." After that she burst into sobs.

I didn't even think before I took her into my arms and held her as tight as I could.

II

Lara Gonzalez

When Wopper's mom finally decided to cross the street and come inside, I thought she looked different. She was heavier and all pale, and she'd been sweating a lot from walking around outside. Her makeup was starting to streak, so she was wiping her cheeks and wiping her eyes, and she probably felt self-conscious or anxious or something. I'd never seen her like that before. But it was more than just the way she looked. She seemed almost desperate. I even felt bad for her. We didn't say nothing for a moment, and so I asked her if she wanted something to drink. She said no and then blurted out, "Can I see him?" I told her he was asleep in the bedroom, and I walked in that direction thinking she'd follow me. But I didn't hear her move, so I turned around and saw her standing still, as if she couldn't move forward. She was just clenching her white leather purse in front of her with both hands.

"Come, follow me," I said. And so she did.

I opened the bedroom door real carefully and opened the shade partway so that light came in. Mrs. Barraza stayed close to the door. I approached the crib and eventually so did she. We watched him sleep, both of us quiet. I looked up at one point and saw that she was biting her bottom lip as though she was about to cry. I looked away. I didn't want her to cry. I wouldn't have known what to say. After a while I looked up at her again, and she seemed calmer. I could tell that she was thinking of Wopper because Wopper as a baby must have looked exactly like this, the same lips, the same nose. If only he would've woken up and she could've seen his eyes. His eyes stared at you just like Wopper's.

After a long while she said, "Mija, can I hold him?" She called me mija, my daughter, which maybe she didn't even think about, but I sure did. I was going to tell her not right now. It had taken me so long to get him to sleep. But then I realized that he would fall asleep again, and I couldn't say no. So I reached into the crib and lifted him into my arms. I handed him to her, and she held him to her chest and let out a deep breath. As if for all the time she'd been standing there she couldn't breathe, not until she felt him against her. He began to move, and she rocked him gently and said, "*Shhh*, mijito, *shhh*." I watched them. It was dead quiet in the room, and we could hear his breathing, heavy, raspy. She looked up at me, and I saw that her eyes were alarmed. I told her that he had asthma, and that I had it too, but the alarm in her eyes didn't go away. She stuck her neck out so her ear was closer to his head. She was trying to hear him, to feel him. "Wopper had asthma as a baby," she said. I told her I knew already. She shook her head and said, "Mija, this is something else. This is worse. His breathing is not right."

I told her that it was just asthma. "Don't worry," I said. "The doctor has checked him plenty of times." But she continued trying to feel his breathing. She kept pressing her ear to his chest and listening closely, until finally he woke up crying. I took him from her and rocked him back and forth. She told me again, "Please, mija, there's something not right about his breathing." And I repeated that I already knew that, that he had asthma, and then I started to get a little angry because I don't like how older women feel as if they know everything there is to know about caring for children and always feel the need to instruct you. But she didn't say anything more. I don't know why she stopped, knowing now what happened. If she knew something was wrong, she should have screamed at me until I listened. But then maybe I wouldn't have listened, and she probably knew me better than I thought. She knew that if she pressed too hard I'd not give in just to spite her. But if she walked away, maybe I'd give in eventually. So she left, and I told her to visit soon, and she said she would, even though both our good-byes were strained.

He fell asleep and I placed him back in his crib. I tried to ignore what she'd said, but I kept thinking about it. He had lost a lot of weight. His breathing had gotten worse. I just thought it was the season, the quality of the air, I don't know. I had stuff to do around the house, but every now and then I'd go into the bedroom and watch him sleep. I'd watch his back lower and rise, until finally I thought that maybe Wopper's mom was right, and then I became sure that she was. I called my mom at work and told her to come pick me up right away.

The doctor told us he had been born with a hole in his heart. A little tiny hole that grew bigger as he did. After that it felt like there was nothing but tests, tests and drugs, and consultations, and visits to specialists. It seemed like there wasn't anybody or anything that could keep the hole from growing.

I knew it was his girlfriend as soon as she said hello. I guess it could've been a secretary, any woman there in the government building, but I knew right away who it was. Wopper's mom had given me his office number. She'd found it on some letter. It was the only number she had for him. She said she'd left messages, but he hadn't returned her calls. She said maybe it'd be different if I tried. So I did, but only after an entire day of thinking about it, not wanting to do it, and then an entire night of tossing and turning, knowing that I had to. He had to know. So I woke up and called and immediately hung up. Called later and hung up. In the afternoon I called again, and before I could hang up someone answered. "Hello," the person said. I froze. What was it about her voice that told me it was her? I really don't know. Maybe it was the pride I assumed she'd have as the woman who won. But I was the only one who knew about the competition. Even if she knew about me, she didn't know yet that I was on the other line.

I didn't say anything. She repeated, "Hello." This time it was the iciness that hit me. Prideful and cold. I could see her there in his office—Wopper's office; how did Wopper Barraza have an office?—sitting there answering his phone calls, treating everyone like she didn't have time for them. How could Wopper be with someone like that? I wanted to scream into the phone. I don't know why I didn't. She deserved it. Then I remembered the reason I called, and I started to cry. The bitch hung up the phone!

So I called back and now I was pissed. I was pissed at myself for crying, but I was even more pissed at her for hanging up. After several rings, she picked up and said, "What do you want?"

I told her, "This is Roberto Barraza's girlfriend, Lara. Has he told you about me?"

She was silent, and for a second I thought maybe I'd messed up my Spanish, but I replayed what I'd said in my mind and it was fine.

Her tone was softer now. "You must be mistaken," she said.

"And why would that be?" I asked her.

"Because I am his wife," she said.

"His wife! I'm *sure*," I said. But suddenly I wasn't. Would he have married her? It made me mad to think that she was lying just to one-up me. Well, I was the mother of his child and so that's what I told her. She was silent on the other end. I kept going. I told her my son's name. I told her that he looked just like Wopper—and then she asked me who I was talking about, and I repeated, "Wopper, Wopper! Don't you know that's his name?"

She let me go off. She was silent on the other end. It was almost creepy. I would never have stood for someone talking to me like I was to her. But eventually I ran out of things to say, and she waited for it to be quiet to speak.

"What do you want?" she asked.

I told her that Wopper needed to come home. She told me that Roberto wouldn't leave La Morada. "He's happy here," she said. "He has nothing to return to there." That's how she said it. He had nothing to return to in the United States. "Not even you," she said, her voice calm. "Because he has me, and I wouldn't ever let him leave." Then she stopped for a second and said, "What makes you think he'd ever go back? For you?"

I was too shocked to respond right away. I couldn't think of anything. So I said the truth. Told her what I hadn't wanted to tell her because it made me sound helpless.

"It wouldn't be for me. It's his son. His son is sick. He has a heart condition. They . . . they"—I couldn't even say the words— "it's serious. We don't know long he'll . . . we don't know."

Then she shifted and moved something, or the door opened and someone walked in the room, because her voice changed. "Thank you, Señora, we appreciate your call," she said. "I will pass along that information as soon as possible." Then she hung up.

CHAPTER SIXTEEN

THE EVENING OF THE PHONE CALL, MIJA AND WOPPER TRAVELED HOME from the municipal council meeting in silence. They should have been in a festive mood, excited that their efforts were now paying off.

The representatives had voted unanimously to approve the second phase of the reservoir development project. Every representative wanted to follow La Morada's model, and they wanted Roberto Barraza to guide them. Once Mr. Gregory came, everyone started talking about the construction that was sure to happen around the reservoir, and they hounded Wopper about it. He told them that if they wanted a share they had to get in quick. So they gave him money—nothing pro bono, nothing promised; it was no longer pointing toward the future. The money was real. Mr. Gregory's commitment even surprised Don Elpidio, who found out when the permit fees were paid in advance. Upon receiving the funds, in a fit of anger he quickly dispatched a note downstairs to be left in Wopper's mailbox. *Fees received, invoice on its way*, it said. *Don't get too confident, understand? You don't want to get ahead of yourself in this game. Who knows, you might find yourself tripped up.*

Wopper immediately ripped up the note without sharing it with Mija. He didn't want to think too hard about what it meant.

He and Mija didn't talk until they arrived at the house. "Do you want tea?" she asked him. He nodded his head and sat down at the table. She placed the water and cinnamon root to boil and brought pan dulce on a platter to the table. Then she removed her heels and took off her plaid sports coat, laying it over the chair. She wore a satin blouse underneath, and he could make out her bra. He quickly averted his eyes as if worried about being caught. Just weeks before he wouldn't have hesitated: he would have stood up from the table and embraced her, or kissed her, or simply removed her shirt, and he would have been sure that she would be willing. But those days felt remote. He only waited for her now.

"What pan dulce do you want?" she asked. He pointed to the white concha. She cut it in quarters, knowing he liked to try a little piece of each one. She placed one of the quarters in front of him and then rose from the table to pour the tea. When she returned to the table, she placed his mug in front of him and asked, "Why are you so quiet, Roberto?"

He blew on his tea and shrugged. "No reason," he said.

Even if he had wanted to he wouldn't have been able to explain. The projects moving forward, growing larger by the day, Don Elpidio's note, his suspicions about Mija: these bothered him, of course, but it was something else. Something larger than any one thing. It was a sense of unease that he couldn't let go. Mr. Gregory had talked to him about good momentum and bad momentum and hitting the ground running. All that implied a direction. And after all this time in La Morada, after all the work that he'd done, Wopper finally realized that he was headed toward something. But he didn't know what that was. He didn't know if he could handle it. Even if he found the words to explain this to Mija, he knew that she would just reassure him, tell him that of course he could handle it. Hadn't he handled everything so far? She would tell him that he didn't need to worry, that they had each other. What he couldn't figure out, she would help him through. But how could he tell her that she was part of the unease?

When Wopper didn't offer any more, Mija rose from the table, put on her red-checkered apron, and started washing dishes.

He watched her as he slowly sipped his tea. She stood at the sink, her back toward him, and she was silent and tense in a way that made Wopper wonder if she felt his eyes on her. He noticed that she was washing the same aluminum pot over and over, so many times that it had to be clean already. Finally, she shut off the water. A last trail of drops fell loudly into the empty pot. She didn't move. She just stood there with her back facing him. After a long silence, without looking his way, she said, "Lara called at the office when you were gone this afternoon."

"What?" he said. He was unsure he heard her correctly.

"Lara. She called." She turned around to face him, crossing her arms and staring at him with her lips tightly pursed. He tried to think of a lie but then decided against it. He could tell in her face that she knew everything already.

"My ex-girlfriend," he said.

She nodded. She took several steps in his direction and then stopped in the middle of the kitchen, as if she didn't know where she wanted to go.

"What did she say?" he asked.

"You have a son," she said.

"Yes," he said. He set down the piece of pan dulce he held in his hand and tried to think of something else to add, but nothing came to him.

"Why did you never tell me?"

"I don't know."

"What do you mean, you don't know?"

He thought for a moment before answering. "I guess I thought if I pretended he didn't exist, he wouldn't. I don't even know his name."

She looked at him, her eyes hateful or sad, he couldn't tell. "That's horrible," she said. "That's horrible."

"I know it is, but what could I do?"

"You left home so that you wouldn't have to face being a father. You left your girlfriend because of that. You—"

"No, no, that's not why."

She waited for his explanation. So he told her about the drunk driving and the deportation. He didn't think she understood. Somehow it made more sense that he had left because he was running away from something. But that wasn't the case at all. He had been kicked out because he was a drunk and a danger to society. Is that what he was? That's what it sounded like as he explained. He knew it was a shitty explanation, especially because it had nothing to do with Lara and the baby. It was clear he had disappeared from their lives and they had disappeared from his.

When he finished, they were both quiet for a long time. He felt judged and defensive.

Suddenly, he heard himself blurt out, "And what about Lucio?"

She moved from the middle of the kitchen and walked into the bedroom. She uncrossed her arms but remained standing. "I thought you knew about him," she said. "I thought that's why you dislike him so much."

"But you never told me about him. We never talked about it."

She sighed and looked at him wearily. "I didn't know that you wanted to talk about that kind of stuff."

"Yeah, well, I guess I wasn't the only one hiding things."

"I wasn't hiding anything," she said, sitting down on the edge of the bed. She paused for a moment, and then, in a low and hurried voice so that he could barely hear her, she said, "I was embarrassed to admit it. I didn't want to talk about it, and there was nothing really to talk about. We didn't see each other for very long. It wasn't a relationship. I didn't love him. I'm the one who ended it, and it's not my fault that he couldn't take it."

Hardly listening to her answer, realizing he didn't care anymore about Lucio Barraza, he said, "Then tell me what happened between you and Don Martín?" He forced the words out, terse and mechanical.

She looked up at him, alarmed. "What are you talking about? Where's this all coming from?"

"What happened between the two of you?" he demanded. "Why is everyone afraid to speak about him?"

"I can't speak for everyone else," she said, her voice sharp and irritated. "If you want to know why they're afraid, then you should ask them."

"They won't talk about it, you know that."

"I told you over and over: they're silly."

"But silly about what? What is it they're afraid to talk about?"

"Gossip," she said. "They probably don't even know themselves what they're afraid of."

Wopper shook his head, frustrated. He didn't know how to continue. Mija could talk him in circles, he knew that. At that moment he understood that it wasn't just his inability to ask that had kept him in the dark this entire time. She had avoided his questions, deflected them over and over, and only now did he realize the extent.

"Fine," he said. "Then what happened between the two of you? Were you together?"

"What do you mean by together?" she asked, an expression of disbelief on her face.

"You know what I mean," he said.

"I worked for him. I cleaned his house. After his wife died, I started going there. He was all alone, and we became close."

"And what else? There's more than that."

She looked up at Wopper. "How long have you wanted to ask me all this? Why is it coming out now? Just because I found out what you've been hiding all this time?"

Wopper was silent, feeling the rage rise into his chest, into his throat. He looked at her. Her eyes stared at him, cold and distant.

"Fine, if you want to know," she said. "He was another father to me, and yet he wasn't anything like my father. He was much more than a farmer in La Morada. He showed me everything. He taught me more than I could've ever learned . . . he showed me everything I've shown you—"

"Like what? What did he show you?" Wopper asked.

"About the workings of the municipal council and La Morada," Mija responded, scowling at the insinuation. "What did you think I meant?"

"Why would he care to teach you about that? You were just there to clean."

"His eyes were bad, and so I started reading his papers to him. I was always good at reading. Eventually I began to understand what was going on, and I started asking questions, and it was as though he had always wanted that, just someone there to listen to him, who cared as much about La Morada as he did. And even though I just read to him, he made me feel as if we were working together—"

He cut her off. "Well, then how did he die?"

"I told you, he was old. He had a heart attack, a stroke. I don't know."

"So then why is everybody so afraid to talk about him?"

She sighed and shook her head. "Because they believe in rumors and gossip! I don't, especially in La Morada where there's nothing to do except invent stories to entertain oneself, especially when it involves the misfortune of others."

Wopper abruptly rose from his chair and stood in the doorway. He looked out the screen door into the night. In the distance, he saw a group of dogs huddled under a patio light. He could hear crickets, and for a brief moment he thought he heard the buzzing sound of Lucio's four-wheeler. He was confused. He didn't know what else to ask. Was there more, or did he just want there to be more? Why couldn't he let go of his suspicions? He felt Mija's eyes on him.

"Lara said you need to go home, Roberto," she said.

He turned to her. Her face was sympathetic, but he didn't trust it. "What do you mean?" he asked.

"Your son is sick," she said.

"Sick?"

"Yes. Lara says he's dying."

Again, he thought he didn't hear her right. She repeated herself. He still thought he had misunderstood. Sick? Dying? This son he never wanted, that he tried never to think about, that he hadn't ever imagined as living, was now dying?

"He has a heart problem or something. She said that—"

"Shut up!" Wopper cried. He grabbed his head and then placed his hands behind his neck. He began to pace back and forth from the kitchen to the bedroom. This was why he had never asked her anything before. He knew it would only make things worse. He couldn't think straight. He didn't want to be inside the house. He didn't want to be around her either.

"I'm going to La Piedad," he said. He turned around to look for the truck keys.

"Roberto, stop," she said, walking toward him, reaching out for his arm.

He moved away from her and grabbed his coat and searched in the pockets for the keys, finding them.

"Look at me, please. You wanted to know," she said. "Don't leave right now. We need to talk. Are you going to go back?"

He waved his hand as if to dismiss the question. "I'm going into La Piedad," he said. He slammed the screen door behind him.

"But where?" Mija cried.

Without answering, Wopper climbed into the truck Ernesto Maya had lent him and drove as fast as he could toward the city. Halfway there he looked at his hand gripping the steering wheel and realized he was trembling. He tried in vain to control it. "Fuck!" he cried at the top of his lungs.

CHAPTER SEVENTEEN

I

Don Cirilo

SO MY DAUGHTER COMES TO MY DOOR AND SCREAMS, "APÁ, APÁ! WAKE up!" And I call back, "I'm not sleeping! I'm watching television!" So she yells at me to shut it off and come outside. I did, even though I liked the program I was watching. Daughters don't always come screaming at nine o'clock, or was it eight o'clock? I lose track of time during the long days of summer. I walked outside and she says, "Get dressed, you have to go to La Piedad and follow Roberto. I have a bad feeling!"

"How did he take off?" I asked her. She told me that he was very upset. I said, "No, no, in his truck?" She screamed back at me, "Of course! What else is he going to take?"

And I explained my predicament of only having Don Jaspero to ride, but as Roberto could've attested, the donkey had had a rough day and was in no shape to go into town. My daughter left me there, and just when I thought she'd given up on me, she returned on the back of a four-wheeler. Lucio Barraza was driving.

"You two go into town and make sure Roberto doesn't do anything stupid," she instructed.

I looked at Lucio. He appeared to have been sleeping—his eyes were puffy, his hair was tangled, and his clothes looked like they'd been grabbed from wherever he could find them. I felt bad for him. I was her father; I couldn't say no. But what relation did he have to her? Just a neighbor with a motorcycle. I hopped on and placed my arms around him, which felt strange because I hadn't touched any-one in years, let alone a man. But who was I to fall off and create trouble for everyone? I held on tightly. He revved the engine and we lurched forward, and soon we were down the street, and I looked back through the dust cloud to see my daughter standing with her arms crossed at the front door.

On the way Lucio tried talking to me, but I couldn't hear him too well being as I'm just about deaf. I'm surprised I could hear him at all over the engine. "Where to?" I made out. I told him to head to El Castillo, for that's where I heard he liked to go. Rather, that's where he himself told me he liked to get a beer and watch billiards. When we arrived at El Castillo we found the bar full. We had to enter and push through the crowd. A couple of people gave us odd stares. I assume this was because I was old and wearing my after shower clothes and Lucio looked like he'd hopped up from a nap. We asked the bartender if he'd seen Roberto Barraza around that night. He nodded his head and indicated that he'd been over there in the corner. We turned to the corner. There was a tall man playing billiards. We turned back to the bartender and he said, "Go ask Rooster, that man over there—he was talking to him."

We approached the big man. I'd heard of him of because he was now the coach of La Morada's soccer team, but I'd never actually met him. "Rooster," I said, "have you by any chance seen—" and that was when the coach cut me off with a wild grito, a long loud cackle that brought the attention of the entire bar. A few others close by followed his grito with their own variations, and so I had to wait before continuing. When everyone settled down, I asked the man again, "Excuse me, Rooster," and once again he cocked his head back and let out a grito that could've been heard in Morelia. I felt much too old at that moment. Lucio looked like he should've stayed asleep.

I decided we should buy a drink, and maybe that'd wake us up to the challenge of finding Roberto, because he clearly wasn't in El Castillo. I approached the bar and asked for two shots of tequila. When the barman brought me the shots, he told me that when Rooster got really drunk, the only way to approach him was to announce yourself with a grito. Then, if he approved, maybe he'd talk to you. So I assumed right then that that's why he was called Rooster. I sure wasn't going to go up and make a fool of myself, so I explained what needed to be done to Lucio. Lucio agreed to do it. Rooster was in the middle of hitting a bank shot, so we waited until he missed before approaching. Lucio let out a grito that sounded like Don Jaspero when stung by a bee. I had never heard anything more pathetic, and it seemed neither had Rooster. In fact, he looked like he'd taken personal offense to the squawk, and I couldn't tell whether his next move with his pool stick was to break it over Lucio's back or his face.

I decided my pride meant little, and what mattered was finding Roberto and preventing whatever it was that my daughter wanted us to prevent. I quickly downed the two shots and let out a grito I'm sure woke up my great-grandfather a hundred years dead. When I finished, without pausing for a breath, I cried, "Rooster, I am the father-in-law of Roberto Barraza, at your service. Will you do us the favor of telling us where he's disappeared to on this night?"

Rooster approached me, and before I could step back he hugged me. "Why didn't you say so!" he cried. "The father-in-law of Roberto Barraza is like a father-in-law to me because we are brothers, me and him. The Licenciado from La Morada!"

And then, just like that, he told us that Roberto had come by briefly, found the bar too crowded, and took off for La Palapa on the corner next to the eye shop and the market.

On the way there I asked Lucio what he knew of the situation, and he said that he knew nothing except that my daughter was a prideful and domineering woman and that she wished to have complete control over anything and everything that related to her. I took offense to this because what did he know? Having such a harsh judgment of my daughter, as if he'd suffered his part because of her! I told him he should know better than to speak of that which he didn't know firsthand. That was when he told me that he did know firsthand, that he and my daughter had been together for almost one year and then some. He couldn't believe I didn't know. I thought he was trying to lie himself out of a hole. "Look," I said, "I'll forget what you said about my daughter this one time, but you don't have to start inventing craziness." He insisted that he had loved my daughter and that she had driven him crazy. He was still crazy for her. Why else would he be out at this time of night looking for her new lover? "So she still has you in her clutches?" I asked. And he nodded in a way that told me he really was, and that was when I felt bad for him because he would've done better to stay in bed. But love will do that to you.

The rest of the way to La Palapa, Lucio told me about my daughter and his relationship, which seemed to have escaped my notice. I didn't realize that Lucio had tried to kill himself twice. He told me that he was asked to resign his position on the municipal representative council. Once that had happened, my daughter had no use for him. "Why not?" I asked. "Because she wants to own La Morada, Don Cirilo!" he said. What could I do but laugh at this idea? My daughter wanting to own the rancho! I told Lucio that he really had gone crazy.

We arrived at La Palapa and found it empty. We went straight to the bartender and asked if he'd seen Roberto Barraza around that evening. He was drying glasses and placing them below the counter. "Who?" he asked. Lucio started describing Roberto, going on and on, as if he'd spent whole afternoons observing him. Finally, the bartender cut him off. He leaned over the counter and whispered to us. But with my bad ears and his whispered words running together, I couldn't hear a damned thing he was saying, so all I could do was hope Lucio's ears were better than mine.

I watched Lucio's face for a reaction. His eyes widened first with surprise, then concern, and then horror.

"What's he saying?" I cried, unable to wait.

Lucio reached for my neck and pulled my head toward his and spoke right into my ear, so close that I could feel the bristly hairs of his mustache. He told me that two men had been there with Roberto. They bought him drinks. They were clean cut and dressed as cowboys. They were watching him the whole time, though Roberto didn't have the slightest idea, because he was so lost in the bottom of his glass. When Roberto got up to leave, they followed him out to where two Suburbans were waiting. One of the men knocked him over the head with a gun or a club, then they carried him into one of the Suburbans and took off.

I shrugged off Lucio's hand and asked the bartender, "Do you know who the men were?"

You could tell that he knew, without a doubt he did, but he shook his head. "Never saw them before," he said.

"Don't be a coward," I said.

He looked at me and half-smiled, as though he felt bad for me, and continued drying glasses and setting them below the counter.

Then, get this, the son of a bitch said, "A drink on me?"

II

Lucio Barraza

We didn't talk the entire way back to La Morada. I, for one, was afraid of giving the news to Mija. She never liked bad news, and it didn't matter that we couldn't have done anything to prevent what happened to the Licenciado. I knew she would look at me and see that once again I had failed. Never mind that her father was with me, and that it was his idea to get the shots of tequila at El Castillo, and then the bartender's kindness to give us two more shots at La Palapa. I knew she would hear the bad news and then smell the tequila on our breath and blame me for failing her once again (and probably for getting her father drunk).

When we arrived back at Don Cirilo's house, I shut off the engine, and the old man said, "Well, do I tell her or do you?" He was slurring.

I thought he should tell her, being as I was just there to provide transportation. That was when he called me a coward just like he had the bartender.

"Why would that be?" I asked. But he just mumbled something that made no sense and then turned to walk inside. I saw Mija's silhouette appear at the screen door. Her face moved into the light, and I could see the worry and fear in her eyes. Of course, I couldn't help but wonder if she ever once felt such concern for my well-being. I knew the answer. At that moment, despite not knowing whether Roberto Barraza was dead on the side of the road or alive only to be held for ransom, I envied the man. How she loved him!

Don Cirilo told Mija what we'd learned at La Palapa. She seemed to know exactly what had happened and who was behind it. She said she knew that as soon as the waterfront project got underway, it wouldn't be long before Don Elpidio got nervous and did something like this. She shook her head and said, "He didn't waste time finding his opportunity."

Even though she spoke quietly, barely a mumble, I assumed she was talking to me. Her father had already collapsed on the sofa and was grunting loudly as he struggled to remove his boots. I was happy to be included once again in her confidence. "Yes, Don Elpidio is probably behind this," I said. "He probably—" I stopped midsentence because she shot me a glare that told me that if I wished to stay I had to shut up. I should have left. I didn't deserve that kind of treatment. After all, hadn't I brought her father all around La Piedad looking for her lover? I was about to remind her that when we were together, I had never gone off drinking by myself, but then thought better of it.

"What are you going to do?" I asked, finally.

"Tomorrow I'll look for Roberto," she said.

I wanted her to ask me to use the four-wheeler. Actually, I wanted her to ask me if I would take her on the four-wheeler. And then I would refuse! This was the last time I would go out of my way to help her. I deserved more. I would tell her exactly that. "I deserve more. I'm not your chauffer!" But she didn't ask to use the four-wheeler. So of course I found myself offering it, and then I had to suffer the indignity of her refusal. "No, I'll be okay without it," she said. Then she asked me to leave.

I insisted she use it.

"Lucio, I don't want to use your four-wheeler," she said. "Thank you for bringing my father to look for Roberto. Goodnight."

"I see. I'm not good enough for you!" I cried. "My four-wheeler is beneath you!"

She sighed and gave me a look I remembered well. It said, *Here he goes again.* And so I was!

But then suddenly she turned away from me, and I saw that she was wiping tears from her eyes and trying to hide it. I knew to be quiet then. I said my good-byes to Don Cirilo, who was passed out and snoring gently, wished Mija luck, and left the house. I knew the next day she would go directly to Don Elpidio and demand Roberto's release. But Don Elpidio was not going to let him go so easily. She would have to give up something, and I wondered what that would be. *Maybe that's why she is crying*, I thought to myself. Just like her disappointment when I went crazy. How far would this set her back?

CHAPTER EIGHTEEN

I

WOPPER'S HEAD FELT LIKE HE HAD BANGED IT AGAINST A CINDER BLOCK WALL.
For a second he thought he was right next to Mija, and he reached
over to feel for her, but as his eyes adjusted he realized the vaulted
ceiling wasn't theirs. He rose in bed and looked around the room.
It was large and filled with oversized, expensive-looking furniture
with matching mahogany finish. There were Spanish tile floors,
glass vases in each corner, and rustic religious paintings on the
walls. In front of him, on a flat screen television, he stared at his
reflection and tried to remember what had happened to him the
previous night. He had stormed out of the house. After that, all he
could remember was drinking at La Palapa.

He removed the covers and slowly moved off the bed. His head
throbbed. He was still wearing the clothes he had on the night
before. He must have kicked off his boots. He saw one and then
found the other on the far side of the bed.

Wopper opened the bedroom door and peered down a long hallway. He didn't know which way to go. He headed toward what
looked like a living room. The hallway was dark and cool, but the
rooms off it, including the large area where he was heading, were
filled with sunlight. He entered what looked like a living room, and
the bright light sent a jolt of pain through his head. He squinted his
eyes and continued walking.

There was a woman on the other side of the room. "Good

morning," she said cheerily. "I will be right back. Have a seat, young man."

His eyes began to adjust to the blinding light, and he saw that she was mopping the floor. She leaned the handle against the glass door, wiped her hands on her apron, and walked toward the hallway and disappeared.

"Where am I?" he called after her. She didn't answer.

The entire room was nothing but windows and glass doors. There was a pool and garden outside, and in the far distance the tops of other large homes on the mountainside. Wopper couldn't figure out where he was. He wasn't even sure if he was still in La Piedad.

A minute later the maid returned and said, "Breakfast will be ready in a minute."

"I don't need breakfast," he said. "If you could just show me to the door."

Again she ignored him. He could hear her on the other side of a wall, in the kitchen, he assumed, turning on the stove and opening cabinets. "Sit down," she called out.

Almost mechanically, he pulled out a chair and sat at a long black marble table with a place setting at either end. A moment later a man walked into the room, tucking in his pants.

"Breakfast coming up!" he said with a cackle.

Wopper recognized him. It was Pilimón, Don Elpidio's right-hand man. He knew for sure this wasn't Pilimón's house. It must be Don Elpidio's.

"Man, were you drunk last night!" Pilimón said as he took his seat at the other end of the table. He spoke in a high, tinny voice. "Slobbering, couldn't even keep your face muscles together. You looked like this—" He made his face limp. "What made you drink like that? That's what I want to know! A slut, huh? I bet it was! Only a slut will make a man drink like he wants death."

Wopper didn't remember drinking that much. He had a few beers, a shot or two, that was all. He was almost positive of that. He caught a glimpse of himself in a mirror across the room and saw that his hair was standing on end. He made a motion to smooth it down and instantly felt a large lump on the back of his head. He winced in pain. He remembered now. The men at La Palapa. On his way out one of them had hit him and knocked him unconscious. He remembered the black Suburbans too.

Pilimón began to laugh. "Oh yes, that's right. The blow to the head, that didn't help much. We didn't want you struggling and making a scene."

Wopper had never seen Pilimón talk so much. He always just stood there, or at the meetings he sat there with his boots up on the table, his very silence intended to be threatening.

"I need to go," Wopper mumbled absently. He rose from the table and looked around as if searching for the door.

"No, no, please, stay for breakfast," Pilimón said sarcastically. "It should be ready any minute now." He called past Wopper into the kitchen. "Hurry it up with the breakfast. We have a hungry man!"

"I'm coming right now, right now, don't worry," the maid responded. She emerged holding a pan of steaming eggs and chorizo. She piled them onto Wopper's plate and then rushed over to serve Pilimón.

"Now hurry up with the tortillas!" Pilimón said. He looked at Wopper and pointed at the chair. "Sit, please. I said please."

The maid returned to the kitchen and brought out two stacks of tortillas wrapped in white cloth.

Wopper sat down. He thanked the woman.

"You should be thanking Don Elpidio," Pilimón said, chuckling.

Wopper didn't say anything.

"You'll be seeing him soon enough," Pilimón continued, his mouth now full of food. He held a strip of tortilla in either hand. Again he began to laugh. "Do you know that we have been waiting for this moment for a long time now, and look here, you arrive on our doorstep, easy as that."

"I didn't arrive here," Wopper said.

"Oh, well, yes, that's true. When Rubén and Osvaldo called us from El Castillo and said you were leaving alone, we couldn't believe our good fortune! We thought you'd never leave La Morada by yourself. Always someone around you, goddamn it! What matters now is that you're here, and you are ours until you decide that you're going to play our game."

Pilimón stopped talking and eyed him closely.

Wopper remained silent.

"You understand what I'm saying, right?" Pilimón said. "You're going to be on our team, not anyone else's."

"I'm not on anyone else's."

Pilimón burst into cackles, small pieces of food spitting out of his mouth. "Whatever," he said. "Whatever you say." He returned to eating and gestured that Wopper should do the same.

Wopper felt sick. He couldn't take another bite. "I'm going to leave," he said.

Pilimón slammed his hand down on the table, his face instantly transforming from cheerful to livid. "What about what I just said did not make sense to you?! You fucking backward country idiot! Before you leave this place—*if* you want to leave this place—you are going to cooperate with us."

Wopper leaned back, his head throbbing. The numb feeling upon waking had given way to confusion. This was too much for him to think about. He wanted to talk to Mija. She needed to be there with him. Now he felt nauseous, and he turned and threw up what he'd just eaten.

From a distance he heard Pilimón say, "That's not going to get you out of this." Then came his muffled laugh.

Wopper was collapsed over his chair, the armrest digging into his ribs. He couldn't look away from the vomit on the pristine tile floor. Still laughing, Pilimón called the woman to clean up.

When Pilimón escorted Wopper to Don Elpidio's office, his nausea had subsided, but his headache was so strong that it was difficult to keep his eyes open. As they walked down the hallway, Wopper kept fighting the urge to shut his eyes, and twice he bumped into Pilimón. The second time Pilimón threatened, "Watch yourself, or you'll find yourself on the floor."

They reached the end of a long hallway. Pilimón knocked on a set of ornate wooden double doors and waited several seconds. "Enter," called Don Elpidio's raspy voice. Pilimón opened one of the doors. "Go inside," he said to Wopper. Then he gave him a slight shove, backed out of the room, and quietly shut the door.

Wopper was relieved to find the shades drawn in Don Elpidio's office. He barely even noticed Don Elpidio, who sat in a large chair with his legs propped up on a massive desk that occupied half the room. Only the shape of Don Elpidio's cowboy hat was visible above the silhouetted form. As Wopper's eyes adjusted to the darkness, he saw a wrinkled hand adorned by large gold rings reach across the desk to turn on a lamp. The dimming light slowly became brighter until the room was lit in a muted golden glow.

"I don't usually sit in the dark," Don Elpidio said, his face still lost in the shadows, "but I imagine this is a little better for your headache, am I right? Sorry about that. I told my men to be gentle. Put a little pill in his drink, I said, easy as that, but what can one expect from men hired to be rough? A pill *and* a blow to the head!" He chuckled. "I myself prefer sunshine, as you might have guessed from the layout of my house. I told my architect, plenty of windows, windows everywhere! This architect was an expert in—"

"I want to go home," Wopper blurted out.

Don Elpidio knit his brow and appeared amused. He removed his boots from the desk and leaned forward in his chair until his wrinkled, craggily face appeared in the dim light, his eyes lost in the shadows of their sockets. "Well, I want you to go home, too," he said, chuckling. "Believe me, young man, I would like nothing more. However, first we must discuss business. In my opinion, *this*, my friend, is the only way to do business. The only way! Why have an even playing field when you can skew the results in your favor? Believe me, I would like nothing more than to assist you in your desire to go home. But I guess what it comes down to is what home we're talking about. . . . Am I right? You see, I finally decided to do a little research. I found out about your legal problems back home. I know why you're here, deported no different than your average wetback. Of course, your average wetback wouldn't have been given as many chances. You, on the other hand, made quick work of four. That's called not learning your lesson!"

Wopper shifted in his seat uncomfortably. His head continued to throb, and he felt the nausea returning. He placed his hand across his face and began massaging both temples.

"Are you listening to me?" Don Elpidio asked.

Wopper looked up and nodded absently.

Don Elpidio stared at Wopper as though he didn't believe him. After a moment, he began again. "Well, I didn't stop there, young man. I continued my research, and I discovered that beyond your trouble distinguishing the appropriate time to get behind the wheel, you also held no job. None! I thought maybe you were a full-time student—too busy studying for work!—but your academic record doesn't exactly reflect a young man dedicated to his studies! Believe me, after learning about your life in the North, all I could ask myself was, *How did the Licenciado manage to accomplish all that he has so far?*"

Again Don Elpidio stopped and looked at Wopper as if expecting some sort of reaction. When all he received was a blank stare, he scowled as though growing frustrated. "Maybe you think you're the only one with connections in Woodland, my friend. But I also have cousins and nephews and friends of friends who have moved there. Many of them know you, some of them even know your so-called councillor from the North, this Arnulfo Beas that you brought to my office several months ago. That was quite an impressive stunt, I have to give you credit—even more impressive coming from such a fuck up as yourself. That is, if you even came up with it on your own. Of course, getting Maya and Moreno those contracts, that was the real coup."

Wopper was now sweating heavily. He moved forward slightly and felt his shirt stick to the back of his chair. "It doesn't matter what I did then," he managed to say.

"Hah!" Don Elpidio cried out, slamming his hand on the desk, his rings clanging loudly. He seemed happy to finally get a response. "It does! It does! What you were then *does* matter, if only because I can't quite accept that a deadbeat such as yourself suddenly finds himself maneuvering around a system I've been establishing for more than forty years. *My* system. You understand that, right? No? You seem confused. Well, how about I let you think about that for a few minutes." Don Elpidio held his finger to his lips and added, "Seriously, think about it. Both of us. Let's give it a few minutes to settle in and see what we come up with."

Wopper shook his head but said nothing. He didn't know what he was being asked to think about. Don Elpidio waited, staring at Wopper as if willing him to understand. After a long pause, Don Elpidio said, "Well, what have you come up with?"

Wopper shrugged. "I don't know what you're asking me."

"That's about what I expected," Don Elpidio said, shaking his head. "Know what I think? You're a Don Nobody. Have you heard of that before, a Don Nobody? It means you exist to be used by others. Back home, no one had any use for you, so you did nothing. Maybe your friends had a use for you, a drinking buddy, and you filled that role. Your father, I bet he wanted his boy to come claim the land he never had a chance to work himself, so you were nudged in that direction. You were deported, I know that, but you could've ended up in far more exciting locations than La Morada, am I right? I would've gone to Puerto Vallarta! But no, your father wanted you to live on *his* land! Then Don Cirilo, he needed a helper, didn't he? And look who drops from the heavens just in time for harvest! So you were used for that, too. Otherwise it never would've occurred to you to work, let alone hard work like that. Hell, you could've worked less and made more money working with Lucio at the car wash!" Don Elpidio laughed, then he sighed and leaned back in his chair. "But it was Mija who recognized your true potential as a Don Nobody. She's used you, you realize that. None of this was your idea. Not one part of this scheme. *A municipal representative!* you probably cried. But I give you credit, I really do. At least you allowed yourself to be used well. Am I right or am I right, Don Nobody?"

Don Elpidio again kicked his boots up on the desk and stared at Wopper, squinting his eyes and furrowing his brow, as though divining Wopper's thoughts. After a pause, Don Elpidio asked, "You know she killed Don Martín?" He grimaced as though it pained him to reveal this. He began shaking his head. "She seduced him, son; had him eating out of her hand the old-fashioned way, the only way a woman has ever dominated a man, with her charm and youth, and of course with what's between her legs. But you know more about that than I do . . ." Don Elpidio's voice trailed off. He clasped his hands and stared off pensively.

"I wish you had known Don Martín," he began again. "I was lucky to have known him, I truly was. Even though I knew from the very beginning that I couldn't ever be the kind of man he was, that we were breeds entirely apart, that we were destined to fight for opposing sides, I still could respect him. That's why when I heard what happened to him it made my neck hair stand on end. Did she tell you this? Stop me if you know this already. Did she tell you that they found him naked on his bed, his eyes wide open as though he'd seen the devil himself. He'd shit the bed, and on top of that, he had an erection you could hang a wet towel on—"

"He had a heart attack," Wopper said.

"Yes, exactly. And I believe she knew what she was doing. That so-called heart attack served her well. She inherited a good chunk of Don Martín's money. How else do you think she and Don Cirilo built that house? They used to live in your pathetic hovel"—he stopped briefly as though to gauge Wopper's reaction—"but you know that, of course."

Wopper didn't respond.

Don Elpidio continued. "And what about Lucio? Do you think he knew what he was doing?"

"I wouldn't know."

"Well, how about you? Do you know what you're doing?"

Wopper shrugged.

A smile slowly emerged on Don Elpidio's face. "You're nothing to me, you realize that? You don't exist except as some annoying splinter in my finger. And right now I'm about to root you out. I'm going to remove this splinter because I'm tired of dealing with it. But before I do I want to ask you what it is that girl wants. What is she after?"

Wopper's mouth was dry. He swallowed. "The same thing I'm after," he said.

"I could give a flying shit what you're after. I already told you, you're a splinter in my finger. What I want to know is what she's aiming for?"

Wopper stared hard at Don Elpidio. His heart was pounding.

"She wants La Morada to be a better place to live," he said. "She doesn't want it to disappear because everybody left for the North. It's her hometown, and she wants—"

"Go play with yourself all you want," Don Elpidio interrupted him. "However, don't play with me. Are you telling me that after two years of living with this girl you don't know any better than that— than some feel-good slogan? Of course not. You're a fucking idiot, a simpleton. You're as oblivious as poor Don Cirilo. I'm saving you from harm, my friend. One day you'll thank me for the favor I'm about to do for you. I don't want to see you like Lucio, screaming from the roof of the municipal palace, threatening to kill yourself, and I don't want to see you like Don Martín either—his eyes bulging out, his face drained of blood, his manhood touching his belly button, the room smelling like his last shit, the result of a fright we can't even begin to imagine. I'll say it again: the residents of La Morada believe he saw the devil, and I must agree with them! I'm saving you, young man. Go back to your worthless life in the North and forget you ever came here. Forget La Morada, forget that vicious bloodsucker; go back and consider yourself among the lucky, because that girl will stop at nothing until she gets what she's after."

Wopper found it difficult to speak. He swallowed, trying to generate enough saliva to say something, but he couldn't think of what to say.

"Don't be mistaken; I'm not afraid of her, just wary," Don Elpidio added, more subdued. "Wary. And if you had known Don Martín, you'd be too. He could take down wild stallions, but the poor old fool probably never saw this coming. And soon she'll devour you. Take it from me. Sign over the contracts to us. We'll take over the work paving La Morada. We'll pour the foundations for those homes you envision, don't you worry. We'll even send you home with appropriate compensation for your trouble. You'll cross the border like a citizen of that country."

"You have every other contract out there," Wopper said finally. "Why can't you just let these be?"

Don Elpidio stared at Wopper for a long time and then shook his head. "You poor kid. It's called principles. You never know what might set precedent." Then he picked up the phone and called

Pilimón. "He's ready for you," Don Elpidio said. He set the phone down on the receiver and stared at Wopper in disgust.

"I'm ready for what?"

"You'll find out."

Pilimón brought Wopper to a windowless room, empty except for a folding table and a chair. A stack of papers lay in the middle of the table.

"Well, these are the contracts we'd like you to sign," Pilimón said, pointing to the table. Then he stopped and looked around himself. "Damn it, there's no pen," he muttered. "I told him to make sure and leave a pen."

Wopper stared at the papers, the words just a blur. Pilimón continued grumbling about the pen, walking from one side of the room to the other. Suddenly, he rushed at Wopper and shoved him in the back of the head. Wopper stumbled forward, knocked against the table, and fell to the white tile floor. The blow didn't hurt, but when he turned around to face Pilimón he was met with another punch that hit him squarely in the jaw. After a few dazed seconds, he lost consciousness.

When he woke up he could barely move his jaw, and he felt dizzy. He looked up and saw a ceiling fan slowly turning, emitting a creak with each rotation. A light bulb flickered inside the fixture's frosted globe. He didn't know how long he'd been out. He couldn't tell the time of day. He rose from the ground and stared at the stack of papers on the table. He noticed there was a pen now. Afraid of losing his balance, he cautiously took a step toward the table, his hand out to steady himself. Pilimón had left a note. Wopper strained his eyes to read it: *Sign, or I'll be back to make you sign.*

Feeling steadier, Wopper walked toward the door and tried the knob, but it was locked. He hung his head and stared at his indistinct shadow on the tile. He wondered how it was possible that all of this was happening at the same time. Didn't he have enough to think about? He looked down at his hands. He opened his right palm, and with his left index finger he felt for his calluses. He took his nail and dug into the rough skin below his pinky. For a moment his headache and his fear and his confusion disappeared. He wasn't even in the room. He was back in La Morada, working the fields, waiting for Mija to call him in for dinner. But just as soon as the thought entered his mind, it turned on him, and he felt a surge of emptiness come over him. He didn't know what to believe anymore. He thought of his and Mija's conversation the night before, then Don Elpidio's rant, then his own ignorance all along. Then he thought of Pilimón coming back to knock him out again. He sighed heavily and leaned against the door, pressing his entire weight against it. He thought he felt the door shove open.

He looked down and saw a small opening. The knob had been locked, but the doorframe was warped, so the door hadn't closed all the way. After listening for footsteps, he pushed the door completely open with his shoulder and peered in either direction. He stepped into the hall and walked quietly, sure that at any second Pilimón or one of the guards would spot him and drag him back into the room.

It was afternoon and the sun had shifted to the other side of the house. Through a window, he noticed two guards on the roof smoking and talking to one another. He reached the end of the hall undetected. He recognized the hallway leading to the living and dining room where he'd eaten that morning. He stopped when he heard voices at the end of the hall. One of them was Don Elpidio's; the other voice belonged to a woman, a girl. He thought it sounded familiar. He wondered if it was the maid. He listened more closely, but she had stopped speaking. He walked slowly and deliberately, one careful step at a time, and stepped into a darkened entryway leading to a bathroom. The voices were easily distinguishable now.

He was short of breath. He calmed himself, steadying his hands against the wall, and listened in on the conversation. He could hear Don Elpidio's voice, then Wopper heard the girl speak. It sounded like Mija. Could she have found him that quickly? He found himself relieved. He almost had to fight the urge to rush out to greet her.

"And where is the Licenciado now?" he heard Don Elpidio say. "Does he know you've come to me?"

"He's at home, that's where he is," Mija answered.

"At home?"

"Yes, in La Morada."

"In La Morada?"

"Yes," she said.

Don Elpidio chuckled. "What if I told you he was here in my home, and I plan on getting what I want whether or not you tell me about all your business dealings?"

"Where he is," she said, "is not why I've come. I've come to tell you how to undo your company's losses."

Wopper thought he hadn't heard right. He almost doubted it was Mija. But he knew her voice. He poked his head out of the entryway. He would be exposed if anyone should happen to pass by, but he didn't care. He wanted to hear everything.

"And just why would you want to do that?" Don Elpidio asked. His voice sounded as incredulous as Wopper felt at that moment.

"With the contracts going to Maya Brothers, many more are sure to go his way," Mija said. Her voice was calm and unwavering. "Valentín Moreno is catching up, too. There's plenty more to be had, especially with the buildup around the reservoir, and I can tell you how to maneuver yourself so—"

Don Elpidio cut her off. He sounded angry or impatient. "Look, little girl, I know you're not here to help me out. You have some plan and this is one move in it. Now, if you don't tell me how it benefits you to sabotage your own efforts these last months, hell, these last years if you count all you put into place with Lucio Barraza and Don Martín, God rest his soul."

"Don't worry about my efforts," Mija replied.

Don Elpidio laughed. "Don't think for a second I'm worried about your well-being, and I speak on behalf of the departed Don Martín when I say that, but I don't know why you think I should trust you. I'm telling you right now that I don't. You can tell me whatever you're going to tell me, and I'm going to take it for what it's worth, and then I'm going to go into the other room and make sure that my right-hand man, Pilimón, breaks your boyfriend's or husband's or whatever he is to you, breaks the fingers on his left hand until the fingers on his right-hand pick up the pen and sign the documents that give me title to the properties and turn the contracts over to me. I hadn't wanted to do this, because it makes it messier for me, but you two have given me no choice. I couldn't just sit back and watch while you maneuvered through the municipality, playing everybody off everyone else with your promises and plans. So I've taken matters into my own hands. Now tell me what you wish to tell me and then get out of my home."

"You need to buy up all the properties along the water," Mija said, her voice still calm. She seemed unaffected by Don Elpidio's threats. "They're going to develop those and have buyers from the North who'll use them as vacation homes, but the homes need to be protected from flooding, so an embankment will have to be laid as well. The construction of the homes and the construction of the dam will be years' worth of work. If you want to screw over Moreno and Maya, I mean put them out of business, because they're committed to these projects and they are sure the deals with northerners will put them past you, way past you, then you need to be there before the northerners come in and invest in these homes . . ."

With each cold and detached word Mija uttered, Wopper felt his heart clench tighter and tighter. He felt choked, suffocated. He couldn't understand why she was doing this. What had he done to deserve this? Was it because he never told her about Lara and the baby? Was this her revenge? Suddenly, Don Elpidio's warning came back to him. She would devour him, too, he had said. Was that what she was doing?

"You need to invest first using dummies, fake investors," Mija continued. "Just enough so that the northerners who come down will be too late. And just when they've gone through with the project, put in enough money that if they're not reimbursed they're sunk, then you pull out. You pull out your investors. They won't be able to sustain the amount that they've put out, and it'd take them too long to gather the northerner's interest again. Also, once the northerners hear that five, six, seven, however many investors have pulled out and left the project midway, then they'll lose interest. They won't want to invest in a project that others have abandoned."

Wopper couldn't stand to hear any more. He left the entryway and ran down the hall, away from the living room, away from the voices. Frantically, he began opening every door he passed, as if expecting one of them to lead to an exit out of the house and past the guards. An exit that would take him as far away from there as possible.

II

Don Elpidio

She came to me, all the way out to my house in La Colonia Nueva. Must have taken her an hour of bus rides and then longer to walk, because the only way to get to La Colonia is in your own private car, or a taxi, I guess, but from the look of her—sweaty and dusty— she hadn't taken a taxi. At first I was upset because I thought for sure we had Roberto Barraza right where we wanted him, that we'd found him alone, kidnapped him, and now held him hostage until he agreed to our terms. But if she knew, then someone else must have told her, and if two people know in the municipality of La Piedad, then every fucker and their mother knows. But when my man Alfonso came in and told me that Barraza's girl was at the door and she wanted to speak to me, I asked him if she had asked about her man, and he shrugged. I asked him, "Does that mean yes or no?" He shook his head. "No, she didn't ask," he said. "She just asked to speak to you, sir." So I was left wondering what this visit would bring. I knew that Pilimón was having his fun with Roberto at the back end of the house, so I told Alfonso to bring her around the side. I'd see her in the living room.

When she entered the room, I noticed that she wasn't as sure of herself as she was when we last spoke after the municipal council meeting. Maybe she was tired from the walk. Anyone would look pretty haggard after the steep climb to where my house sits over-looking the city. She was wearing heels, I noticed, but I was sure she'd taken them off and only put them on at my doorstep. I thought this was funny, picturing the slut walking barefoot on the side of the road, carrying her heels in hand. I chuckled and asked, "Mija, why didn't you take a taxi? No one walks up here!"

She didn't even flinch. "I thought it was closer," she said.

I stopped laughing. She didn't have a sense of humor, that's for sure. People without a sense of humor unnerve me. They do, I can admit that. Because what's the point to their life? What's the fucking point?

So I decided to skip all small talk and dive into business, if that was all she came for. "What can I do for you, my little girl, walking all the way up here?" I said.

"I'm not your little girl," she told me.

"Don't get offended," I said. "At my age everyone is my little something." She paused for a second, staring at me like she could see right through me. She stared so intently that I had to change my position in my seat. It was like staring at an alley cat and realizing it had thoughts of its own. If she had continued staring like that I would have stood up and walked around the room. I was relieved when she began talking, but only momentarily. What she said unnerved me even more. She told me that she wanted to reveal Roberto Barraza's business dealings. She would tell me how to undo the damage already done to my company.

Of course, I had my suspicions immediately. Why would she want to screw over the man she'd propped up so expertly? I thought she was fucking with me. In fact, I was sure she was. But then I thought, *Maybe she's willing to fuck herself over just to get him released.* If so, then by all means, I would reap the benefits.

But suddenly I realized this was too easy. We kidnap him, she then tells all in order to secure his release. Such is the extent of her love and devotion! This was too simple for her. All this time I had struggled to discover her angle, and now I was going to fall for so simple a trap? This was a decoy, it had to be, and she was trying to pull me into another of her schemes. The more I thought about it, the more I was sure that this was her plan and that she must think I was really a dumb fucker if I was going to fall for this game so easily. I wouldn't be surprised if she knew our plan before we even knew it was a plan. She was probably the one who encouraged him to go off drinking alone, made him fall into our hands knowing we'd hold him hostage until he signed over the contracts, and then I'd be primed, ready for her, ready to fall prey to whatever her scheme was. Was that even possible?

Well, whether it was or not, she did tell me. The slut told me everything.

I listened to her and it all made too much sense. It made too much sense. So much so that I had no way to answer, not right away at least. I had to think it over. She really did tell me how to screw over my competitors. And all I could ask myself was, *Why?* What was her angle, goddamn it? After a brief moment of digesting what she'd laid out, I told her, "Look, I'm still going to break his fingers until he signs those contracts, because I really don't fucking believe that you're telling me this against your best interest."

She cut me off like I was the fucking idiot. "Oh, believe me," she said. "This is in my best interest." She explained that if I forced him to sign over the contracts right then, I would end things too quickly and miss out on the real money to be had down the line. I couldn't wrap my mind around what she was telling me. It made sense, but it was too damn hard to believe. Or maybe I really was the idiot in this conversation.

"Listen," she said, looking me right in the eye. "I have no alliance with Maya and Moreno. This will benefit me and me only."

"You mean the two of you?" I asked, indicating with my head her man in the other room.

She didn't say no, but she shook her head slightly to indicate the same thing. *Cold-hearted slut,* was all I could think to myself.

I called Pilimón and told him to let Roberto go and to be sure and rip up the contracts. He had been asleep, I could tell. "Are you sure?" he asked groggily. "Of course I'm sure!" I said. But of course I wasn't at all.

That was when I thought I heard footsteps in the hallway and doors opening and closing. I looked up, confused. I didn't know who it could be. Somebody must have been listening to our conversation. The footsteps became less distinct, and I heard a door slam and commotion on the other side of the house. Someone called out, "Get him," followed by, "I got him!" Then Pilimón called me and I picked up. All the while the girl was staring at me with her beady black eyes, I assumed because she was waiting for me to go fetch her man. Pilimón told me that Roberto had escaped and had tried to run out the door, but they caught him.

"It doesn't matter. He's free to go," I said.

"Let him go?" Pilimón asked.

"Yes, and tell him his woman is here," I told him.

I heard them talking, then Pilimón said to me, "He knows that, sir."

"Well, then tell him I'll provide a ride back to La Piedad for the two of them," I said.

After a jumbled exchange I couldn't make out, Pilimón said, "He doesn't want a ride. He just wants to leave."

"Well, let him leave then, goddamn it," I said.

I turned to the girl and smiled widely. I told her, "Strange, offered the two of you a ride, but our man wishes to leave on his own."

I can't even begin to describe the expression of confusion and apprehension on her face, as though she were imagining the consequences of some grave error she'd just committed. I knew exactly how she felt. Why? Because I had him just where I wanted. He was ready to sign, but I second-guessed myself and let the son of a bitch go. I should've known better.

III

Don Cirilo

I was relieved when I saw him get out of his truck just as he had that first day when I was eating my tacos out there with Don Jaspero. But this time I didn't have the donkey with me, because the donkey was sick, throwing up bile, and I didn't have any tacos either, because my daughter had gone off somewhere without making me lunch. She left without even answering my question, which was, "Where you off to, Mija?" Well, Roberto looked about how I felt. I had a headache that made me think maybe I'd fallen off Lucio's motorcycle. I didn't have any scratches or bumps, so it must've been the tequila—just a few shots we had, but never has a hangover left me in such a bad state. I almost couldn't get out of bed, and if it wasn't for my daughter waking me and bringing me water and a ham sandwich, I probably would have just stayed there all day.

When I saw the look on Roberto's face—like he wished to die rather than walk the remaining yards to his house—I told him, "Me and Don Jaspero are sick, too!" I thought he'd at least nod his head or ask, "Is there anything I can do to help?" But clearly work wasn't on his mind that day. He just walked toward his house, dragging his feet so that the dust kicked up around him. I called after him, "Were you really kidnapped? They said you were kidnapped!" He didn't even answer. So I said, "It was just friends of yours messing about, isn't that the truth? They got you to drinking, didn't they?" Again he didn't answer. He just kept walking as if he was carrying some awful weight. I figured then that the previous night had affected him many times worse than any hangover. So I said, "Well, I'm glad to see you're safe, whatever it is that happened!"

A shovel was on the ground about ten feet in front of him, and I saw him heading straight toward it. I assumed he saw it, but as he got closer I realized that he wasn't paying attention to anything, let alone the ground in front of him. So I called out, "Watch out for the shovel!" But I was too late. His feet tripped over the handle, and he fell to the ground like a bag of cement. I rushed to help him rise to his feet. But he didn't want to. He just lay there with his face pressed into the dirt like he was trying to breathe it in. I grabbed his arm and said, "Come on, help me, lift!" But he stayed put, like he'd been knocked out. I noticed a purple bruise on his face. "Did that just happen?" I asked. I saw his body begin to shake, and then I heard the snorts of a painful sob, and now I really understood that something terrible had happened.

I put his arm around my neck and shoulder, and I lifted him and said, "Ought to be ashamed of yourself—missing work, Don Jaspero sick and can't help either, the two of you leaving everything to me, an old man!" But all he did was blubber and sob as I dragged him home. I put him in bed and brought him some water to drink. Then I told him that Mija would be home any minute to tend to him. I thought if anything that would make him feel better, but he only moaned louder and said, "She screwed me, Don Cirilo. It's too much. I can't take this anymore. This is too much. She screwed me."

I didn't understand what he was talking about, and he was in no shape to answer me properly, so I let him be. Who screwed him? I didn't have to wait long to find out. Soon after, Mija arrived in a taxi—I just about fell over. My daughter would rather walk five miles than waste money on a luxury like that. So I knew she must have been in a desperate rush to get home. Well, as soon as she paid the driver, she asked me, "Where's Roberto?" I could hear a tremble in her voice. I pointed to their little house and said, "Over there, of course." She marched toward her door, and I followed, curious to know what was going on.

I stood outside the door, wondering if I should walk inside or not. I was about to knock when I heard Roberto scream, "I heard everything! You told that bastard Don Elpidio everything!"

Then I heard Mija's cries to match his: "I was only trying to get you released without losing everything we've worked for! I was only trying to get you out of there. I know Don Elpidio will never believe me; he won't allow himself to trust me. I could tell him anything and in the end he won't go for it! I know that for sure. I didn't ruin anything. Please, Roberto, you have to believe me!"

"I heard you," he said. "I know what I heard."

"How could you think I would be capable of something like that?" my daughter cried. I had never heard her voice so desperate.

Then Roberto said many things that I didn't completely understand, but I remember his words well because it's not every day one hears the secrets of a pained man. He said that he didn't know what Mija was capable of. Everyone seemed to know except for him. He said that he was the only idiot walking around not knowing anything about who she was or what she did or why she did it. He just blindly followed her every order and listened to every explanation, but he still didn't know why they were doing any of it. Why he was negotiating the contracts, or working with the concrete companies, or dealing with all sorts of people he didn't care about and never would. He said that he didn't care about paved roads in La Morada or La Morada's soccer team or building houses along the reservoir. He kept saying that he never asked for any of this. That he had a life back in Woodland and that he had never asked for another one. I was about to interrupt and yell,

"Well, why did you come down here, then?" But I kept quiet. I was frozen, to tell you the truth.

The way Roberto made it out, my daughter was to blame for everything. My daughter! And at that moment I decided he was a poor excuse for a man. He said it was Mija who had decided his fate for him. She made him what she wanted him to be. Then he started saying that he was just Wopper Barraza. "*Wopper fucking Barraza*," he said. He was no Licenciado and he never had been. And he never wanted to hear about Don Elpidio or Pilimón or the concrete companies or those stupid contracts again. He said that Don Elpidio could have all of them for all he cared. The old bastard could even own La Morada. Then he called La Morada a piece of shit rancho. After that I thought I heard him crying. "I don't care, I never cared!" he yelled. "I just did it for you, because you asked me to, and I trusted you, and look where it's got me! I don't know my ass from a hole in the ground!"

He went on like that, yelling and yelling, and after a while I could hardly understand him, even though he was yelling loud enough for me to hear every word. Mija kept trying to interrupt him. She kept apologizing and saying, "I didn't, I didn't know. I'm sorry!" What didn't she know? I wondered. What was she sorry about? I decided eavesdropping at the door was no place for an old man like me.

I fell asleep watching television only to wake up to them screaming some more. Which meant they were yelling loud enough to wake the dead, if I could hear them over the television. It was Roberto yelling his head off mainly. I heard my daughter say, "No! Please, understand! It's not true!" but other than that it was Roberto's voice I heard most, though I couldn't understand him, his words running together so it sounded like one long bellowing growl. Later, I thought I heard the truck drive off in the middle of the night, but I was too tired to think much of it. But the next morning I woke up and my daughter was sitting at the table, her head cradled in her arms. When she heard me rise, her head shot up, and I could see that her eyes were red and that she'd not slept at all.

"What's wrong?" I asked as I put on my boots, and I wondered to myself whether Don Jaspero was feeling any better.

"He left," she said.

"Who did?" I asked. Then I asked her to get me some water because my mouth was dry. Then when she started to fill up the glass I told her, "Better yet, give me some coke because my stomach feels a little upset."

She set down the glass and burst into tears. I told her, "Mija, there's no need to cry! I'll take the glass of water then, if it means so much!"

But then she told me that Roberto had left late that night. "He'll be back," I told her, not seeing what the big deal was. He'd left in the middle of the previous night, too, and I'd seen him again the next day. In bad shape, but I'd seen him. And she just shook her head and said, "I don't think so. He thinks I've done something horrible. Don Elpidio somehow turned his head around."

"Well, did you tell him that you didn't do it?" I asked.

She didn't answer me. She went to the refrigerator and pulled out the liter of coke. She poured me a glass, and as she handed it to me she said, "How could he think I would do something so horrible?"

"I have no idea what you're taking about," I said, and I grabbed my sweater and walked outside. I stared out at the fields before me. Roberto wasn't there to help, and Don Jaspero was sick, and I thought about all the work that awaited me. I picked up a bucket and took one step in the direction of the reservoir, but then I set the bucket down. A breeze picked up, and a cloud of dust passed in front of me like a ghost. I didn't know what happened. All I knew was that I had never in all my life seen my daughter so upset. My poor little girl! I turned around and walked back inside. She was sobbing on the floor. I picked her up just as if she were a child—and she's the size of one, as light as a feather!—and I carried her to the bed where she used to sleep, and I said, "Now, now, my daughter. He will come back. Don't you worry."

"No, he won't," she whimpered.

PART IV

CHAPTER NINETEEN

I

Jorge Barraza

I CAME HOME FROM WORK, AND HE WAS THERE SITTING ON THE FRONT STEP in front of our door. His head was bowed so all I could see was his full head of hair and his rounded shoulders, which before had been so shapeless. But I knew it was Wopper. Yet I stood there in the walkway, carrying my lunch pail and thermos, staring as if I didn't really believe it could be him.

"Mijo!" I said.

He looked up. "Dad," he said.

He didn't have any bags. His clothes looked dusty. He looked like he hadn't slept in days. His hair was oily, his face strained. "What happened?" I asked, walking up the pathway toward him. "What happened?" I asked again.

"Nothing, Dad. I came home," he said, as he rose from the step. I fumbled in my pant pocket for the key, and my hands were shaking so it took me a moment to get the door open, but as soon as I did I turned toward him, and there he was, ready to hug me, and I hugged him, and of course I felt the tears streaming down my face, and I was ashamed of them. I didn't want him to see, not again. But I looked up and there wasn't any shame in his face, just concern or confusion or exhaustion, I don't know, just that it wasn't shame. And so I let myself cry for all the times I wanted to over that year and a half, two years, was it? I let myself cry, and I blubbered out questions, not even giving him time to answer.

"Come in, come in," I said, stepping back and looking at him again.

I knew he had suffered. And I felt for him. I wondered whether he'd suffered on his journey home, whether he'd lost himself in the desert. A million possibilities ran through my mind. No bags; I wondered if he'd been robbed. So skinny; I wondered if he'd starved. I told him that he smelled like a wet dog in a trash heap, and I thought that this at least would make him smile, but he didn't. He just pulled his shirt to his nose to verify if it were true. I told him that he should shower and change, that his mother shouldn't see him so dirty, like he'd been lost in the wilderness, in the desert. "How did you cross?" I asked him. And he told me, "Easily."

"No problem whatsoever?" I asked.

"No," he said. "Just nerves."

"Any close calls?" I asked.

"No, just a lot of waiting," he said.

"Yes, always waiting!" I cried. "I remember, waiting and waiting. Did you have to run at all?"

"No, no running," he said.

"That's good," I said. Then I asked, "One attempt or two or three?"

"Just one," he answered.

"You found good smugglers, then!" I said, clasping my hands together, unable to believe that my son, my Wopper, had crossed the border. I couldn't picture him running across highways or crawling through barbed wire fences or huddled on the floors of safe houses. Yes, I had done it so many countless times, but I was of a different generation! Yes, he was home, he was safe, but that didn't seem to matter. All I could think then was that I would've crossed a thousand times if I could have saved my son just this one.

He went into the bathroom to shower, and I sat in the living room, listening to the patter of the water in the bathroom, and I kept rocking back forth and clasping my hands and removing my cowboy hat and putting it back on all because I didn't know what to do with myself. When he came out of the bathroom he was wearing his old clothes. They hung on him like sheets. I laughed and told him, "Wait till your mother sees you! She will force food down your mouth for weeks!"

He walked into the kitchen, and I followed him and took a seat at the table. He mumbled something about making a quesadilla, and then he stared at the stove and the comal as if he'd forgotten how. I told him not to eat too much because his mother would be home soon and she would not like the privilege of stuffing him taken away. He made the quesadilla, put it on a plate, and sat down with me at the table. I wanted to ask him so many questions. *How was the land? Wasn't it a difficult time to leave, no? He must have a whole bunch of workers on his payroll, eh? How was the politics, the life of an official? My son the Licenciado! How had he done it? How long was he to stay?* But I didn't ask him a thing, I don't know why. I just kept clasping my hands together and saying, "I can't believe it, I can't believe it!"

The truth is I was scared that the suffering in his face, which hadn't gone away even though he looked less exhausted, told me the answer to all my questions: that everything had fallen apart and there was no going back. I felt it. I saw it in his face. So I asked no questions. He asked me instead about his mother, about work, about his sisters who'd both moved out and were living with their boyfriends, about my compadres, about his friends, about changes in Woodland, and I answered them as plain as could be. "Other than your son, mijo, everything is the same," I said. "Everything." I wanted to tell him, *It is you who has journeyed far. We here just got a little older, that's all.* But I didn't say this, because I didn't yet know how far he'd traveled. I thought he had gone and found him- self, but his face was not that of a man found.

When his mother came in the door and saw us there in the kitchen, I thought she was going to have a heart attack. I wanted to laugh with joy, to share the happiness and relief she felt, but honestly I thought that maybe she couldn't stand the shock, such was the surprise on her face. I waited to see that she began breath- ing again. She did. I was sure the entire block heard her scream!

After she recovered, she told Wopper, her face dead serious, "I don't know how long you plan to be here, but you're not leaving until your son is healthy. You hear me? I won't let you leave. He needs you too much."

Then she asked him if he was hungry, and without waiting for an answer she started pulling food out of the refrigerator and heating up tortillas. So we all ate. Well, Wopper and I ate. My wife just sat and watched him, this smile on her face as if she had missed seeing him eat most of all. I joked that she was thinking he was going to fatten up right before her eyes.

Ten minutes after dinner we were crammed into my little Toyota and driving to the hospital. My wife didn't even complain about the broken air conditioner. We just rolled down the windows, all of us silent as though in disbelief that we were together again. The truth is, it didn't even feel real at that point. If he disappeared and someone told me it was all just a dream, I would've believed it. I kept looking at my son in the rearview mirror, waiting for some sign that he was okay, but he looked weary and lost, lost in his head, as if something wasn't letting him rest. He stared out the window, and I wondered if he was just nervous about seeing his son for the first time. Of course, I wanted to ask him about La Morada. I wanted him to tell me about my land, what it looked like, what if felt like to work it. What kind of crops did he grow— just corn like the old days—or something else? Who was still around? But I kept quiet.

When we arrived at the hospital we went directly to the room, knowing our way through the halls as if it were our own home. My wife walked fast, her footsteps clacking on the linoleum floors, and I tried to keep up with her, but Wopper didn't hurry, walking as though he were a patient himself out for prescribed exercise, and soon we were well ahead of him. I kept looking back at him, wondering why my wife was walking so fast and why my son was walking so slow, and there I was torn in the middle, not understanding anyone or anything, as if confusion was a state I must get used to. "Just this way," I told Wopper. "Room three fifty-four, just around the corner and to the left." He nodded his head and I turned to my wife, who had already rounded the corner. "Raquel, slow down, for the love of God!" I yelled after her.

We waited outside the room for him to catch up. He stood several feet away from the door, reluctant to enter. We prepared him for what he was about to see. This wasn't a baby in the nursery. We told him about the monitors and machines, about the baby's condition, and we would've continued as if we were the doctors themselves, but he stopped us.

"What's his name?" he asked.

"Whose name?" I asked. "The doctor's? I haven't any clue," I said. "It's something like . . . Wash—Wash—"

"Dr. Washburn," my wife finished for me.

"No, not the doctor. My son," Wopper said.

"You don't know his name?" my wife cried, and then she looked at me as if this were somehow my fault. "His name is Roberto," she said. "Robertito, we call him."

And I added, "I call him Junior! I always wanted a junior, but your mom wanted to name you Roberto, so I didn't get my junior, but at least now you get to have yours."

Then after a long silence we watched Wopper walk into the hospital room, or I watched him, because my wife was staring at me with her eyes bulging out, as if everything that came out of my mouth was either inappropriate or irrelevant. I mean, what father doesn't want a junior?

II

Lara Gonzalez

I felt someone at the door, but I didn't turn around. I thought maybe it was a nurse or doctor. I was listening to a mix of Spanish music from the eighties on my CD player. A Leo Dan song was playing, "Pideme la luna." When I was growing up my mom always cleaned house to this music. It reminded me of weekends in the spring. The songs made me happy, I don't know why. Those last couple months I must've listened to that CD a thousand times. So I was lost in my thoughts, holding Robertito's hand, and suddenly I felt someone close. A hand touched my shoulder and I heard my name, "Lara," in a muffled voice. I backed up, kind of startled, thinking it was a nurse, wondering why he or she was standing so close, but then I looked up and saw Wopper's face. I pulled the earphones out of my ears, my heart beating faster and faster. And all I said was, "You came."

I didn't expect to see him so sad. I'd never seen his face like this. Wopper was always so hard to read. You never knew when he was upset or tired or angry or just bored, but this was sadness. Was it because he felt sorry for me, was that why he looked like that? I rose from the chair, and we stood there staring at one another for a second, and then we kinda moved toward each other, like we were unsure if we should hug or not. I held out my arms and so did he, and it was as if we came together in slow motion, but once we did we held one another tightly. Maybe it was just me who held him tight, but I didn't care. I wanted to hold him tighter, and if there was a way to hold him even tighter I would have. I think in that hug I realized how empty everything had been without him.

"You named him after me," he said.

I nodded and felt tears coming to my eyes. I lowered my head and pulled away, and that was right when Raquel and Jorge walked in the room. "Oh, we're sorry!" Jorge said, as if he'd caught us making out or something. "We didn't know you were here!" he said. But they didn't make any move to leave the room. They just stood there all awkwardly, Jorge holding his cowboy hat in his hand and Raquel clutching her purse, and we were all silent until Wopper said to his parents, "Can you give us a minute?" They nodded their heads and shuffled out of the room. "We'll be in the cafeteria," we heard Raquel say. When they were gone, we were both quiet. I wanted to say something, but I didn't know what, or I didn't know how to begin. So we just turned to the small crib and watched our baby in silence.

"He used to look more like you," I said finally. "But you lost all your baby fat."

He chuckled a little and then said that he thought he looked like me. "Really?" I said, surprised. "No one thinks that." He nodded and said, "I think he does." I stared at Robertito and wondered what part reminded Wopper of me. We were quiet again. Wopper looked around the room, first at the get-well cards on the counter and the balloons and a large white teddy bear in the corner. Then he stared at my night kit that I kept there for when I stayed over. He briefly looked up at the television screen before he turned back to the baby.

"Will he be okay?" he asked.

"The doctors say that he's not in the clear," I told him. "They don't know when he will be."

"What can we do?" he asked.

"Wait," I said. "Just wait. Hope that the hole closes rather than opens wider. Right now it's just stopped growing."

I looked up at Wopper and watched him as he stared at Robertito. Except for that moment when he first walked in, we had yet to look into each other's eyes. I don't know why that seemed important, but to me it was. I kept looking at him until he looked up and our eyes met.

He tried to smile, but that's what it looked like, as if he was forcing himself to. As if he thought he had to be gentle with me. Then he said, "I missed you, Lara."

"No you didn't," I heard myself say.

He stayed quiet.

"I heard about your girlfriend," I said. "It seems between her and your life as a politician, you didn't have much time to miss me or your son."

Again I felt my heart beating faster, and my voice started to tremble. I didn't want to get angry, but I couldn't help myself. If he tried to tell me differently, I would have told him he was lying.

But he paused for a long time and then said, "Maybe you're right. But knowing I was going to see you again, and seeing you right now, I realized how much I missed you."

I didn't respond to this at first. I didn't know how. I thought for a second and then asked, "What about her? Are you going back?"

He looked down at his hands, which were gripping the edge of the crib, and he shrugged.

I remembered a time when I would've let that go, when I wouldn't have cared to figure out his shrugs, but I had to know this time. "What does that mean?" I asked.

He looked at me, still with his eyes so sad, and he said, "I'm not leaving anytime soon," and I wouldn't have known how to take that except he put his hand out for me, and he held it there, waiting for me to hold it, and I could see the top of his hand shaking just a little as if he were nervous. As if he feared that maybe I wouldn't give him my hand to hold. But I did. I gave it to him, and he held it, and I felt myself breathing easier.

Then Robertito stirred, and I went over to the baby's side and gently caressed his back. "Do you want to hold him?" I asked.

"We can do that?" he said.

I laughed. "Yeah, of course we can," I said.

He nodded like he wasn't sure and slowly took a few steps toward me.

I picked Robertito up, careful to move aside the tubes connected to his nose and wrist. "Here," I said, and I reached for Wopper's hand, and I placed it at the back of the baby's head and then shifted him into Wopper's arms. For a moment Wopper looked frightened, as if he was afraid of dropping him or crushing him, but then a look of relief crossed his face, and he smiled. "I never guessed it would feel like this," he said.

I knew then that I didn't want to raise my baby alone; I wanted to raise him with Wopper. And maybe it was simply a relief to have him home, a relief to not feel so alone anymore, but for the first time I had hope that everything was going to work out.

CHAPTER TWENTY

Raul Leon

I WAS SITTING IN MAIN EVENT WAITING TO GET MY HAIRCUT, READING *SPORTS Illustrated*, when I looked over, and who walks in but Wopper Barraza. I couldn't believe my eyes. He was skinny as fuck and he had a fro, but I recognized that fool immediately. "When the hell did you get back, man?" I said.

He looked as if I had scared him.

"Oh, hey," he said. "What's up, Raul?"

We shook hands, and then he sat down, and then a second later I sat down too. That's it. Just like that, as if we'd seen each other just last weekend. As if I hadn't thought about him for two years straight. I swear to God. I'd be in bed at night, unable to sleep, and I'd think to myself, *I wonder what the fuck Wopper Barraza is doing right now.* And I'd imagine him riding a horse or some shit like that. I'd be at work and suddenly Wopper would pop into my head and I'd think, *I wonder what the fuck that fool Wopper is doing for money down there.* Stuff like that, all the time. And I couldn't ever figure out why. I never told anyone either. I'd just wait for someone else to say it, like at the bar, Frankie or someone would say, "I wonder what Wopper be up to now." And I'd just say, "I know, huh." That would be it. I never told them I thought about what Wopper was doing all the goddamned time. And now there he was, waiting at Main Event for a haircut.

"What are you doing back, man?" I asked.

"You hear about my little boy?" he said quietly, as if he didn't want anyone else to hear.

I lowered my voice too. "Naw, man, naw. I didn't even know you had a kid. When did that happen? Some chick down there?"

"No, no, with Lara. Before I left," he said, and then he added, almost in a whisper, "He got sick. He'll be all right, I think, but I came back to make sure he was okay, you know?"

"So you going back, then?"

He looked at me all strange. As if I just asked him the craziest thing he could imagine. "I don't know, man. Probably not," he said. Then he stared down at the magazines on the table as if he'd rather pick one up and read about '56 Chevys and chrome rims or what team was gonna win the West rather than answer any more of my questions.

Then Big Tonio called out my name. I'd forgotten all about my haircut. I didn't give a shit about my hair at that moment. I just wanted to keep talking to Wopper. I wanted to hear everything, from Day One to whatever day it was then. I wanted to ask him all the questions that had come to my mind in the last two years. I didn't even need a haircut; I just got one because that's what I did every other Sunday. What I needed was to talk to Wopper. But then Chuy called out Wopper's name and he got up from his chair. That fool did need a haircut.

So I got up, too, and went over to Tonio's chair, and then because my hair was so damn short anyway, Tonio finished it in ten minutes. Chuy wasn't even finished with one side of Wopper's head. So I paid Tonio his money, and then I said to Wopper, "Hey man, the Niners are playing tonight. Let's go watch it over at Zitios."

He looked at me for a moment as if he was trying to imagine what it would be like, all of us at the bar getting drunk and watching the game just like we used to. Then he said, "Yeah, all right, you'll be over there? I'll try to make it."

"Cool, cool," I said. Then as I walked out, I thought to myself, *That fool isn't going to show.*

But he did come. And I don't know why, but no one else came around, so it was just the two of us. I was glad of that because it gave us a chance to talk. We hardly watched the game. I could give a fuck about the Niners, but I was surprised that Wopper didn't seem to care either. "I almost forgot about them down there," he said. "Oh, yeah," I said. *Oh, yeah*, as if even this was important information. There was so much I wanted to ask him, but for one reason or another we never got around to my questions. All we talked about was when we were kids. We talked about when we met in Ms. Martinez's class, and we talked about all the fools we'd grown up with and who had done what with who and when. The same old shit we always used to talk about. But Wopper seemed happy, and he was laughing, and he didn't look all in a daze like he did when I ran into him at the barbershop. So I just went with it, and finally he said, "You know what, Raul? When I was down there I didn't have any friends," and then he laughed as if that shit was supposed to be funny.

And I laughed as if I thought it was funny too. "No friends?" I said. "Not one friend?"

"Naw, man. Not one," he said, and then he got all quiet and stared at his beer.

"But you had a girl, right?" I said.

"Yeah," he said.

"Well, that's something," I said.

"Yeah, but it's not the same," he said.

"It's fucking not," I said. "I hear that." And then I held up my bottle and said, "Salud, man. To you being back. It's good to see you."

Then he asked me where the other guys were, and I told him I didn't know. I told him I hadn't been to the bar in a long time, probably six months, because I was working sixty hours a week and just wanted to sleep whenever I had a free day.

"Where you working now?" he asked.

"Same place," I said. "Over there at the Walgreens warehouse. Shit, I've been there long enough that they made me a receiving manager."

"Oh yeah?" Wopper said.

"I get to hire *and* fire fools," I said.

After that we watched the game for a few minutes and sipped

our beers. Then out of the blue, Wopper asked me, "You get me a job?"

"Hells fucking yeah," I said.

He got serious again and all fidgety, as though he was nervous or something. Then he said to me, "You know I don't got any papers, right?"

I started to laugh. Fucking Wopper. "Yeah, fool, don't even worry about that," I told him. "You just be one more wetback I got on the payroll."

At least then he cracked a smile.

CHAPTER TWENTY-ONE

Arnulfo "Arnie" Beas

I COULDN'T LET WOPPER BARRAZA GO. I KNEW HE HAD RETURNED. I KNEW that he and Lara took up right where they left off (my bet was on the couch watching television), and I heard that he worked nights at the Walgreens distribution center off Road 102. I guess he found a way to get the paperwork processed correctly. I assumed he was just performing menial labor and there wouldn't be much opportunity for him to do much else. Moving up the ladder, moving around, he risked detection and possibly deportation. I knew from my own family members without papers that, whereas it wasn't a constant and imminent risk, it was still a risk one didn't want to take lightly. So I had to picture him monotonously stacking boxes every night, certain that his days as a politico maneuvering around La Piedad's concrete companies were long gone. In fact, those days must've felt like a dream. But I hadn't spoken to him in person, so I didn't know the whole story. And I preferred to keep it that way. Wopper Barraza had already dominated enough of my thoughts.

But then one day Mr. Gregory arrived in my office at the college and asked to speak with me. He was wearing a suit, his white hair parted, not a strand out of place. He shut the door behind him, a concerned look on his face, and asked, "What's become of Wopper?"

"He came back," I said.

"I know that," he said. "But he hasn't visited me or anything. I figured he'd come by and update me on the project. I just recently got back from La Piedad, making sure the development is progressing on schedule, and it is, but without Wopper! I asked around, but no one seemed to know what had happened to him. It wasn't until I came across that girlfriend of his that I found out he'd left. She told me that construction was underway, as I had seen, and that I shouldn't worry. But I told her I'd gotten involved because I thought Wopper was attached to the project. She just shook her head and told me she didn't understand. With my limited Spanish and her limited English, that was as far as I got."

I had heard about the project months ago while Wopper was still in La Morada. In fact, my friend's parents were considering buying one of the homes, and I thought it was a ridiculous venture. They sent a down payment anyway. "So the waterfront house project is really going forward?" I asked.

"His house is just about finished!" Mr. Gregory exclaimed.

I shook my head in disbelief. From the moment I heard he'd come back, I assumed that everything had collapsed and that was why he ran off. "Well, I think he's back for good," I said. "His child was sick, but he's doing better now. The child, I mean. And Wopper is working here and everything."

"Where is he working?" he asked.

"At the Walgreens distribution center," I said.

Mr. Gregory knit his brow. "What's he doing there?" he said.

I shrugged my shoulder. "Who knows?" I said. "Stacking boxes, I presume."

"Stacking boxes, hell," he said, placing his hands on his hips and shaking his head, a look on his face that said, *Isn't that the darnedest thing!* Then he asked, "What's he doing wasting his time there for?"

Until then I didn't think it so farfetched that Wopper was working some minimum wage warehouse job. At least he was working, I thought. But Mr. Gregory helped me see something. He and I were the only two people to have known Wopper before he left for Mexico who also witnessed him once he was there serving as the influential municipal representative. Meaning, we were in a position to know just how far he'd risen in such a short period of time, and

Mr. Gregory had arrived at a conclusion that deemed it preposterous that our Wopper was no longer the esteemed Licenciado Roberto Barraza. And I guess I had to agree with him. I say *I guess* because I couldn't shake my reservations, my prejudices even. Sure, I had encouraged some of my struggling students to take "spiritual voyages" to their homeland, relating the story of a "former student of mine" who had discovered himself in Mexico. All the same, I still wasn't willing to give him credit where perhaps credit was due. But Mr. Gregory had no prejudices, it seemed. He respected Wopper's competency as one would respect a business partner. Why couldn't I? Did I prefer to see Wopper as a loser? Did it fit better into my worldview that he was now working where he should've always been working, unloading tractor trailers with a bunch of other meatheads?

I didn't share these thoughts with Mr. Gregory, of course. Instead, I gave him my aunt's address and told him he'd probably be able to find Wopper there in the afternoons.

When Mr. Gregory left my office, I met with a counselee named Gabriel Ramos, a nineteen-year-old who had enrolled in classes for three straight semesters and, without fail, had never properly registered and therefore had only half the credits he deserved. I figured he wanted to see if he could receive those credits retroactively; though, of course, he didn't know how to ask for that, nor if something like that was possible, nor even what retroactive meant. He just asked to meet with me. This was our first session, so I started in with the usual questions about educational plans and career goals and aspirations and general interests, hobbies, and passions, and I was met with the same perfunctory shrugs and the all-encompassing, "I don't know." As I was asking these questions, I had Wopper in the back of my mind, slowly pushing himself to the front of my mind, and soon I wasn't even paying attention to Gabriel Ramos's monosyllabic answers and inscrutable shoulder movements, because all I could remember was Wopper's counseling session years ago and his answers then that were no different than Gabriel Ramos's now, just shrugs and I don't knows, and it made me wonder, made me really wonder, what I expected my counselees to answer? Should they say, "I want to be a lawyer!" Should they say, "I want to be a heart surgeon!" An artist, an elementary school teacher, a biologist, an agronomist, a social worker, a counselor, a restaurateur . . . Because what if they did? Would having an answer to my question account for the obstacles thrown their way, the unpredictability of life, the dramatic changes that forever alter our course? I considered Wopper's deportation as the greatest thing to happen to him if only because it woke him from a senselessly inane existence—yes, that's what it was—but six years ago, when he sat in my office and shrugged his indifference to his future, could there have been any way to predict it would happen? Of course there wasn't. So what was the point . . . what was the point to any of this? Why was I talking to Gabriel Ramos? Why did I talk to any of my counselees? My sessions should go like this: Student enters; I say, "Good luck in this crapshoot life"; student leaves.

God, was I ever pessimistic at that moment.

Maybe I don't believe that any man can be transformed. Either a man rises or he falls on the sharp stake of his own habits. Wopper rose. So I guess the question is this: If he did it at twenty-five, could he have done it at nineteen, when he first sat before me in this office? Was his potential already within him, and I just couldn't recognize it? Would it have been possible to recognize? In my defense as a counselor, I say of course not. And then I looked at Gabriel Ramos in front of me, staring at his cell phone, waiting to get the hell out of my office so he could go home and play video games or smoke weed with his homies, and I wondered if he too had the potential to move beyond this mindless stupor, a potential that would never be reached if it weren't somehow forced out of him, beaten out of him. But right then I didn't care about Gabriel Ramos or any of my counselees. What mattered was the fact that six years ago I had seen a young man going nowhere, with no future, and I had accepted it, but I had been wrong, simple as that. Because Wopper had gone somewhere, and that fact was unequivocal.

I didn't sleep that night. At six in the morning, without showering or shaving or drinking coffee, I put on a baseball cap and drove to the Walgreens distribution center on the outskirts of town. I waited for Wopper to emerge from the gigantic warehouse. It was a cold fall morning, and I stayed inside the car, shivering. I was in such a fog that I'd forgotten to bring a jacket. After freezing for half an hour, I saw workers start to exit the building. I watched closely for Wopper, afraid I'd miss him and suffer another sleepless night. Finally, I spotted him. He was alone. He walked slunk over, carrying a blue vinyl lunch bag in his right hand, his left hand tucked deep into his jacket pocket. I wondered if he carpooled or if he risked driving without a license. I sat there watching him, as if that's what I'd come to do, just watch him. I'm the first to admit I don't function well without sleep. I snapped out of it just as he was leaving the parking lot. I quickly started up my car and followed him. I found him waiting at the bus stop. I rolled down my window and asked, "Wopper, you want a ride?"

"What?" he said.

I corrected myself. "Roberto, do you want a ride?"

He hesitated. He looked down the street as though hoping the bus was visible so he could reasonably decline my offer. I wondered why he would be reluctant to see me. He walked around to the passenger side and got in. "Thanks," he mumbled.

"Why did you come back?" I asked, not wasting any time.

"What do mean?" he said.

I turned on the heater. I was shivering uncontrollably. "Mr. Gregory came by and asked about you," I explained to him. "He told me that he'd returned to La Morada and talked to your girlfriend, and she told him that you had backed out of the project but that it was still pushing forward."

"I don't want to hear about any of that," he mumbled.

"But why?" I asked.

He was silent for a long time, and I was about to ask again when he said, "It got to be too much for me."

I said, "But you were doing so well—"

"Mr. Beas, really, I don't want to talk about it," he said.

"I don't understand. What could've happened?" I asked.

He scoffed, but he didn't dismiss me completely. "I just needed to get out of there," he said. "I didn't know what I was doing."

"But you *did* know what you were doing," I exclaimed, more emphatic than I intended. It was something I'd thought a great deal about over the course of my sleepless night: the extent of Wopper's role in his own fate. I remembered the constituents happily shaking his hand. I remembered the secretaries listening to his instructions. I remembered how *I* followed his instructions. And to top it off, I remembered full well how he spoke to that lowlife Don Elpidio.

"How do you know that?" he asked.

"Because I saw you," I answered, and then I said, "I saw you in action!"

He was quiet for a moment, and I regretted saying "in action!" if only because the last thing I wanted to do was come across as patronizing.

He stared out the window in silence, and I wondered what he was thinking. Finally, he said, "Why did you come by, Mr. Beas?"

"I wanted to see how you were doing," I said.

He chuckled. "As you can see, I'm doing," he said, and he held up his vinyl lunch pail as though it were evidence of how much his life had changed.

"I want to help you, Roberto," I said abruptly.

He looked at me strangely, and for a second I thought that maybe what I said sounded perverse. I quickly clarified. "I know you're illegal here and that limits your options," I said. "But I've had a lot of undocumented students, believe it or not, and some of them manage to get by, go on to Sac State and get their degree, and, who knows, after that maybe other options will open up."

"Like what?" he asked.

"I don't know, Roberto," I said. "But you'll at least be in a position to take advantage of those options."

"School's not for me, Mr. Beas. You know that," he said.

"I don't think that's true," I replied. "Maybe at one time it wasn't. But I wouldn't have ever guessed municipal council meetings in La Piedad, Michoacán, were your thing either, but you did it and you performed well."

"That was different," he said.

"I don't think so," I told him. "I really don't. You just have to set your mind to it. You just need to have the proper—"

He cut me off. "Mr. Beas, she helped me," he said. "Everything was her idea. She was the smart one. I just followed her instructions. She propped me up and just as easily tore me down."

"How did she do that?" I asked.

He shrugged. "I told you, I don't want to talk about it," he said. "Can't I just forget it? I'm trying to, and you're reminding me all over again. Look, Mr. Beas, I appreciate you wanting to help me out, but I think I'm better off just seeing where this job takes me. I can at least hold down work, save money, take care of Lara and the baby. Isn't that enough right now?"

"It is," I said, feeling deflated as I turned onto Fifth Street. We arrived at his house in silence. He reached out to shake my hand.

"You know I still feel bad about what happened when you came down," he said. "I already apologized to Lara's mom and I'm paying her back, but I'm really sorry that I had to do that to you."

"I'm over it," I said.

After I dropped him off I went home and got ready for work. It was another distracted morning in the office, half-listening to my students. I took an extra long lunch break and went home to eat. I continued to think about what Wopper had said about the girl directing everything and how he had just followed along. I guessed that was possible. Maybe she was a rare bird in whose hands he had fortunately or unfortunately ended up. But it didn't account for everything. So he had followed her instructions, but he had still followed them well, or well enough, and was that any different from what one needed to get through school or perform favorably in a job? How often did I go out on a limb and try something new? Never, actually. I was always following instructions. My entire life I had done so. Well, then, if it was instructions he needed, then instructions I could provide. I just needed to set the ball in motion.

When I returned to my office I called the secretary and had her reschedule the next hour's appointments. Then I pulled up Roberto Barraza's record on the computer and enrolled him in the upcoming spring semester. I even picked his classes, choosing the most engaging instructors. Some were already full, but I had ways around that. I printed out his schedule: Pre-algebra and English 115 on Mondays and Wednesdays, Mexican-American History and Intro to Speech on Tuesdays and Thursdays, all in the late afternoon so he could get to work in the evening.

I know, I know, I kept saying to myself. *It's not exactly municipal politics, but it's something. It's a start, right? Yes, it's a start.* And I kept telling myself that for the rest of the day, doubting myself the more I said it, until finally I'd convinced myself of the absolute futility of the idea. You can't do something for someone if he doesn't want it for himself. I'd at least learned that in my twelve years of counseling. It was aggravating me so much that I finally had to tell myself to let it go. You know what I actually said? I said, "Fuck it!" I really did.

At 4:50, unable to wait ten minutes more, I left my office without saying good-bye to my colleagues and walked out into the crisp fall air, feeling relieved that I was away from my desk and computer, not to mention no longer staring at Wopper's schedule printed out before me. I walked through the staff parking lot, and in the distance I saw someone standing by my car. I wondered who it could be. More so, I worried why this person had decided out of all the cars in the parking lot to lean against my silver Honda Accord. But as I approached, I thought the person looked familiar. My heart leaped as I thought it was Wopper. Could it really be him? Had he really come to seek out my help? But just when I was sure it was him, my heart beating, a smile already on my face, the man got inside the car and drove off. It wasn't even a Honda.

That evening I made myself a simple dinner—a few spinach and squash quesadillas—and then I tried watching television, but I was just flipping through the channels. Nothing held my interest. Finally, I shut it off and sat on the couch, not doing anything but listening to the room's silence. I don't know how long I sat there, ten, fifteen minutes, a half hour, all the while my mind racing, unable to stop thinking about Wopper, about my job as a counselor, about what I used to want out of life and what I wanted now. One thing was for sure: I used to dream much bigger. It was strange to me, to follow the train of my thoughts in this way and for them to begin with Wopper and end with my own hopes and unfulfilled expectations.

Something made me get up and walk to the closet in my bedroom. I opened the door, moved aside my dress shirts and slacks, and stared at the filing cabinet. I stepped forward and opened the middle drawer and removed the hanging folders. I was surprised that I remembered exactly where it was, as if I had subconsciously been thinking about it for seven years. At the bottom, pushed to the very back, I found the seventy-five pages of my masters' thesis. I half-smiled, half-cringed when I read the title: *Leadership Strategies to Confront the Latino Educational Crisis.* As if I had any clue what was I talking about. I pulled it out slowly, unsure why I was so hesitant. I turned to the last chapter and began reading.

It all came back to me. I remembered writing the words. I remembered my state of mind. It was me, and yet it wasn't. It was Arnie Beas seven years ago, working full time at the high school, taking night classes, dreaming of getting his PhD. I couldn't wait to be called Dr. Beas. But I was promoted, given a raise, and then a position opened up at the college, another raise. I bought a house, and, needless to say, I didn't go back to school. I read quickly through the first ten pages of the final chapter. I recognized my attempt at a straightforward and orderly summary, but then abruptly the tone changed, and I was no longer so careful. I made careless mistakes, misspelled a word or two, and the sentences became long and unwieldy. Errors that instinctively made me cringe. But I recognized the voice as my own. It was a desperate voice. Or I should say, it was a voice desperately in search of something. What's strange is that I never thought of myself that way, but it was so apparent now. I continued reading. I was describing my work up until that point, first as a counselor at Douglass Junior High and then moving to the high school and comparing the differences in the students' mentality, their approach to their future, the way they talked about what was important to them. I had forgotten most of the stories, but they came back to me now, even the faces of my students, though I had changed their names. Of course, I tried relating these personal anecdotes to arguments proposed in the thesis, but more often than not I deviated completely from the paper's premise. It had nothing to do with leadership, nothing to do with the Latino education crisis. In fact, I mainly just went on and on about how our parents' dreams were wholly dependent on an imagined future, while my generation was incapable of imagining any future whatsoever.

Still carrying the paper, I walked back to the couch. I sat down and read through the last twenty-four pages again, repeatedly surprised by the audacity of my voice. Of course, I had removed every word of it, and no one but my advisor and I had seen it, but I had still written it, thought it. The ideas had come from me alone. In fact, what stood out so clearly was that I wasn't just talking about second and third generation immigrants in the abstract. I was talking about myself. I was defending myself, critiquing myself. I was basically saying this: Our parents' generation, for all the difficulty of their sacrifice, for all their years of struggle, had had the easier task, if only because their dream was more fundamental. They could say, "I am working toward a better life," and that was the simple, enduring truth. What a powerful feeling that must have been, to hold inside, always. But it left my generation wanting, struggling to find its own simple enduring truth, a truth that could and would never exist, at least not until the day we faced again the decision of staying and rotting or leaving and hoping that out there was something better. Was that what I was saying? Did I really believe that? But I guess, more importantly, why was I thinking of it now after all this time? What did it have to do with Wopper Barraza?

I knew what I had to do. I rose from the couch and walked to my desk. I opened my laptop, and as soon as the blank page was before me I began to transcribe the twenty-four pages I had discarded and tried all this time to erase from my memory. There was something there, something I had to understand. I had been full of dreams at one time, but it wasn't just my students who suffered from a lack of imagination. This numbing stupor had caught up to me as well. I was trudging through that malaise now, and I hadn't even realized it, going about my job as if it were just a job, as if I had no responsibilities outside those that earned me my paycheck. My students didn't need someone to just grease the wheels. As ridiculous as it sounded, I felt as if they needed me to find my own enduring truth, as if somehow it were the key to our collective release.

I kept typing and typing, reading the words and transcribing them as fast as I could. Then something powerful came over me. I remembered the feeling clearly. It was the same as that night my writer's block broke and I'd written the pages before me. But suddenly I realized I couldn't waste this inspiration on mere transcription. So I moved the pages aside. I pushed them off the desk. I didn't want to look at them again. They had served their purpose. This wasn't seven years ago; this wasn't some manic outpouring to be added to yet another run-of-the-mill masters' thesis. No, I had to start over, from the beginning.

I stared at the screen before me, the daunting blank page. And the only beginning I could think of was imagining Wopper as he stood before the judge and learned that his life was about to be changed forever. I kept thinking of that image, kept imagining it as if I'd been in the audience that day. But I couldn't go forward. I couldn't imagine beyond that moment. So I went backward, and I imagined Wopper spending the night in jail. I saw him getting pulled over by the cop, I saw him at the bar, drunk, downing one beer after another, and I kept going backward, the beers disappearing out of his system until I saw Wopper enter the bar, sit down on the stool, and ask for a Tecate or a Bud Light. I saw him as he stared at the full glass before him.

I imagined this moment, Wopper Barraza stone sober, but no matter how vividly I saw that moment, as vivid as if I had actually been there at his side, I couldn't enter Wopper's thoughts. I couldn't know what was going on inside his head. And I realized that I would never know. That was when I pushed myself away from the computer and placed my forehead on the edge of the desk, and I said to myself, *Damn it, Arnie, you don't know anything at all.*

Epilogue

Mija

I STILL WAIT FOR HIM EVEN THOUGH I NO LONGER EXPECT HIM. THERE ARE days when I see a truck like his coming around the bend and my heart stops, or maybe it pounds harder, or maybe I feel it in my throat, only to realize that it's not him, just another man with a similar truck. There are days when my father comes and tries to comfort me by telling me Roberto will come back soon, that a man doesn't leave such a big house unfinished without returning to finish it, and even though I know he doesn't know a thing, I wish that he was right. Sometimes our house feels so lonely that I go back to my father's and sleep there, just as I did before, but after a couple of days I miss the little house if only because I miss the memories of what we had. I prefer the memories. I don't mind remembering. I think about him all the time, and I sometimes wonder if he thinks about me, or if he knows that I think so much about him, if it's possible for one to know they consume another's thoughts. I didn't know for sure that Roberto had returned to Woodland until Señor Gregory, the old gringo, showed up one day and told me that he had a few more investors interested and that he'd like to start construction on his house as soon as possible. He told me he was disappointed that Roberto wasn't going to be around, but that Roberto had told him the project was still going forward. And when I asked him where he'd seen Roberto, the old gringo was confused. "Woodland, of course. Didn't you know?" he asked. "He told you were the one in charge now." And he gave me the full installment of his money, and I contacted Maya and Moreno, and the reservoir projects were once again underway. Don Elpidio stayed out of it, just as I knew he would.

I had a dream the other night, an unsettling one. I woke up and felt sick with a numb grief. In the dream Roberto and I were lying on a bed, napping, I think, because it was light, or maybe we had just woken up. It was our house, but it wasn't our house. Maybe it was the one we were building together, because even though it looked familiar, it was bigger and there were many rooms, and it had partitions instead of complete walls. Roberto rose from the bed, and I watched him leave the room just as he did the night he left for good, but this time I followed him. In each room I saw him just as he left and entered the next one. I kept wanting to call out to him, but I didn't, as if there were some reason to be quiet. I had the sense that others were asleep, though I don't know who, or maybe I just kept thinking he would stop, but he didn't. Just when I thought he was going to turn around, he would disappear into another room. Finally we came to the last room, and I don't know how I knew it was the last room except it once again resembled our home, the bedroom leading to the living room, the kitchen just around the corner. Just as Roberto opened the door and was about to disappear again, I called out his name, and he turned around, and he stared at me as he sometimes did when he was someplace else, far away in his thoughts, thinking about a life I didn't know, a place I'd never seen. A look that scared me, not then, but now it scares me, because his distance was so evident. Only I didn't realize it when it mattered. He stared back at me, waiting for me to say something, to state why I'd called out for him, and even though I knew what his answer would be, I still asked him, "Can we talk?" And I can't remember whether he merely said no or he shook his head or both. And then he disappeared out of the room and closed the door.

There are days when I think that I should go to Roberto, when I think I should just take some of this money, pay for a coyote, and find my way to Woodland to see Roberto in person, see the new life he's created there. And I wonder if he's back with the mother of his child, and I wonder if his child is okay, too, and I wonder what we would say to one another if we were to stand before one another, if there would be any point in seeing one another again and talking about what had happened, asking him why he had left so suddenly, asking him if he was happier there or if he ever thought about returning. Because I would take him back. I want him to come back. I would tell him, "Please come back to La Morada, please come back. We don't have to do anything you don't want to do." And if he didn't, he didn't, and then I would know. Because what's hardest is not knowing. What's hard is waiting and wondering and hoping, always hoping, because there is no end to hope like this. I know that now. Maybe today, I think to myself, maybe today he'll show up on that bus, the same bus he arrived on, and when it comes and stops and opens its door to let the passengers off, I pause what I'm doing and I wait until the old ladies get off, and I wait for the school children to get off, and I hold my breath waiting to see if there's anyone else, and then the door closes and the bus turns around and leaves La Morada, and I return to whatever it was I was doing.

MACEO MONTOYA grew up in Elmira, California. He graduated from Yale University in 2002 and received his master of fine arts in painting from Columbia University in 2006. Montoya's paintings, drawings, and prints have been featured in exhibitions and publications throughout the country as well as internationally. Montoya's first novel, *The Scoundrel and the Optimist* (Bilingual Press, 2010), was awarded the 2011 International Latino Book Award for "Best First Book." In 2013, *Latino Stories* named him one of its "Top Ten New Latino Writers to Watch." Montoya is an assistant professor in the Chicana/o studies department at UC–Davis where he teaches a community mural workshop and courses in Chicano literature. He is an affiliated faculty member of Taller Arte del Nuevo Amanecer (tana.ucdavis.edu), a community-based art center in Woodland, California. More information about his writing and artwork can be viewed at www.maceomontoya.com.